PRAISE FOR
QUINT

"Irving's impressive debut follows a set of quintuplets born in Canada in the 1940s and based on the historical 1934 Dionne quints, freshly reimagining their exploitation from several points of view...The well-paced plot includes arson, an attempt to escape from Quintland!, a fatal accident, and more, all handled with aplomb. Much has been written about the real-life quintuplets, including another recent novel, but Irving does justice to the novel's inspiration."
—*Publishers Weekly*

"Dionne Irving's fascinating novel begins as an exploration of the ways in which innocents can be exploited, perverted, and victimized by rampant commercial exploitation. From there the story broadens and deepens to become a poignant and ambitious meditation on the human condition itself, particularly as it relates to our relationship with love or its absence. *Quint* is a compelling read and Dionne Irving is a writer on the rise."
—**Wally Lamb, author of** *I Know This Much Is True*

"*Quint* is an expansive novel of multiple births, motherhood, siblings, celebrity, exploitation, loss and connection; this story truly contains the world. Dionne Irving is a fantastic writer; she tells this unique story with honesty and precision and playfulness, and this novel compels with her vision, which is original and vast."
—**Karen E. Bender, author of** *Refund*

QUINT

a novel by

Dionne Irving

7.13 Books
Brooklyn

Cover art by Gigi Little
Edited by Hasanthika Sirisena

Copyright ©2021 by Dionne Irving
ISBN (paperback): 978-1-7361767-2-6
ISBN (eBook): 978-1-7361767-3-3
Library of Congress Control Number (LCCN): 2020953038

For Aaron, even though the world intrudes.

The ceremony of innocence is drowned;
The best lack all conviction, while the worst
Are full of passionate intensity.

—William Butler Yeats

PART ONE

MOTHER

WHEN SHE STARTED BLEEDING, she thought for certain she'd lost the child. The blood was bright red, the kind the midwife had warned her about. The kind that meant surely this child, like the others before it, had died inside her. Again, her body had failed her, had shown her that she wasn't really a woman. In a month or so, he would climb on top of her and do it again. And she would get pregnant again. And they would do this *bebe/non bebe* ritual again. At least that's how it'd been before. She looked to the picture of the Virgin on the wall and was reminded of how *Notre Dame* had failed her time and time again.

So, she was surprised an hour later when, after she had hoisted her mass into the kitchen for water, she felt that flutter. The hint of an elbow or knee, she couldn't be sure, pressing against her from the inside. That thing that told her that this was life. She looked again to the picture of the Virgin Mary hanging over the bed. She could see her from the sink, like the Virgin was calling to her, like she was beckoning her and she floated, wet hands, back onto the bed where she spent most of her days.

The next thing she remembered, he was shaking her, and, when she opened her eyes and saw him, her husband, standing there, it was like she had been waiting for him all her life. Or at least waiting for someone like him.

"Are you alright?" he kept saying, and then finally, "Answer me!"

"Yes," she said. "Of course, of course."

But she couldn't get up, couldn't sit up in the bed. She remembered the blood and her hand flew between her legs. She drew that hand up to her face to inspect it for any hint of red, but there was none.

"What is it?" he asked. The hard edge in his voice gone. He sat at the end of the bed smoking a cigarette and watching her.

"There was blood today. Earlier. But I think I felt the baby move after that."

He stared at her with large, unblinking eyes and she couldn't tell what he was thinking, or what he understood.

"This happens with the cows too." He dropped a bit of ash on the floor, and she tried to imagine when and how she would be able to clean it up. "Sometimes they bleed a little at first, a little blood, but then later on, a perfectly healthy calf."

There were only two rooms in the little house, and his cigarette smoke filled them both. She wanted badly to open a window, to breathe in clean, crisp January air that cut right through her lungs in a way that both stung and felt delicious.

He got up finally and went into the front room, lighting a second cigarette on the stove, a wedding present ordered from Sears & Roebuck. It was the newest thing in the house and took cord after cord of wood to heat. And while the house was wired for electricity, money came too infrequently to leave it on.

She watched him pull a hunk of bread from the larder and slather it with butter. She wondered if the Virgin's husband ate like this. Sloppily, hunched over the sink, like an animal. No, he didn't. She knew that, even though Joseph knew that the Virgin wasn't carrying his child, he was attentive, devoted and gentle. He wouldn't smoke a cigarette in front of her. He wouldn't jam bread into the gaping maw on his face, never offering her a bite.

She could see him from the bed, wiping the knife on the seat of his trousers after each slice, and she felt the bile rise in her throat.

She turned and vomited all over the floor, feeling the heat from the contents of her stomach splash back onto her face as she wretched and wretched. And when she finally stopped, when she looked up, he was just standing there, staring at her.

"What should I do?" he asked, still clutching the butter knife.

"The doctor," she murmured. "You better call the doctor."

And then it all went black.

SISTER

In the beginning, there were six babies. That sixth baby—the dead one, the one whose face you don't know—is me. Time can whisk away a half-century's worth of television, film, and cultural spectacle. Much of the memory of my sisters' lives may be crowded and created by what was in the tabloids. Visualize a photo. It is a portrait of my ignominious father, my long-suffering mother and the passel of gnarly-haired brats they spawned who were copies of the original. Me again!

We weren't the first, you know. There is a statue in Hamlin, Germany, commemorating seven, all with identical death dates and hours—as if the Pied Piper himself had taken them away. And, of course, Aristotle wrote of quintuplets as early as ancient Rome. The bane of the Roman Empire, some kind of curse, the children of multiple births rarely saw adulthood. But we were special. We were the first that you've ever heard of. We were a medical marvel, one in the hundreds of millions, a monozygotic miracle, our mother's egg splitting into six even pieces, creating the world's most perfect matched set, with identical DNA coursing through us *in utero*.

Six little babies all alive,
One kicked the bucket and then there were five.

Five little babies imagine they were poor,
One tumbled in the public eye and then there were four.

Four little babies on a shopping spree,
One overspent her cash, then there were three.

Three little babies, darling little chou,
One caught quite a cold and then there were two.

Two little babies frolicking in the sun,
One got a nice red burn then there was one.

One little baby all alone.

I close my eyes before the story even begins. I was buried in the backyard by our father and not mentioned again—to anyone, not even our mother—outside of his single deathbed confession to his priest.

Five little girls instead of six. Fifty little fingers and fifty little toes, thick black hair and button noses. No, not perfect, but good enough, more than good enough when multiplied by five…

TÈMISCAMING

OUR TOWN WAS TWO hours north of Toronto by motorcar, but it might as well have been another planet. It was one of those company towns, every pebble, every house, every bit of bread and butter the property of the Canadian International Paper Company. If you worked for paper in Témiscaming, you worked hard, but if you didn't, you never had enough. Some of us ate and lots of us didn't.

Because Témiscaming was a factory town, and because it was mostly French and mostly Catholic, it wasn't ever a tourist destination. It was not the gateway to the North like North Bay. No vacation cottages, no pie stands, no lake to swim in. There was nothing in Témiscaming but loggers and employees of the paper mill and a handful of farmers. If it hadn't been for the Quints, you would never have known its name.

THE HOUSE

SHE HAD BEEN A girl desired by men and boys from the time her body told her, at age thirteen, that she was no longer a girl. She was thin-hipped and had thick, dark brown hair, heavy-lidded eyes, and a nose that was only a little bit too big when compared to the other features on her face.

Her father had disappeared when she was a child. (Rumors persisted that she was a bastard.) There were also rumors that her mother was promiscuous, which led to murmurs concerning the borders who stayed from time to time in the room above their stable, that they were her mother's lovers and not just loggers who came to town to work through the winter season. So, when August Phalene, a farmer's son, started to show an interest in her, she was surprised. He was no catch, with one leg shorter than the other and a badly scarred face—a remnant of an adolescence spent picking blemishes. But still, he had the bright blue eyes of a movie star and a few extra *sou* in his pocket, which was far more than most boys in Témiscaming had. So they courted, mostly sitting in what passed for her mother's parlor, which was comprised of an over-stuffed chair and several apple crates. He didn't talk much; instead, he listened to her. She spoke quickly, steadily, and at length about her hatred of the town and her desire to go to new places and to meet new people.

She could tell that August liked her cooking and the way she looked. He told her that he liked the idea of a wife. For her, it seemed good enough that he worked steadily and saved a little money. And most importantly, he promised to take her far from her mother, far from Témiscaming, and to give her a better life somewhere else.

And his family, even though they weren't a "paper family," made a good living working their land, though, in fact, *they* hadn't worked the land themselves in nearly a decade. Instead, they hired out farmhands and the occasional rancher from out west. But then came the Depression and they had to put their hands in the earth again—to remind themselves where they came from. English boys married managers' daughters, while farmers' sons, mostly French, settled for farm girls. But she was neither, and when in her senior year of high school she was without a steady boyfriend or a husband, she had assumed, much like everyone else, that she would end up a spinster.

She took the offer of marriage because it was the best that she could hope for.

She hadn't been told anything about love or boys.

It had been the shock of her life when, after their wedding (a ceremony in front of the priest, his mother, father, and his three older brothers), he had come at her, snatched at her clothes and her hair. Oh, she wasn't a total naïf. But like all the good girls she knew, she understood when and where to stop, knew how to put her hand on a boy's arm and say, "Please, don't." Or to whisper, "I can't, I'm sorry," if a hand drifted up her blouse or down her skirt. When it was over, her husband (*her husband!*) rolled over and she lay still in the bed, running over the events of the previous two minutes.

As if it had been someone else underneath him, she closed her mind and observed. Her wedding dress was balled up in a corner and—worse yet—her brasserie, panties, the garter and stockings were in a heap on the floor, and she felt shock at what they had just done. She wanted to pull the bedclothes over her head, to hide from the shame of it, but he had pulled her roughly to his side and then fell asleep, snoring deeply.

She and August had travelled to Montreal from Témiscaming a day later. He was to pay taxes on his newly acquired farm and they were getting a kind of honeymoon. They'd been married early in the morning to give his brothers time to get back to work after the ceremony. She liked seeing the pride that came from his family's industrious nature. They were hard workers, all of them. He liked to remind her of that when they were courting. That he wasn't afraid of hard work. That he would work hard, as hard as he could, to take care of her.

The first morning in the city, she watched the minutes tick past on the clock and wondered how much longer she was going to have to lie there. She shifted slightly and he stirred next to her.

"Where are you going?" he asked, grabbing her and pulling her closer.

The room felt stifling hot, but she liked this, being close to him and smelling the way her own scent mixed with his.

"What are we going to do today?" she asked.

She had never been to Montreal before. She'd never been any further than North Bay.

He groaned and rolled away from her, pulling the blanket over his eyes.

"I'm going to sleep. And you should get some sleep too. Tomorrow it's back to work!"

"Tomorrow? I thought we were going to stay two days."

"I can't afford to be away from the farm for two days. Who do you think is going to take care of it while I'm gone?"

She had imagined eating in a restaurant or seeing a picture show, or...something.

She didn't know what to imagine, really. She waited for a moment until she heard the steady pacing of his breath that indicated sleep. Then she put on the rumpled slip and went over to the little sink and splashed some water on her face.

She had spent weeks thinking about these days, and now she was stuck in this tiny, hot room. The window faced onto a narrow little street lined with bricks. She unlatched the window and opened it up, bringing a bright breeze into the room. She leaned out, feeling it caress her skin, as she watched men and women moving up and down the lane, dressed in all kinds of colors. And the stockings. At first she thought the women weren't wearing any at all. Then she saw a seam or two. She leaned out as far as she could, trying to take it all in.

"Shut the goddamn window," he roared from the bed. "Can't you see I'm sleeping? It's so loud out there."

She shut the window with a bang and he sat up.

"Fine," he said. "Fine. If you aren't going to be quiet, then go." He pulled aside the quilt and shoved his fist into the pants he had thrown hastily on the chair next to the bed, yanking a few coins from the pocket and tossing them across the room at her.

She pulled on her dress before he could change his mind and snatched the coins from the floor.

Outside in the street, she paused. She hadn't been able to find the Innkeeper before heading out, and now, in the middle of the street, she had no idea where to go. She looked left and right before finally settling on a left-hand turn and heading down the curved street, hoping it would take her somewhere to find something she had never seen before. She spent the day wandering, getting lost, stumbling upon a picture show, buying *bonbon* from a shiny, well-lit shop in Vieux Montreal. And she felt free—so very free—for the first time ever.

After the honeymoon, she found that being a wife was easy. She spent any extra money her husband gave her on movie magazines. She liked to spend summer mornings lying in the grass drying her freshly washed hair in the sun and flipping through their pages. She made dinner in the evenings, breakfast in the mornings, did her best to seem pleasant when he came home at the end of the day and let him climb on top of her most nights. And if she did all those things, he was pleased.

And after four years of marriage, she got used to doing *it*, although she had never learned to like *it*. And she liked *it* even less because *it* seemed to always make her pregnant. And although there had never been a baby, she hated a baby's uncertainty in her body. The slip of its life there, a succubus, and then again, not there.

There were a host of pregnancies in those four years. She could not remember how many. Only that her body did not seem to be a habitable environment for a child. When she found herself pregnant yet again, after years, she hadn't paid much attention to it, assumed it would go the way the others went. But by the third month she already had a good-sized belly.

"Are you pregnant?" August asked her one night once they had finished dinner.

"I think so," she said.

He hoped for a son who would help to relieve the burdens of farming, who might help him to break even in subsequent years and, hopefully, maybe turn a profit. He knew his wife wanted to spend money with both hands, as fast as she could. He knew he was pretty and he knew he had better hope for more income in the future so that he could try and keep her happy. Or at least keep her amenable to his needs and her situation.

She went to see the midwife who said she was a little fat, her only advice to not eat quite so much. It was important to keep her husband's interest during this time, she was told. Did she understand? She didn't. But nevertheless, she took to skipping dinner even though she continued to get bigger.

TÈMISCAMING

AT TWENTY-FIVE CATHERINE PHALENE was one of the oldest pregnant women in Témiscaming. By her age most women were working on their fifth or sixth child. We whispered about her, and had full-blown conversations in the company store (where the Phalenes were not allowed to shop) and even in the women's auxiliary sewing circle. The pregnancy was a topic of conversation because of her age, but also because of her size. The woman was fat. Obscenely fat.

"It is the French," the mayor's wife said. "One baby and they are ruined."

"And you know they never have just one," said the Postmaster's wife.

And we laughed.

MOTHER

THOUGH SHE WAS ONLY in her second trimester, she looked ready to pop. She grew so large that August looked at her like she was the main attraction at a freak show. The midwife couldn't figure out why she continued to swell.

"What are you eating?" she asked. Doctor LeFevre asked the same thing after she stepped onto the scale. He repeated it again when he clucked about her blood pressure.

But soon enough, she stopped skipping meals. She was so ravenous that she dreamed of eating the sawdust and bunting in the mattress. During the day with her husband gone, she ate entire loaves of bread smeared with bacon grease and bowl after bowl of porridge. It seemed like there was never enough. Her breasts grew to a wide expanse—too large to be titillating for her husband—eventually expanding well beyond the confinement of any brasserie. She took to wearing an old sheet in the middle of which she'd cut a hole to put her head through. She imagined this was the way the women must've been pregnant in Biblical times. It was so cool and so loose. And when she stopped being able to bend over to shimmy into her underthings, and to fasten her girdle, she stopped wearing those too.

She had never been a thin girl, but men had always liked her shape, and she had imagined that her long arms and her strong calves made her look dependable. But with each passing month, the weight seemed to come in somewhere new. Zaftig and billowy, her hips spread flat and wide, her face ballooned as though she'd stuffed her cheeks with cotton balls and her fingers swelled so fat that she awoke one morning to find her wedding band snapped in half.

By the time she was six months pregnant, she couldn't so much as walk. Her ankles exploded overnight, it seemed, blooming like angry red grapefruits atop her feet and making it impossible for her to stand. Her hair came out in handfuls so she stopped brushing it, resorting to patting it into place to make it look, in dim light, presentable. And eventually, when she stopped even leaving the house, she let it get matted and dirty, allowing it to snarl in tatty swirls around her head.

Marooned on their bed in that tiny back bedroom, she some days relied on the scant kindness provided by her husband. And on other days, she shimmied across the floor on all fours like an obese raccoon, chafing her hands and knees so that she could have a glass of water or empty the chamber pot out the door so the smell didn't make her wretch again. The effort usually exhausted her and August returned home more than once to find his wife sprawled on the kitchen floor. Moving her was no easy task. He'd been unable to help her to stand up in well over a month, so he finally worked out a pulley system. He wedged a quilt underneath her and dragged her on her back through the front room before both hoisting and rolling her thick body into the bed. They would both lay there panting, each trying to figure out what was wrong with her and wondering—silently, resentfully—why she was so big.

SISTER

ON THE DAY OF our birth, Mama came out of a dead faint and screamed for nearly three hours, until her voice was hoarse and broken, before Papa finally sent for the doctor. It was a point that was cited in the later trial as evidence of his apparent cruelty. But the only births he'd ever come close to were all animated by screams. How was he to know any better?

Dr. LeFevre arrived just before the birth of the first. He grimaced at the shrieks and quickly washed up in the cracked metal basin in the kitchen before attending to our mother.

News stories say a lot of things, some of which is invented or imagined. But I was there and I will tell you that our births were far from hygienic, far from miraculous, and far from quiet. The moment our tiny bodies came into the world is now the stuff of legend. The branch that scraped the windowpane, the towels used to wipe us, the way the last child's cries—my cries—filled the room...all became the cornerstone of what would become a thriving gynecological practice.

I came last and let out one small cry, the rallying moment of my life before I died, right there, in Dr. LeFevre's hands. And he wept. Both for me and for the miracle of my sisters.

I know of the doctor's many sins, of the blackness in his heart. But this isn't his story, and while his tears were for me, they were

remarkable only because they were the only ones that came. He
handed me to my father and never gave me another thought
beyond that day. By the time I arrived, my mother had fainted and
my father was in the corner on his knees, praying fervently to any
Saint who might help them, and then to God Himself, quietly at
first, and then louder. And then louder yet.

Later, LeFevre would take too much credit, as though he
himself had conceived us all. But, in that moment, he said, "My
God, it must be some kind of curse," and stood staring for a
moment, before he even thought to cover my sisters' tiny bodies.

My five sisters were placed in a wicker basket by his nurse,
who arrived around the time that Calendre, the penultimate sister,
made her appearance. I was the runt, weighing in at a little under a
pound. Blankets were heated in the oven by the nurse who turned
up shortly after the doctor, to keep my sisters warm while my
father wrapped me in butcher's paper and went about burying me,
in a fairly shallow grave, near a Sycamore behind the house where
now sits a museum dedicated to my sisters' birth. He was the only
one who knew I was there. The burial was without ceremony or
sentimentality. Was without much thought at all. He placed me
there delicately. But beyond that gentle gesture, my father never
extended any other kindness. He heaved a mound of dirt on my
tiny body and went about his day. And his life. For this, I never
forgave him.

The basket with my sisters was set in front of the open oven
door to keep them warm, and one by one they were taken out of
the basket and massaged with olive oil by the nurse. They perked
up at the touch, their hearts beating double time when the doctor
or the nurse laid a finger on their doll-sized bodies. Our parents
didn't lay a hand on them for over two days. The doctor was
worried about contamination, because my sisters looked so small,
so fragile, barely resembling life at all.

My sisters weren't as charming at first as it was later claimed.
Their heads were misshapen after being wrenched from our

mother's womb, and they suffered from jaundice, making them look more like overripe squashes than children. But there is no photographic evidence of such things.

The doctor prescribed water sweetened with corn syrup every two hours for the first twenty-four. By then he had called in the local wet nurse. On their second day in the world, my sisters were moved to a slightly larger basket. They had three hot water bottles (which were enough to cover all five) laid across them to keep them warm. The doctor, his nurse, and the midwife kept a vigil. They prayed to Mother Mary, to St. Gerard, to God Himself, to please save these poor, little unbaptized souls. No one knew to say any prayers for me.

The nurses and the doctor took turns watching them. The vigil was constant, uninterrupted. And when it became apparent that the job of feeding my sisters would be too much for our mother—even with the help of any wet nurse—the doctor invented a formula of milk, boiled water, two spoonfuls of corn syrup, and a drop or two of rum, a concoction fed to my sisters using an eyedropper. Each of them clamored for life and food in a way that eluded me. I was jealous then, because they had achieved what I never could.

TÈMISCAMING

IN LATE JANUARY, 1940, just weeks after their birth, August Phalene came into the birth registry office smelling of liquor. But that was nothing out of the ordinary. We all knew that he liked a drink now and then. Now and then being a literal statement, not an expression, in his case.

Because the birth registry office was a government building, there was a telephone and heat and even a fireplace in the rear office in case one of those notorious early January winds should sweep through and make the already cold place colder. The bureaucrat—he was not from here—sat hunched over his desk, writing birth records for the area in government registries, when Phalene came through the door.

The bureaucrat did not like the French. Had never liked the French. He was from Toronto and didn't care for the country or the loose and free way in which these French, these Catholics, conducted themselves. He was in this northern outpost at the behest of his superiors. When Canada had entered the war the previous September, and every able-bodied man had been snatched to fight, he—because of a right foot that was missing five toes—was sent north to cover this office, a government post to keep track of the mewling French Canadian brats, who would be shipped off, too, (he hoped) as soon as they hit puberty. He had wanted to enlist; even a war in the furthest reaches of Europe was better than that post.

August leaned across the counter and asked the bureaucrat how much for one birth certificate. He intended to record all five births on it. The man leaned back theatrically, wanting August to take notice of the fact that the bureaucrat smelled the alcohol on him. August wasn't so drunk as to be able to ignore the fact that he did not approve.

"Certainly, sir, you are mistaken. Cats, and dogs—they have litters. Humans do not," he said slowly and carefully in his most perfect French so that August wouldn't misunderstand him.

He thought that that was all those people seemed to do: drink, fornicate, and pray.

"Is true," August slurred, but in English. "My wife gives five baby just three days ago. Ask Dr. LeFevre."

His English wasn't great and it got worse when he'd been drinking. He messed up idioms and dropped pronouns.

The clerk stared at him for a moment, unsure of what to do.

"Wait here," he said.

The doctor was called and it was confirmed, and five separate birth certificates were presented. The bureaucrat assured him that he would need to pay separately for each in spite of August's protestations for a discount. And it was this bureaucrat who issued all five Phalene birth certificates. This bureaucrat who hoped for bigger and better things. Anything bigger. Anything better. Any reason whatsoever to get out of Témiscaming and back to civilization.

ARCHIVES

Témiscaming, January 7th 1940 – The stork was prolific when he visited a farmhouse two miles from Témiscaming last Friday morning.... Before he winged his way homeward, he delivered five baby girls to Mr. and Mrs. August Phalene.

It is admitted to be a record for Canada, if not the world.

These are the first children to be born to the Phalenes. All five babies were a picture of health, and Dr. Emile LeFevre, who attended Mrs. Phalene, pronounced them fit.

This morning, all was quiet at the Phalene residence. Mr. Phalene, who is 31, was not sure of the weight of the children. A potato scale was produced and each of the youngsters placed in the pan and weighed. Their total weight amounted to 14 pounds, 4 ounces, with the first-born leading the list at three pounds 6 ounces. The two lightest tipped the beam at 2 pounds, 5 ounces.

Asked how she felt, the pretty, brown-eyed, dark haired mother asked the reporter in French, "Are you English? You speak no French?" And "Are you Catholic?" And then in English, "Pretty good. Thank you."

Not one whimper was heard from the little ones during the entire proceedings. They blinked their eyes and squirmed, but seemed quite satisfied with their lot.

The family may be eligible for the 'King's Bounty' of three pounds, it was learned at the Department of Secretary of State today.

The qualifying provisions for the bounty specify mothers of triplets. If their regulations are fully met, officials of the Department intimated they see no reason why the mother of quintuplets should not be eligible also.

TÈMISCAMING

IN THE WEEKS FOLLOWING the birth of the five babies, as news spread, women in the French community volunteered as wet nurses. They were farm wives mostly, Catholics who were both superstitious and suspicious. But they knew that in the Phalene house, they would have access to the miraculous, the spectacular. And on that basic, shameful level, each woman wanted a chance to be involved, to take part in the miracle. They wanted to jump into that spectacle breast-first, to feel the tug of life and nature in its gaudiest, most freakish outing. It would make them feel not like poor, bedraggled farm mothers, but rather like handmaidens to greatness, like mothers to humanity. Like the Virgin herself.

Three days after the birth, Dr. LeFevre and his nurses packed up and left and were replaced by a steady stream of women coming and leaving Madame Phalene's front parlor. Many of us got called forward at the trial later as witnesses. Madames Tremblay, Gaultier, Bergon, Nadeau, Beaulieu, Grenier, Landry, Blais, Lachance, Michaud, and Bedard all trooped through the tiny house in those first few weeks. They each believed they did their good Christian duty—offering more than twenty breasts to feed the children—as they were all new mothers themselves. While noting the deplorable state of the house, they brought covered tin pie plates of supper for the Phalenes. They brought hand-knitted blankets for the new mother, for the too-tiny babies. They noted that she was still quite large. They brought wood to keep the stove going. They mentally recorded that the Father smelled of liquor. They tried to be patient with the Mother, who cried often. They noted the absence of her own mother. But the reason they were there most often and most of all was to stare into that basket, afraid even to touch those…babies?

They would look chastened years later when a barrister questioned their motives, but by then they were able to admit to the wrongdoings of their spirits and bodies. They had been to confession and absolved themselves of all misfortune that had come to those girls. They blamed the Phalenes. They said that the Father rarely picked them up, choosing instead to stare at them as if he couldn't believe they were his, couldn't believe they were real. They said that the mother couldn't seem to do much but cry. These women admitted to being motivated by a perverse desire to marvel, to stare, to gaze, not by the pure desire to help. They knew that God had forgiven them for their sins.

ARCHIVES

From *the Globe and Mail*: "...these latest arrivals will arouse fresh apprehensions regarding French-Canadian ascendency in Northern Ontario. Quoting Reverend Dr. C.E. Silcox of the United Church, who was advocating for birth control: "... a part of the whole problem is the extraordinary fecundity of the French-Canadians and the suspicion that the French are deliberately trying to outbreed the English, even though in so doing, it may involve the lowering of the standard of wages and living and all that depends on such standards."

FATHER

He had not wanted children. He made himself believe that he'd all but perfected that method of birth control he liked to imagine was pioneered by the Catholic Church. It hadn't always worked. That wife of his seemed to get pregnant as easily as she blinked. But there had been no babies. So, he lived only for today, the farm, the drinks, and sometimes, yes, on the better days, for his wife. And he lived with the urgency of a fatalist imagining that, any day, some sort of happenstance might strike him dead.

In the days after they were born, he imagined—hoped even—that they would die. From lack of sleep, from the incessant, endless tears and shaky sobs flowing through the two-room farmhouse, a cacophony of human misery. And after a while, it seemed like there were always women in his house. Women at the stove, women in the front room washing nappies, women in the bedroom tending to his wife. Women everywhere. Watching. Jesus, God. Where was a man supposed so sit, to stand, to eat? To be a man, for Christ's sake. He took to coming in the door and going right back out again.

He hadn't seen many of these women since pulling their plaits in the one-room schoolhouse where they had learned to do sums, to sign their names and to play at being grown up. But now they were everywhere, staring at those children, and he wasn't sure if they were regretful or relieved that he hadn't married one of them instead.

It was winter and there wasn't much farm work then—mostly just tending to the animals. So even though it was freezing outside, he spent as much time as he could in the barn. But even that didn't take up much of the day, and eventually he'd wander back up to the house. And then once, as he'd stepped inside, there was Madame Bergon—or as he had known her, Ada. Ada, standing in his kitchen. Seeing her in the late afternoon light, he remembered kissing her once—only once—when they were just twelve, some Sunday after Mass. Most children avoided him because of his leg. They made fun of the way he walked, with a slight limp. The shorter and slightly deformed leg always lagging behind its strong and muscular sibling. Oh, the things that they had called him; *bossu, boiteux, le impotent.* But she had never seemed to notice. She would sit with him under the trees after Mass, singing to him softly and propping up the leg on a stump in her childlike way of playing nursemaid. Even letting her hand linger on the leg a moment or two, as if in awe of the power it might possess. All the while the other children ran around and he imagined that it was only the two of them.

"*Bonsoir, Monsieur,*" she said, drying her hands on a tea towel. "*Comment ça va?*"

"*Bien, et toi?*"

He hated these forced pleasantries—the formality of titles and last names, of having to pretend that she was here to help and not just gawk at the spectacle of his life, of these lives.

His wife and children were sleeping, she said. She motioned toward the closed door of the bedroom. It had been a tough morning, and the babies were in bed with his wife so that she could keep them warm.

"*Déjeuner?*"

The questioned startled him and he grunted in response. She ladled some stew into a bowl from a pot bubbling on the stove.

He ate quickly, his hand curved around the bowl, the broth sliding easily down his throat, the hunks of meat juicy and tender after hours in the pot. It was good. He had to admit that it felt good—to be warm, to have a woman looking after him.

When he was done she cleared away the bowl and served him a slice of *Tart au Sucre*. He had forgotten how tasty it was, and he reached back in his mind to her parents' maple syrup farm, the fun they'd had there as children.

She sat across from him at the table and watched him eat.

"I still remember you as a little boy," she said. "Charming and brave."

He shrugged. And she sighed and folded her hands in her lap.

"But this," she said. "How are you going to get out of this?"

He thought about the question for a moment. Out of this. He hadn't thought past these moments. Hadn't considered what would become of them all when those five lumps stopped needing to be fed from an eyedropper. And not even one boy in the lot. No one to help him run the farm.

"It's going to take money, I guess. Where I'll get it from, I don't know."

She looked away as if embarrassed that he'd alluded to money, and her cheeks turned pink. She wasn't bad looking after all these years, he thought. Her face was a little wider and there was more loose skin on her lower arm. She had four children of her own and a husband and farmhouse. What was she doing here? he thought. In his house, in his kitchen? Cooking his food? He wondered how she might respond if he asked her to run away with him. Could either of them leave their families and start over? Somewhere warm. He could get a suit. A car. Could get away from the problem of these babies. With her. With Ada.

"I should go," she said suddenly. "Leave the plate in the basin. One of the women will come for it tomorrow. And you can have more of the stew for supper."

"Thank you," he said, wanting to say something more but unable to find any words that might persuade her to stay, to look after him. Today. Tomorrow. Every day. To be looked after.

Instead, she plunged through the doorway and stepped into the cold, blustery afternoon air. After the door latched, the house was silent for a few minutes. He could hear the wind whipping and then, finally, the first of many cries rang out from the bedroom. When he pulled the door open, he looked for his wife in their bed. He followed the sound of her voice and found her curled up in the corner, crying, her face wet with tears.

In the basket at the foot of the bed, the babies had started to make the snuffling sounds that he knew would become cries.

"Get up!" he yelled. He grabbed her arm, trying to wrench her off the floor. "Get up, damn it! Take care of your babies. What kind of woman are you?"

She wrenched her arm away from his and again curled into herself in a ball on the floor. When he touched her again, more gently this time, she turned and looked at him, her eyes wild with something he'd never seen before. Maybe rage?

"No," she said. "No, no, no. I can't. I can't. I can't."

Her voice was flat and she gazed at him without blinking.

"Get your hands off of me."

The mewling from the basket had reached a crescendo and he turned his attention to the babies. He touched each of their chests, feeling the patter of life beneath the skin of each in turn. They were all still alive. They must have been hungry. Who knows when that woman had fed them last? What monster was she, who had been neglecting her responsibilities as a woman, as a wife? As a mother?

He watched them for a moment. Watched each of them, their heads no bigger than an apple, watched as their lungs inflated and deflated under the soft muslin cloth as they screamed, and screamed, and screamed.

What was he to do? He had no breast for them to suckle and he felt helpless for a moment, watching the children, his children, desperate for food. He remembered finally the way his mother had fed the barn kittens when the mother cat had been trampled by a horse, soaking bits of cloth in milk and letting the kittens suckle. And so he did the same and dipped his shirt sleeve in milk and fed his children one at a time, holding their small bodies against his chest and feeling their life thrum back against him. They sucked greedily, falling asleep one at a time, until he put the final one down and realized that his heart had been racing. He watched as the gentle wave of breath moved through each of their bodies, their sleep twitching and agitated, and he realized for the first time that these were his children. His flesh, his blood. This would be who carried on his legacy. If they survived.

SISTER

Later, these early moments were immortalized at *Quintland!* (that opulent, yet rustic, shrine to my sisters' spectacle) with a series of tiny wax replicas, my sisters shrouded in a glowing light, smiling beatifically, while, with the exception of Mama, the other models in the room—our father, Dr. LeFevre and an assortment of midwives—are stooped, hunched, with die-cast heads that only a phrenologist could love. Artistic license that went eerily well as far as I can tell.

The diorama was a commissioned piece, which has long since been relegated to some government archive in Ottawa. In the mold, Mama, her arms out of proportion with the artist's rendering of her body, manages to wrap them around all of my sisters at once, as though drawing them closer to her. There was no hint of the sixty-five pounds of pregnancy weight that would linger well into her old age. Instead she looked like a young maiden fawning over her brood. The artist was paid in cash.

TÈMISCAMING

IN THE SHED IN Detant's pasture, where the farmers went to drink, we listened to Phalene's stories, which were always more boastful than we could understand a man in his situation being. We imagined those children as some kind of curse. We wondered how he had angered God enough to get five babies at once. And five girls. In spite of what the local priest said it was no blessing. No blessing at all.

We wouldn't tell stories in this piss poor shed.

But, we drank our whiskey and listened. Listened to him tell about the harem of women who showed up to cook and clean and take care of his offspring. He bragged on the children's looks, on his own virility.

We drank some more.

It was only his wife that seemed to give him pause. He leaned in one night around the rickety table where we all sat. When he did, the glow from the kerosene lantern illuminated what only then had become apparent: the clothing crusted with dirt, the beginnings of a beard, the hollows of his cheekbones. The man hadn't slept, bathed or eaten in quite some time.

"That wife of mine," he finally said to the other farmers. "Every little tickle in the throat and she needs to see a doctor."

It was the way he said it, both proud and disgusted, that made us uncomfortable. We nodded, didn't say much, and were glad it wasn't us. Glad we had only our own problems. We clapped him on the back and poured him another drink.

During the trial the local men would tell this story, but in ways that tried to make it sound less callous, less cruel. But it never did. Even then, so many years later, as men, they wanted to be loyal to him, even if they didn't feel that way.

MOTHER

WHEN SHE WAS PREGNANT she talked of wanting to name the child after a film star, a Joan, a Katherine, perhaps even an Ingrid. The battle over the names had lasted for weeks after the birth. August wanted sturdy French names, and she wailed that these were both boring and old fashioned. It only ended when August, whose religious and legal duty it was to declare the births, picked the names of his two grandmothers and three female cousins and registered their births with the local magistrate. Calendre Adele, Fabienne Clemence, Eliane Collette, Madeline Valerie, and Anglette Helene Phalene. And she started to hate him a little then, for taking away her choice.

She could not remember when she started crying and when she stopped, only that the babies wouldn't stop screaming. As much as she wanted to refute the story about the milk and the shirtsleeve, she really couldn't remember. Something inside of her was screaming and screaming and wouldn't stop. She remembered putting the babies down and curling into herself as far away as one room would allow. She tried to make her mind go quiet, but she couldn't, though eventually it seemed as if everything was so very far away.

When she came out of it, Dr. LeFevre was at her bedside.

"Do you hear me, Madame Phalene? You were missing for a moment but you are back with us now, aren't you?"

She nodded and wiped her forehead on the back of her hand. Her skin felt clammy and her bedclothes were saturated with milk and sweat and urine. What kind of husband let someone in their home with her looking like she was? She saw him standing there then, at the end of the bed, his hat in his hands, looking down at her.

"She'll be fine," the doctor told him. "Just get her doing some work, and she'll bounce right back."

He called his mother to come round the next morning and two of his sisters-in-law and they dragged her out of bed. The birth had nearly torn her in half and she wore a folded towel between her body and her britches. The blood coming out of her had soaked the towel and as one sister-in-law pulled off her clothes, the other picked up a corner of the hardened, blotted, clotted thing with the tips of her finger. She felt empty and so she let the women pull and push and prod at her. They inspected her body as though she was a cow.

"*Mon Dieu*," her mother-in-law finally muttered.

And one of the sisters-in-law drew water into a basin and warmed it on the stove before giving it to her. The woman told her to wash herself. The directive wasn't delivered unkindly, but it was an order nonetheless.

She turned her back to them, her cheeks growing hot, the embarrassment spreading up through her scalp and down through her hair. She squatted over the basin in a corner of the small room, her back to the three women as they fussed with the children and washed the windows and made the bed and swept up the small room.

She could hear them trying to pretend she wasn't present. There they were, all of them acting as if that splash of water over her chest and back covered the things those women said. She washed the crusted blood from herself until the water in the basin was silt-y with her. And when she was done, her sister-in-law handed her a new towel, again just with the tips of her fingers, and she couldn't imagine having been more ashamed in all her life.

The other sister-in-law helped her into a housedress and a pair of her husband's work slacks. And, as she was standing, inspecting her body in the new clothes, feeling like she was watching herself from outside, he came into the room and took her roughly by the arm, walking her out onto the porch. She woke up for the first time then and screamed and screamed and screamed.

"No, no, no, no, no, no, no!"

He screamed back at her that he was saving her life, that these were the doctor's orders, and his family watched from the porch like she was the one who had lost her mind.

He put her out in the yard to chop wood. And when he gave her the axe, she thought for a moment about coming after him with it. But she attacked the wood instead. Pretended it was him. She did it for hours, until the towel was saturated and a trickle of blood began to make its way down her legs. She chopped until her hands were pulpy and raw. She watched the woodpile next to her grow. It helped her in this way, knowing that sixteen chops would lead to eight pieces of kindling, and so on and so on. The methodical counting and swinging of the axe helped her to forget the mewing, need-filled children inside. It helped her to imagine another kind of life.

When years later, in print, she pointed out that this was a kind of cruelty, the doctor fervently denied that he advised work. She didn't know it then, but it was dropsy that had swelled her body to twice her normal size. The result of that testimony was that she was branded as unwomanly and lazy by the Catholic League of Young Mothers.

Soon after the wood chopping, she was taking care of the babies. They demanded constantly. The crying was a constant. The dirty diapers, a constant. The need to be fed or soothed was a constant. They were so fragile in those early days. Their hearts raced in double time when she picked them up. They wriggled with palpable excitement when their heads were stroked. They groaned with pleasure like adults when they were fed. This scared her, the weight of their desire.

She nursed as much as she could, sometimes nearly passing out from sheer exhaustion. In a matter of weeks, her maternity clothes hung from her frame and her face took on a haunted look. But she wasn't back to her old self. Her breasts were still big and uncomfortable, and her belly, though smaller, was marked by layers of excess, folded flesh from having been so distended. She barely recognized herself in the mirror.

She often did less than she should have, letting the infants' cries daisy-chain together while she sat on the front porch and smoked a cigarette or looked through catalogues, knowing that without much effort, they would wear themselves out soon enough. It wasn't that she didn't love her babies; it was that they were overwhelming.

When in the third week the midwife came to check on her, she gasped at the sight of her.

"You can't give those babies all of yourself!" she said.

There was something queer in the way she said it, "all of herself." As if she had a choice about how much to give when they demanded everything of her.

The midwife left and came back an hour or two later with two cases of evaporated milk and a carton of glass bottles and India rubber nipples. She taught her how to clean and disinfect the bottle, how to coax the rubber into the babies' mouth and how to stagger their feedings.

"The most I've ever done this for is two," the midwife said after feeding the last baby. "But you will learn. You will have to."

The midwife stayed through the day and into the early evening when August came back and mumbled a hello.

"Do you want to see?" she asked him. "Do you want to see how to feed your children?"

He watched for a moment or two.

"No," he said finally. "You handle it."

And she tried. As hard as she could, she tried to handle it.

SISTER

THERE ARE STORIES ABOUT those months, before the article in the *Toronto Star*, before the government came in, before they built *Quintland!*, before the trials, and the lawsuits and the lurid news stories. But there is a truth somewhere in there. And I know it.

Historians forget that part when remembering my sisters' story. The whole world saw what came after.

While that first reporter may have noted that my family seemed satisfied, that didn't last long. And far be it from our father to be satisfied with an extra three pounds. No one was going to be satisfied with one little story: not the town, and certainly not a certain bureaucrat.

It started with that story, absolutely. But then the bureaucrat—not satisfied with his finder's fee from the *Citizen*—tipped off a Toronto reporter, and then the humble gynecologist, Dr. LeFevre, was interviewed, which was followed by an article that was published in a major North American newspaper, and *voila!* Things were set in motion.

By the time we were born, the 1939 World's Fair was gearing up for its second season, beginning in October. The Fair had been doing poorly. People just weren't coming. America was lifting itself out of the Depression and former New York police chief Grover Whalen had been elected to take over operations. But what do police know about running anything?

The Fair had been less of a success than anticipated. Only the Americans could ignore Hitler while he took over another continent and instead focus on the Fair. The corporation that owned the Fair was already $11 million in the hole by 1940, and the goal was for the second season to be focused less with education and cultural uplift and more on spectacle, and my sisters were nothing if not spectacle.

The man sent to take Whalen's place was Harvey Gibson: rotund, loud, and good with numbers. Gibson was a banker who, the Fair's investors hoped, could turn things around. Gibson had been given a budget of up to $9,500 to get my sisters there, but he figured $5000 was as impossible to imagine as almost twice that to poor people, and so he would just keep the rest. Gibson's only job was turning a profit, and he knew people loved babies. At least the kind of people who had the time and money to wander around the Fair loved babies. And what a spectacle it would be.

FATHER

THE CHILDREN HAD BARELY been alive a full month when he was contacted by an American. Calling from Toronto, the man rang the town post office where the postmaster took a message that he later gave to my father. The man wanted to meet to talk about his babies. And there might be some money involved. He ignored the message and assumed it was some prank, until the Western Union Man came with a telegram. He'd never received a telegram. Ever. It was from the American, telling him he would be there the day after tomorrow to lay eyes on the girls himself and to make him a proposition.

That word, proposition, rattled around in his head for the next day or so. He imagined himself haggling with the American until he offered him more money. But money for what? What did he have but a bunch of mouths to feed and a wife who was almost criminally lazy? They had received donations, charity that in another time he would have thought was only for the laziest of Témiscaming, not for him. But the tins of Carnation milk from the Red Cross and the blankets and tins of corned beef from International Paper were too hard to turn down.

When the big black car pulled up two days later, he was at the door, as scrubbed as he could be, his face a minefield of shaving cuts where he'd knicked himself over and over again.

Gibson was the worst kind of American. Cigar chomping, loud and oily. He learned how to say *bonjour* in French only just before he'd arrived at their home, and he kept saying it over and over again, like an over-stimulated parrot, until the interpreter put a hand on his to indicate that he needed to be at least a little bit quiet in this moment. He brushed away her hand and pounded his chest.

"Gibson," he nearly screamed. "Mon nom est Gibson."

"Yes," August said. "I know."

The man smiled at him kindly, muttered something in English. August backed out of the doorway and invited them into the house, which Gibson thought looked cozy and warm in comparison to the blustery March sleet.

"This man is an idiot," the translator muttered in French to August as she stepped through the door, brushing moisture from her coat sleeves and taking his hand. She introduced herself as Elsa and told him that she would translate for the large American. She promised she would do her best to relate everything he said. The woman was petite and pretty and he liked how soft her hand felt inside his. He liked how she mocked her employer.

"And what does he want with us?" he asked her, still holding her hand.

"You mean you don't know?"

He shrugged and released her hand and called his wife from the bedroom. She came carrying the children in the basket and set them on the table. She busied herself making tea for the guests. There weren't enough cups for everyone, and so August gave her a look to let her know that she shouldn't take one.

Introductions were made all around. The translator was called Elsa and he gave this man, this Gibson, both his Christian name and his family name.

"You know of my family, yes?" he asked the American and the translator repeated the question. He shrugged helplessly.

"I think he just wants to see the babies," Elsa said.

They were just beginning to fuss slightly, and when he pulled back the blanket, they howled a bit, feeling the first burst of cold air. They seemed to try to move closer to each other, to feel the wonder and warmth of their sisters' skin pressed against their own.

The American beat his chest again and spoke in rapid fire to the translator.

"He is dazzled by them," she said. "He wants to make a deal with you. He wants to make you rich."

"Let's talk," he said in English. "I'm a reasonable man."

He had practiced this phrase over and over again in his head that morning as he'd put on his pants and a vest, the one he wore on his wedding day. And when the words came out of his mouth, he imagined that he'd been saying them his whole life. That he was a man who sat at the head of the table. A man who had the power to make things happen and that his whole life had been leading up to this moment.

Gibson's terms were these: $5000 to him for a month-long exhibit in the Canadian Pavilion inside the Second Hall at the 1939 World's Fair in New York City.

"But '39 has already passed," he argued.

"It is how these things work," the translator said. "1939 lasts two years in New York City."

And he laughed a little. Imagine, a woman who made jokes. She explained that the Pavilion would focus on the products of Nature's gifts—mining, lumber, and industry—and the most spectacular example, his five daughters. With the girls as an entry point, the world would be introduced to Canada's quality, variety, and abundance. By showcasing his five healthy, bouncing, and identical babies, the Pavilion would draw thousands, maybe millions of visitors, and with those visitors, finally, a healthy profit, not just at the Pavilion but throughout the fair.

The 1939's fair in New York was closing its doors in October 1940, and what a perfect final exhibit for the Canadian pavilion: a way to link the past and the future. For babies, and babies that looked as though they'd been made in a mimeograph machine, certainly bespoke a certain kind of future.

Gibson said all of this loudly in English, while Elsa translated as fast as she could, occasionally rolling her eyes in a way that only he could see. He couldn't make that kind of money in a year, even in two, and now it seemed his prayers would be answered. Someone else could help him provide for those five girls.

As if on cue they began to cry, mewling little cries of hunger, and his wife began feeding one at a time from a bottle. He gave her a look and hissed in a low voice that she ought to keep them quiet. Didn't she understand? Big things were happening for them, right here, at this moment. Gibson planned to exhibit their children and to make them the toast of the world. With accolades came money, maybe even more than the $5000 he was promising. She looked at him with those heavy-lidded eyes and shrugged her shoulders. She turned toward the window, bouncing one of the girls ever so slightly against her shoulder, and he wished in that moment that something would strike her dead.

"It sounds good," he finally said, turning back to the pair. "But let me talk it over with my priest and with Dr. LeFevre. Who knows if the girls will even live?"

This sounded more callous than he'd meant it to, but he couldn't take it back after he'd said it.

ELSA

THE FATHER APOLOGIZED FOR his blunder. "I've just never seen any babies so small," he said. "Of course I want my children to live."

"Of course you do," she said.

She did her best to explain his comment to Gibson, who shrugged.

"If they don't," Gibson said, "we can make plaster casts of their bodies and put them in big jars. Either way, it'll be something to see. Quite something."

He made his hand as big as a jelly jar and nodded at her to translate. She just stared at him, wondering what kind of animal she worked for. She turned to August.

"Go," she said, instead of translating. "Talk to your priest, or your family. We will wait."

"Thank you, Madame," he said. "Thank God for you."

The man put on his coat and pulled a toque down over his ears.

"I'll be right back." He didn't say so much as goodbye to his wife.

Kneeling in front of the open oven, the heat warming the basket of babies in front, the mother glared at Gibson when he lit his first cigar. Two of the babies had begun to writhe.

"Are you English?" she called out to Gibson in French. "You speak no French? You are not a Catholic?"

The babies coughed again. She looked up at him and, in English, screamed, "Out, out, out!"

Monsieur Phalene had been gone nearly an hour, and in light of the hysterical mother's response, Elsa was sure that Gibson had witnessed his investment slipping away before he had even secured it. He stepped out into the snow and she shut the door behind him.

The mother knelt in the corner over what looked like a laundry basket. Elsa's breath caught in her throat when she saw them. They were barely even babies. They looked like the rats Elsa had seen in Paris years ago—squirmy, red and hairy. What was she doing here, in this place? Elsa opened and closed the steno pad in which she'd been instructed to take notes for Mr. Gibson, that lout. The man seemed to have his hands all over her the moment they were alone in any space together. He wanted a concubine, not a translator, not a secretary.

"How are you doing?" Elsa asked the woman as she finished feeding the last of the babies. "You must be exhausted."

The mother shrugged. She was hollow-eyed and wore a dress that was too tight in some places and too loose in others. She stood up, opening a simmering pot.

"This is all they eat," she said. "The doctor calls it Seven-Twenty Formula. Cow's milk, boiled water, two spoonfuls of corn syrup, and one or two drops of rum."

She pulled the pot onto a cold burner and measured it into glass bottles.

"Your home is lovely," Elsa said. "So warm. What a wonderful wife you must be."

The mother just stared at her from the kitchen sink as she rinsed out the pan. When she was done, she smoothed her skirt and checked the seams on her stockings to ensure that they were straight.

"I had a home like this once," Elsa finally said. She didn't know why she kept talking, why she couldn't seem to stop. The woman's silence unnerved her. "I came to America from France to live with my husband."

She told the story lightly now, remembering her big American husband. His massive hands and the dust-filled farm where they'd tried to make a life for themselves. She remembered how hard she had worked to make their two rooms feel like home. It had almost been a relief when two years later, her husband died of pneumonia, his lungs filled with dirt. Stranded in a Kansas wasteland with no money and very little English, she moved to New York. She was small and pretty, which helped her to find work in the city. She worked first as a maid and then as a nanny. She was courted, but had no desire to marry again. She learned English a little at a time through her jobs and eventually saved up enough money to go to school. She lived like that, quietly, for five or six years, and by the time she'd saved up enough money to go back to France, she was already thirty-five and her parents warned her not to come because of the impending trouble.

She kept talking, the sound of her voice seeming to close the space between them until the hollow-eyed woman moved closer, sat next to her, and even took her hand. Finally, the woman burst into tears.

"I'm so sorry," Elsa said. "I didn't mean to upset you! Your life must be an endless list of tasks with five new babies. You don't need to take on my heartbreak."

"It isn't you, Mademoiselle," the woman gasped between tears. "It's me. I am not like you, beautiful and smart. I have no skills, no talents, and no idea what will become of me."

Her words were stilted as she tried to use her most proper-sounding French, remaining formal in speech despite the intimacy of their conversation. The opportunity to take a long bath, the woman said. To linger over a slice of heavily buttered toast, to wash her hair. Such little comforts.

They ended up, somehow, together at the sink. Elsa didn't know if she led the woman there or the other way round. She unpinned the woman's hair. It smelled both sour and greasy, but was long and brown and ultimately pretty.

"Your hair is lovely," she told her.

With Mr. Gibson outside, smoking his second cigar, she helped the woman out of her dress and brought a fresh one from the wardrobe. Elsa recalled wearing the same dress for two weeks after her husband's death. She was so stricken with grief, she couldn't be bothered with changing. She remembered the way she lunged at one of the Kansas farmwomen who had tried to comfort her, how she had cursed at her in French. But this woman spoke her language, seemed to know her, and yielded to her touch.

Elsa pumped water into a sink that seemed identical to the one in the grandparents' house in Toulouse. She told the woman about her grandmother's kitchen and the lilacs that grew in the field near her house. She washed the woman's hair in slow methodical strokes until she felt her beginning to weep. She kept on, and let the woman cry. She rinsed out the soap and squeezed a little lemon into the woman's hair—as her own mother had taught her to do—and brushed it as gently as she could, taking her time and handling the tangles as best she could.

"Does it hurt?" she asked.

Tears gathered in the mother's eyes and threatened to run down her cheeks again.

"Not in the least."

When her hair was dry, she twisted it into a bun and secured it with hairpins.

She unzipped the woman's dress and lifted it over the woman's head; it came down over her shoulders like a pink waterfall. Elsa looked at the network of scars covering her belly and hips, light pink and white. They crisscrossed her body like a railroad map. She had been marked by this emblem of womanhood and Elsa wondered, was this what it meant to be a mother?

The dress was ugly, but a perfect fit. She helped her do up the buttons, watching the woman as she watched herself in the warped looking glass on the wardrobe door.

All of a sudden, they were both embarrassed. They sat on opposite sides of the room and didn't speak again until the Mr. Gibson and Monsieur Phalene came in, grinning and handshaking as though all had been decided, even without the help of an interpreter.

"A man like me should be in jail," August said to Elsa. "I haven't had a nickel in nine years and now here I am with a fortune."

They decided that he would get $5000, with an additional $1,000 going to the Priest. As August explained, and Elsa translated, the priest said the birth was a miracle and so the church deserved to get a share.

Five thousand dollars seemed like a lot of money to her, too, and while she knew that the mother needed help, more help than it was possible to imagine, she wondered what that money would really do. What good could this offer that miserable woman? She looked at the woman as she picked up each child in turn, trying desperately to sooth them as they made minor-keyed snuffling sounds. This woman needed another set of hands—a sister, a mother, a friend—much more than she needed that money. And wasn't it Elsa's duty as a good Catholic and citizen for Christ to find a way to help this woman?

Once the deal had been finalized and Mr. Gibson had returned her to the bed and breakfast in Témiscaming that he'd hired for her, Elsa took a long, hot bath and thought very hard about what she could do, what she should do.

She wasn't much better off financially than those people. She was proud of the small life she'd built for herself, but even she had missed a meal or two when times were tight. She couldn't imagine how different her life could be with $5,000. What did that much money even look like? And what would she do with it? And worse, what would she do for it?

She thought of the times—the second time, really—that she could have married. Certainly, money would have made her life easier. It would have smoothed away things she was having to do now: fill the cracked tub with ruddy brown water for a bath, and later, rinse out a pair of stockings in the sink, stockings so old and so frail that she was half worried they wouldn't last the trip back to New York City. Then there would be a sad cheese sandwich from the landlady, the bread, probably just past its prime. But two hours south of here with the man—*oh, Anthony*—she imagined would have married her, she might have had an entirely different life. She would've had the kind of money to solve all her problems.

But she was a romantic at heart. Her husband, for all his rough ways, had been a tender man. There was no tenderness in this man, Gibson. Anthony had been witty, had made her laugh until she nearly cried. And he'd always given her the best books. Taken her for lovely meals. Had made conversation so bright and so cheery. But she had never been able to imagine any kind of life with him.

In spite of Anthony's kindnesses, there was a sadness that seemed to be with him all the time. She had wanted to help him too, but she hadn't known how. Anthony was the type of man to shut himself off, to mask his feelings with his intelligence. And she could not imagine lying next to him in bed, sharing confidences as she had with her husband, could not imagine the intimacy between them that came with marriage. There was something deep and dark that she couldn't touch. She thought of him now, in the bathtub, letting the water drip through her fingers and down her legs. It had been easy enough to know, he wasn't for her. It had been easy enough, after her husband died, to think about spending the rest of her life alone.

Her parents had raised her to do the right thing. It had been simple to figure out when to help the little girl with the cleft lip taunted by the village boys (well-timed rocks), or to remember not to taunt the neighbor's dog. But this woman, what was the right thing for her? The woman's smell lingered with her. Even as she climbed out of the tub, she could almost catch a whiff of the musky odor that had clung to the woman, as though the smell had settled permanently in her nose. It was like something dead.

She thought of her all evening, nibbling at the cheese sandwich while pressing her dress for her return train trip. It wasn't right, she felt certain of that. Displaying babies like objects in glass enclosures? It wasn't right. They were people—tiny people, to be sure. But she was no one, she had nothing. But who did these days?

In the safety of the little room, she imagined those children in New York, peered at behind thick, dirty glass, covered in the same film of soot and grim that she washed off her face at the end of the day. She liked this about Canada, the way it was so cold and clean. Her lungs had felt liberated the past few days, and she imagined staying here, finding some husband of French extraction, helping those girls.

She found Anthony's number in her address book. Three different scratches marked out his New York address, but there was his final Toronto telephone number, and she waited a moment before deciding to go downstairs and call him. She hadn't seen him in nearly three years. What if he had changed? But what choice did she have?

She made the call that very night. The landlady shut the doors of the parlor to give her some privacy. She placed a person-to-person call to Toronto and she was surprised when he picked up almost right away. She was comforted by his voice. It was the same, a bit nasal and that very clipped British way of speaking as though the end of their words might get caught on their lips if they didn't finish their sentences quickly enough.

She rushed through the story, skipping over the part about the mother. Those girls she said were certainly worth more than $5000, she believed, and even the Canadian government knew that much. And besides, she argued to Rhys Osborne, those children were not animals to be displayed behind glass. Words she would regret for years.

ANTHONY RHYS OSBORNE

He moved from bureaucracy to business as though it was what he'd been meant to do.

He was a man in charge of compiling numbers on infant mortality, who had done his course at Oxford in Economics and Social Sciences, and he'd somehow put himself in the lives of five French Canadian babies.

He was a man with a degree from a language school in New York and a position at the Translation Bureau who somehow became the center of the 1961 trial that investigated those girls' deaths.

He was the engineer of it all, in spite of Mr. Gibson's lofty aspirations. What would have happened to those girls had Elsa never placed that telephone call?

He had himself transferred out of the Translation Bureau, but quick.

He pretended social work had been his passion. He volunteered for the bleakest outpost in Northern Ontario, and within a month of Elsa's phone call, he was at the door of the Phalene's home. He spoke to the father in his best French, which was in truth not very good, and feigned concern.

He would tell his biographer he was gob-smacked by those babies. But not so much so that he didn't return to the office and fill out the appropriate files to petition to have the children removed from their parents' custody.

He'd seen those babies earlier than most. The experience, which he believed in his heart of hearts was most truly divine, resulted in his believing it was his duty to deliver the five to the masses.

ARCHIVES

EXCERPTS FROM THE *PHALENE Quintuplet Guardianship Act, 1935*:

"...Whereas having regard to the special and unique circumstance touching the birth and survival of the quintuplet infant daughters of August Phalene and Catherine Phalene, his wife, and for the better protection of their persons and estates and of their advancement, education and welfare, it is the interest of said children and in the public interest that a special guardianship be created. The quintuplets are declared to be the special wards of his Majesty the King, represented by the province of Ontario by a specially constituted guardian."

"...Any contract with respect to the persons or estate of the quintuplets is declared by the Act to be null and void unless entered into with the consent of the active guardians."

"The father shall continue as the natural guardian but not as the active guardian. He shall be subject to the provision of the Act and to the jurisdiction and direction of the appointed guardian in all things and for all purposes in relation to the advancement, education, welfare and protection of said children and each of them as to their custody, residence, care and attention. Each of the said children shall be brought up and educated according to the religious beliefs and faith of the father."

SISTER

HERE IS HOW A government goes about taking five healthy white baby girls from the poor.

First find a social worker to make unannounced visits to the parents' house. Make sure that he is a man and has a face like Dudley Do-Right.

When he pops in, make sure he finds the mother sitting in the corner, weeping, and name it madness instead of sadness. Then, the social worker should note the half-filled bottle of whiskey on a shelf in the kitchen, the stains on the mother's dress, the lack of food in the pantry, and an indescribable lack of order. At least that is what his notes should say: "A house without any kind of schedule that is mired in chaos."

The social worker will note the incessant mewling and an unclean smell that lingered on clothes and hair for a long time afterward; Bactine, shit, Lysol and vinegar, which is mostly what seemed to come and go in the house.

That Rhys Osborne always had a way of phrasing things. The way the government managed to take my sisters was an act of legislative genius, and unmatched in history before or since. And so my sisters became property of the crown under the *Phalene Quintuplet Guardianship Act of 1940*.

The legislation was a legal marvel, and it acted swiftly to enable both my sisters' removal from the farmhouse and their expeditious careers. It was explained by Rhys Osborne to the Canadian legislature that, due to the special and unique circumstance of my sister's birth, Catherine and August Phalene's infant daughters, for their protection, should became wards of the crown. My sisters' education, advancement, and welfare were all to be at the behest of his majesty, King George VI. Rhys Osborne stepped into the role of guardian given to him by the Minister of Public Welfare for the providence of Ontario (a former Oxford chum) and took full control of every aspect of my sisters' lives and well-being from that moment forward. Any contract with respect to my sisters' person or estate was null and void unless he approved it—until, that is, they turned twenty-one or died. In accordance with the Act, my sisters would be raised based on their father's, and to some extent, their mother's, religious and cultural beliefs. Osborne felt this would be a strong testament to the government's sincere desire to make sure that they were looking out for the interests of the parents.

Those interested later speculated that the government took my sisters solely for the purposes of exploitation. That the aim all along had been to commodify my sisters, to add them to Canada's GDP, falling in line behind lumber and oil. But for the truth, one should look at the court transcripts from the 1961 trial. Give credit where credit is due. The ingenuity of that Osborne. He'd emigrated to Canada only five years earlier, and while not exceedingly clever, in fact, not even the brightest of his family, he had an knack for marketing, for merchandising, for endorsements, for film and television contracts, for spectacle.

TÈMISCAMING

WHEN THE GOVERNMENT FINALLY came to town, the Phalenes didn't look all that disappointed. From our windows, we watched them charge into that farmhouse, and Madame Canarderie said the parents even looked relieved, and though we couldn't see their faces from our vantage point. we all thought it was true.

We saw the picture in the paper the next day, Phalene standing in the corner, hat in hand as a troop of nurses outfitted as nuns (to make for a better photograph) came in and scooped up those babies one by one.

And the picture of the mother as she sat on the bed making bundles of blankets and clothing with no apparent order, her eyes looking shyly—and perhaps suspiciously—at the camera.

We said later that those girls seemed to know that they were destined for something better, for something more than tinned evaporated milk and a two-room cottage.

They were only a little over a month old, but in those pictures in the paper they smiled! You can see how they nestled snugly against the black broadcloth of the fake habits and let themselves be carted into a line of waiting town cars, their heads tilted ever so slightly towards the flashbulbs.

SISTER

THE SWADDLING BLANKETS OUR mother used were burned. The babies were each assigned the unique color and symbol that would follow her for the rest of her days on this earth. They became a brand before they'd even spoken a word.

ARCHIVES

"CHICAGO PROMOTORS TO KIDNAP OUR QUINTS:

WHO WILL PROTECT THE EMPIRE'S MOST FAMOUS
CITIZENS?"

—The Toronto Star

ANTHONY RHYS OSBORNE

ALL HE HAD TO do was highlight the poverty. All he had to do was highlight their lack of education. All he had to do was highlight what five identical white babies could do for the country. All he had to do was lay out a scheme so simple any good capitalist could follow it. All he had to do was show that an accident of nature could easily be transformed into a dollar. All he had to do was highlight the tawdry details of conception that would rankle traditionalists in Ottawa. All he had to do was mention the hall at the Canadian pavilion inside the New York's World Fair, the matching miniature hockey jerseys that Gibson planned to put the babies in as they sat propped atop carved maple cradles, all painted in the colors of the flag.

It was the easiest thing he'd ever done. Then, he could do what he wanted.

MOTHER

HER HUSBAND WENT TO drink with other men that night, and she sat in the house, not quite ready to cry, but turning a freshly laundered diaper over and over again in her hands. They had only been gone a few hours and already she felt like the whole thing had been a dream.

The sink was stacked high with bottles and nipples, and her breasts started to leak as if on command, but still there weren't any tears.

She washed the bottles and put them in the cupboard. She swept the dried mud and bits of dead grass that had been dragged across the kitchen and the dining room out the back door and into the snow.

She scrubbed the floor on her hands and knees until it shone and her hands and knees were red and raw. She waited again and again for the tears to come.

Eventually, she put on her nightclothes and got into bed. The house was so quiet. The noise had been steady for the past week, and, as she shifted on the mattress, she remembered for the first time the howl of the winds coming off the North Bay, the way the house rustled and shifted, the scratches of the mice in the pantry trying to work their ways into the stash of winter goods.

Was this all there was now? After all that had happened, was this it?

When he came home cold, bloodless and sober, he got in bed without talking or touching.

"What happened?" she asked.

"Go to sleep."

She tried, turning this way and that. She got up once or twice that first night, her breasts aching, hearing their phantom mewling cries. But there was just more silence, profound and ostentatious, and in the morning she felt empty when she realized the tears hadn't ever come.

But after that first night, she slept fine. It was relief. Oh, she missed the babies, like she might miss one of the stray cats that hung around the barn. But there hadn't been enough time with any of them to love them, to care for them, to think about herself as a mother.

ARCHIVES

"Quintrains of Témiscaming"

Mebee you 'ear of Temiscam-
Not on de wall - no, no:
I mean de town of Temiscam
An' Monsieur Doc LeFevre, oh.

Mos' heverybody 'ear of Rome
An' Lunnon an' New York;
But no one 'ear of Temiscam
Excep' one burd - de stork.

Wan day dat stork 'e seet alone
Jus' houtside Temiscam;
An 'den 'e swear; "I'll mak' you known
Aroun' de worl', yes, mam."

Dat burd was right - dis leetle town,

She's known where'er you go;
An' heverybody in de worl'
Know Monsieur Doc LeFevr, oh.

De papers now get hextra hout
Eef wan quintuplet sneeze.
An' heverybody send night-gown
To Keep dose keeds from freeze.

An' peoples here and peoples dere-
From Nord Bay to Cape 'Orn
Are telling wat de mamma say
Wen all de chile was born.

An' wat was said by Doc LeFevre
Ees publish heveryware,
But what de poor ole man 'e say
Nobuddy seem to care.

Ay tink 'e 'as been long neglec'
An' so I tell eet you;
'E laugh een joy wen firs' was born
'E smile at nombre two.

"Eet's more dan I hexpec," 'e say,
"But twins dey may be nice,
I'll be good sport, perhaps eet's bes'
Dat I am pappa twice."

Doc LeFevre come walkin' to the den,
An' say: "while looking a ee's knee
You are a fadder once hagain:
Dat make you pappa tree."

An' soon dat doctor whisper, low:
"Oxcoos to me - eet's four."
Sapre, dat man from Temiscam
'E smile heem now no more.

An' den de poor old fellow wipe
Hees forehead on hees cuff,
An' say: "De joke ees good, but pleas',
Henough ess quite henough."

'E feel jus' lake 'e order 'im
Wan nice banan' for lunch:
An' den de waitress breeng heem quick
De whole banana bunch.

Sapre dat door she move again:
She can't keep still somehow.
"Oxcoos to me," said Doc LeFevre,
"You're five times pappa now,"

De paper tell wat mamma say,
An' wat say Doc LeFevre, oh;
But wat de old man say heemsel'

Eet's bes' you shouldn't know,

When Christmas comes, de folk weel send
Dose babbies toys an' frocks.
But pleas' oxcoos, won' someone send
De old man pair of socks...

FATHER

THEY HAD BEEN GONE nearly a month when he received a letter in the mail. The envelope, big and crisp, was stamped with the King's seal. He recognized that, with its ornate crown and the kind of lettering that looked too pretty to have come from one person. But he couldn't read the document, full of English words and confusing language.

"Can you read this?" he asked his wife.

She peered at the thing and held it up to the light. "It's in English?"

He took the envelope back from her and put it under his mattress. He assumed they wanted more tax money. Money he didn't have. The letter stayed there another two weeks, crushed by the weight of his body when he fell hard into bed to sleep at the end of the day. Things at the farm weren't getting any better. Two animals had died, and he worried if winter went on much longer, they too might starve to death. He'd already gone into debt over the babies. This was his responsibility, wasn't it? To care for her even if he didn't care about her? He ate and slept with her every day, convinced that he'd made a mistake in marrying the girl with the best *cul* and the worst reputation. What was going to become of his family's name? It had meant something once in Témiscaming to be a Phalene. And now, he was just a laughingstock.

It was Madame Renaud who made him remember the letter, when after his midday nap on what seemed like the first breezy, muddy day of spring, he found her leaning over the whitewashed fence to hand his wife an article she'd clipped from the paper with a picture of those babies, their cheeks ruddy and fat. His babies. They did not get the paper. He did not like the way it brought the world into his house and made him look at it. He had his own problems, his own worries.

He snatched the newspaper from her, unfolded it, and then read about how the children had cut their first teeth, how they lived in a hospital in Toronto that had been devoted exclusively to their care, a set of nannies available for their every whim.

"These babies will be a credit to their family and to Canada," their guardian Anthony Rhys Osborne was quoted as saying.

And who was he? Only their father. In church on Sunday he'd noticed the extra attention he got from the gaggle of childless young mothers. All of a sudden, they were eager to come by the house, to check on his wife, to offer him a meal. Women who'd never in their life paid him any mind on account of his leg and his family falling on hard times.

And here he was starving, Goddamnit! Starving!

He remembered the letter then, taking it from under the bed to his priest, where he learned for the first time that his children were not his own. That he had no right to them. No rights. And the worst of it, it didn't seem like he ever would.

When he came home from the priest, she was at the sink doing the dishes from the midday meal, humming softly to herself. And it crossed his mind, then, that he could kill her—right there at the sink, he could kill her. Because what had she done? How had she gotten herself pregnant with five babies at once? This didn't make him a man, it made him a joke. He was a joke. He turned this over and over again in his head at night. Thinking about the way those men in Detant's pasture looked at him and the way everyone looked him up and down, like he was magic, like he was a curse. This woman was going to be his undoing. He grabbed the back of her neck, twisting the skin.

"Owww!" she shrieked. "What are you doing?"

He let her go and she stared at him wild-eyed. Was this him? This casual violence. She was disgusting. He was disgusted by her. He put on his coat and went out of the house, slamming the door behind him. He walked down the main road, wrapping the coat more tightly around himself. Was winter never going to end? He kicked a frozen clod of dirt and wondered what to do. His children were gone, and he expected the farm was next. He thought back to Gibson. He could showcase the children himself—if he could get them back. He didn't see how he could make it happen, couldn't create a picture of it in his mind. It was hard for him to even consider.

The wind whistled through his thin coat and his mind cast back. He remembered how, as a boy, he'd walked this road home from school in winters just as frigid as this one. He recalled how the walk seemed endless and how he'd use certain fence posts or barns or trees to mark his progress. He'd said it to himself thousands of times: *If I can only reach the Ballrain's middle fence stake, then I'll only be three hundred steps from home. And then: If I can only pass the Honoree's bull, I'll only be a thousand yards from home. Or: If I can just reach the red silo, only a hundred and seventy-three more steps to go.*

The red silo had always been the last one, and as he strode past it and the other markers of his childhood in reverse, he thought that this might be the last time. Perhaps he would go into town and join up on the lumber barges. He imagined navigating the ice flows on the Saint Lawrence River, travelling, making a new life for himself. He would find some place where the name Phalene meant nothing to anyone but him, where he could find the kind of wife who would appreciate him.

At first, he counted footsteps away from the house, and then he lost count. But he knew he was well into the thousands by the time he arrived at the door of Doctor LeFevre's office.

First to Dr. LeFevre and then back to the priest, a man who, over the next few weeks, helped him convince the government to get them a house in town, to get him a job at the paper mill, to make them suddenly middle class. It was all much easier than he expected.

As long as he agreed not to speak. He signed a paper. He took their money. He took the job and the house they offered.

He was good at staying quiet. Good at keeping still. And when a team of men showed up to move them out of the little farmhouse, he didn't take a single thing. He didn't even lock the door behind him. He wouldn't need the dungarees, the heavy work gloves or the thick, cracked bar of lye soap to wash his hands.

Starting the very next day he would sit in an office. Wear a suit, give that wife of his an allowance and work hard to dress her up so fancy that everyone would forget that she was a bastard. He would make Témiscaming remember how grand the Phalene name had once been. They would know the name August Phalene. He would even stop going to the bar. He would stand straighter, invoke God's name, and carry a pocket watch. Témiscaming would respect him.

MOTHER

THE HOME HAD PREVIOUSLY belonged to a manager of the mill, and it felt cavernous to her. She remembered walking past it as a child when her mother would bring her into town. She would run her hands over the wrought iron gate and try to peek through to see if she could spy anyone coming through the ivy, down the path inlaid with brick. She had imagined the kinds of people who lived in this house when she was a little girl. When she was growing up, she couldn't really imagine how much money they might have. But she knew that they were people who didn't eat beans for dinner four nights a week. They were people who could go to the picture show in North Bay, who drove cars and had telephones. She knew that much. But she wasn't one of those people. The house, and what it meant, frightened her.

The place had been empty for years, and, when they moved in, the place was covered with a thick and sticky dust. The furniture, the house, and the brisk secretary who showed them around the place, all were from International Paper. The secretary told them they were not to change anything, not to touch anything, and not hammer so much as a nail in the wall without consulting the company first.

The secretary pulled back the curtains in room after room, setting off clouds of dust in their wake. Rooms with heavy, velveteen, stuffed chesterfields and tables with ceramic knick-knacks and sets of tiny, intricate silver spoons in the kitchen that the secretary told her she was to polish once a week.

There would be some assistance. A local Irish girl would come to help her with the cleaning and some cooking, too, if she wanted. Her husband looked around, unimpressed, and when they went to move from the kitchen up to the second floor, he said, "You go on. I'll see it later."

There were three rooms upstairs, each with heavy wooden furniture and a water closet at the end of the hall.

"These are linens," said the secretary. "But you'll need to go about getting dishes and drinking glasses."

"Where do you get those?" she asked.

The secretary gave her an odd look, then, "Why, you order them from Sears and Roebuck."

She blushed. It seemed so simple. But she had only ever seen the catalogue, never ordered anything from it. The farmhouse stove had been there when she moved in, an early present from her in-laws.

She sat in the kitchen of their new house that night, painstakingly picking out plates and glasses. Choosing towels as thick as anything she'd ever seen. Serving dishes imprinted with peacocks and a rifle for her husband. She found a snow shovel and a smart skirt suit for herself. She wrote in the numbers of sports coats and ties, of socks and silk stockings, and when she got to the page with the dolls, she picked out five round-faced baby dolls for her babies.

And in the morning, tired and worn out, she handed the form to her husband proudly. She had done it.

"I'll put it in the post," he said without looking at her.

He looked different that morning, odd as it was to see him in a suit and not the pants he wore around the farm. She noticed the way his legs in the trousers were a little bit bowed and that he did not look quite as smart as the other men around town she'd seen wearing these sorts of clothes. But she didn't say anything.

It had been a terrible winter. The snow that February seemed to come non-stop, and she had imagined herself stuck in that farmhouse forever with those babies, the long winter blending the days together into an endless cycle of diapers to be changed, wash to be done, food to be cooked, and dishes to be done. But now she could smell spring in the air, and, for the first time, she felt hopeful. She wasn't sure what she hoped for, but she understood that now something was better. She would have something better. Maybe not the movie posters that she'd hung on the walls of the old farmhouse, but something better than being chained to five babies, something better than having her life bound to an army of children and a husband, which meant, in other words, a life over at twenty-five. She had too much time suddenly. She read some of the books in the room that the secretary had called "the library" but which was really a room with two or three bookshelves built into the wall. Most of the books were about birds or fish, but she found an art book or two. Different, perhaps. But they held no interest for her either, and she spent many more days picking things out of the catalogue and taking walks. There was also a new garden to sit in, complete with a gardener, Jean, who came once a week and cut her an enormous bouquet of flowers.

She had never received a package in her life, so when the deliveries began arriving from Sears & Roebuck, addressed to Mrs. August Phalene, she was terribly excited. It seemed that the deliveryman came nearly every day for two weeks. All those things she had picked out from pictures of them came in crates filled with paper and sawdust. The boxes were labeled "FRAGILE" and her husband would pry them open with a bar, revealing sets of shiny, bright blue dishes, cardboard cartons of shirts, and stockings, and blouses. Box after box of ties and a new dressing gown for her. She'd never seen anything like it.

The clothes didn't fit, and she held them against her thickened body with disappointment, imagining the days when she might be able to wear them. Or, perhaps, she would let them out a bit and try to squeeze into them.

Spring turned into summer, and she followed the babies' lives as best she could, and of course there were periodic updates from Rhys Osborne. These came in the form of monthly letters from his secretary, written on personalized stationery, which included the title "Legal Guardian of the Phalene Quintuplets," printed just below his name.

But also, it would be a lie to say she thought about them every day. She didn't know them, really. She could hardly remember what they looked like.

She was often lonely. For the first time in her married life, she found herself eager for words, if only to talk through and try to make sense of what had happened to her. She lingered at the butcher shop, in the post office, and started going to mass twice a week, hoping to strike up conversation with someone. When she complained to her priest, he suggested she become active in the community—whatever that meant—and that she use her good fortune to do good in Témiscaming.

He came home at the end of the day, looking tired, but not the same kind of tired as he'd been before. There was something else in his eyes, something she did not recognize—and it frightened her, because she felt that something was coming, though she wasn't sure what it was.

There was something new in her, and clearly he had noticed. Unexpectedly, she found herself desperately trying to fend off her husband's advances. He seemed excited by her all of a sudden. In bed, his hands slid under her nightgown, and he kissed her neck and face with an urgency she hadn't ever known from him. All she could think about was: What if it happened again? Twice, she feigned women's troubles, and when she rejected him again, he finally snapped at her.

"You have duties! Wifely duties! What kind of woman are you? What kind of wife?"

She didn't know.

TÈMISCAMING

IT WAS AS THOUGH she didn't understand that we would remember who she was. She joined the social clubs that she could in town: the Catholic League of Young Mothers, the Ladies' Book Club, and a Victory Sewing Circle that mended soldiers' uniforms. But most of the women were wives of Canadian International Paper Company managers and executives. We were from larger cities and towns. Some had been flappers in the '20s, but now were dutiful wives. Some were her age and had young children to care for. None of us had husbands who were overseas in the war, like some of the less fortunate French women. Her sloppy French, her poor English, her ruddy hands and overly formal dresses. Well, she was a mess.

"Practically an animal with all those children."

"And what kind of woman lets her children be taken away?"

"They must live like pigs. Good Christian women don't do those things."

"Look at the way she behaves! You'd think she had no children at all."

"And who wears stockings during wartime? And where in the world did they get money for silk stockings when we've all been without for months?"

But they smiled at her, warmly, offered her teas and bread, and then spent whatever meeting or gathering they were attending talking about her, around her, and behind her.

ANTHONY RHYS OSBORNE

THE DEVIL WAS ALWAYS in the details. Even before the babies had been collected, he had to find a place to put them. And Toronto, the bustling city 250 miles south of Témiscaming, was perfect. There he could indulge his passions and his pleasures. It would be the perfect gateway to the money, the opportunity, the celebrity that the United States had to offer.

He chose the mansion on Queen Street in downtown Toronto—gothic and large but filled with windows, sunny in spite of its heavy oak paneling and rococo light fixtures. The house had once been a home for the mentally ill, and the large, bright, wire-filled windows were the perfect setting for a psychotic or many infants. It had been the kind of place where one (with the money to do so) put an unsavory—a loud or female family member who was causing trouble.

Many parts had been converted into apartments during the Depression, and the staff that attended to the babies' needs would live in these very small apartments, the larger communal areas and the remnants of the hospital setting being left exclusively for the care of the children. It was leased from the provincial govern-ment for $2 a year, with the sum coming from the babies' already growing estate.

The mansion was renamed "Dr. LeFevre Quintuplets

Hospital," and what had once been a dayroom for people to shake and shift under the influence of Thorazine was turned into a brightly lit playroom.

He was as disgusted by Toronto as he was captured by it. The city teemed with soldiers in training camps. Girls got off the bus almost daily from Moose Jaw or Saskatoon to work in the war effort, to put their children in one of the Salvation Army daycare centers in the city, to work in factories, to date soldiers just coming in. He hired not only Dr. LeFevre, but also a troop of staff to take care of the babies' every physical need. He had his pick of comely young girls to work as nurses, secretaries, and whatever else he wanted. He had developed a taste. For them. He took those pleasures where he could. He embraced his newly found power.

Before they had even cut a tooth, those Phalene brats had a staff of twenty at their disposal because of him.

The nuns had been a stroke of genius. The religious element, the desire to protect the children from the worst of this world, to teach them about the best of the next. By the time the girls arrived at the mansion, the evening edition of the *Toronto Star* was plastered with their tiny faces.

SISTER

NOT MANY CHILDREN GROW up in hospitals, and when they do, there is a reason for downcast eyes, frowns, and furrowed brows of concern. But, in a city where everything was in short supply and women were without sugar and stockings, there always seemed to be plenty in the Queen Street mansion. While housewives and young widows lined up at Eaton's Department store, worrying their ration cards, the staff in the Queen Street mansion had coffee to drink, deliveries of meat and produce to the service entrance, and the second-best of everything the government could find after the soldiers got their share.

In that first year, my sisters were absent of the idea of parents in any real way. They had their favorite nurses, of course. And they had Dr. LeFevre. It must have felt paternal in some capacity for LeFevre, doting on the tiny girls he'd ushered into the world himself. He took care of their every need in the way he imagined a father might. But my sisters were really and truly rats in a laboratory, albeit more prized. Studied and touched, peered at and poked, but this idea of love, and what that meant, was as foreign to my infant sisters as was life outside of the hospital.

Their days were extremely regimented. They awoke at seven o'clock and were bathed in lukewarm water in five identical basins. Then they were given a breakfast of oatmeal and bananas.

Diapers were checked and changed when necessary. And then came two hours of tests, where they were pulled and prodded. A team, led by Dr. LeFevre, weighed them, measured their limbs, took their blood pressure, and listened to their hearts. Their scalps were examined and measured. All changes in height and weight were tracked meticulously. Samples of their stool were collected whenever possible and sent to the furthest outreaches of Manitoba to be studied under a microscope. When any of them made even the slightest change that separated them from the pack, they were whisked away for minutes, or hours, or days, to be examined by another team of doctors. Researchers worked to create something that felt like a natural environment. And there is something about those earliest days of life—even for those with five identical faces—that can feel remarkably mundane.

Following their intensive study, diapers were checked again, hair brushed and faces wiped, and then lunch was served promptly at noon. Lunch was meant to take a full hour, to aid in their digestion. They were fed slowly, which not infrequently resulted in bursts of fury and frustration from my sisters. This hour was supervised by a Dr. Theodore Drake from the Hospital for Sick Children. They were fed a diet of Pablum and canned fruit. Pablum, Dr. Drake's own innovation, was a cereal meant to fight off rickets and to prevent deficiencies in Vitamin D, something that my sisters always lacked.

There was next an hour allotted for naps. And my sisters slept soundly, a nurse positioned next to each crib to watch as their tiny chests moved up and down. They spent time after nap in the mansion's garden, with two nurses assigned to each sister. Here, they learned to crawl and later, to toddle about, getting as much sunshine as they could in a half hour. The late fall and early winter winds sometimes chapped their little cheeks, which had the odd effect of making them look even prettier. Rhys Osborne approved.

They were monitored daily for cold, coughs, infections and other childhood ills, and when they came, as they were bound to, the makeshift hospital went into crisis mode, rigorously enforcing mandatory hand washings and sealing itself off from anyone but the staff.

A scare came in December when Calendre and Fabienne both came down with colds. The staff was rigorously questioned and my two sisters were quarantined for a week as they sniffled through the woes that plague every infant.

During good weeks, the mansion, outfitted with state-of-the-art medical equipment, was toured bi-weekly by doctors in training who wore paper masks and gloves, and while they were never permitted to touch my sisters, they watched them as they grew.

ARCHIVES

Nurse's Log 1940

- **July 5th**: Anglette sits up unaided.
- **July 8th**: Calendre and Eliane follow suit.
- **July 27th**: Madeline and Fabienne sit up unaided.
- **October 19th**: All five girls wave goodbye to the doctors with some prompting from their nurses, who encouraged them by calling out "Say bye-bye to the doctors."
- **November 25th**: Fabienne and Dr. LeFevre engaged in a game of peek-a-boo. The nurses had recently taught them this game— two weeks ago. They seem to be learning quickly.
- **December 1st**: Non-compliance episode.
  Time: 4:45 p.m.
  Activity: Play.
  Description of request: To stay in playroom.
  Description of child's behaviour: Ran out, cried for 1 minute.
  Adult treatment: Isolated 5 minutes, brought back.
  Result: Co-operation.

SISTER

WHILE THERE IS NO indication of love or even affection in these notes, some of these researchers did indeed take a favorite. You have to understand that this was the best my sisters could hope for. Because for nearly everyone else in their lives, they were a source of income. Dr. Richard Sleeman of Hamilton, in Toronto for medical training before he ended up being shipped to the front, took no fewer than a page and a half of notes a day on my sister Eliane alone. Betty Jenning, a recent transplant from Ottawa, who was training to become a nurse, wrote giddily in her journal about Fabienne's terrific smile and Madeline's cute habit of hiccupping after dinner.

These remembrances of my sisters as innocents make me happy. It makes me wonder if there would have been a different ending to their story if any of these people had stopped to raise a question about their care, about the troublesome fact that my sisters had never seen any other children, never saw an adult not scrubbed from head to toe in disinfectant and outfitted in medical garb. History is littered with the corpses of unraised questions.

My sisters were asleep by eight o'clock each night, a rotating shift of eight to ten nurses during the evening hours to care for their needs. As the hospital wound down for the day, the task of compiling notes as well as other standard household chores was performed. Laundering my sisters' diapers became the single and specially assigned task of two young nurses who had only recently completed their certification. (Years later, during the trial, one broke down crying and confessed to keeping a diaper as a souvenir of her time working there.) Every space was disinfected as my sisters slept, and the staff began in ten-minute shifts to report to Anthony Rhys Osborne's office on the mansion's third floor to discuss the day's activities.

The whole organization ran with military precision, Rhys Osborne at the helm. And it seemed that any information he released about my sisters only seemed to quicken the world's appetite for knowledge about them.

While there had been articles in a variety of papers, and even a photograph in *Time Magazine* (which dubbed my sisters "the world's greatest news picture story"), they didn't appear in their first advertisement until right before their first birthday.

There they were, my sisters, dressed in matching white nightgowns made of a sheer organza, peering pop-eyed into the lens. They were only seven months old when the picture was taken, all positioned on a tatty bed outfitted with soft white pillows on which my sisters reclined. The ad man placed a brand new can of syrup (label facing perfectly outward) behind each head, so perfectly identical and focused toward the camera that it was as though God Himself had stilled the babies' movement to hock corn syrup.

My sisters, lucky for Rhys Osborne, were extremely photogenic. Our parents' odd collection of features had produced a very pretty result. All five were dark haired with rosy red cheeks and olive-colored complexions and the kind of blue eyes that even in babies felt accusatory.

ARCHIVES

Quintuplet Lullaby
(Fifty Tiny Toes)
By Gordon V. Thompson

Babies five in number, all prepared for slumber
Cuddle down and close your drowsy eyes. God above will send you
Angels to attend you; soon you'll hear them sing your lullabies.

Chorus
Fifty chubby tiny toes! Every cheek a red, red rose!
Here a fairy lingers, kissing fifty fingers, crooning while your dark
eyes close.
In your beds contented lie; go to sleep and don't you cry!
Vesper bells are ringing, Angel voices singing, Quintuplets, your
lullaby.

All a-board the steamboat, Fairyland's own dreamboat,
Sail away to gleaming magic isles. When the sun gives warning,
You will know it's morning—home again to cheer us with
your smiles.

SISTER

I LIKE TO THINK that these were mostly happy times for my sisters. I even felt jealous at certain moments as I watched them grow, tottering around on chubby legs and peering out the windows as soon as they could pull themselves up to look at life on the outside with a mixture of curiosity and fear.

Even in their first twelve months of life, my sisters—whose smiles became brighter every day and who began to fill out— remained delicate to the touch. A washcloth could impart a severe bruise and even the gentlest of hair brushings at times produced a scabbed head. They were treated like delicate china and handed from one gloved individual to the next. But they played with each other, and as soon as they had started to put on a little weight, that monster Osborne had camera crews filming their baths, their diaper changes and, unfortunately for Fabienne and Calendre, a particularly painful round of shots, their faces scrunched in breathless wailing.

But along with these images were pictures of all of my sisters playing with their nurses, pushing balls through the hospital playroom and smiling, first gummy and then slightly toothsome. These all were packaged and ready to be sold as a holiday book in time for December 1940. *A Year with the Phalene Five* was of course a bestseller, and in it, for the first time, Calendre was labeled the shy one;

Fabienne was the comedienne; Eliane was the flirt; Madeline, the most adorable; and, of course, Anglette was fetishized as the one with the mole. Anglette's mole distinguished her from the rest almost right away, and by either nature or nurture, she became the fearless leader among my sisters—crawling first, sitting up first, and the first to eat solid foods. The other four seemed to wait for her lead.

ARCHIVES

Excerpt from Scientific Grant Application

... In my time working on Dr. LeFevre's team at the hospital, I have been honored and excited to have the opportunity to work so closely with the Phalene Quintuplets.

I petition the government of Ontario today for a grant to continue the further study of the children. I am a researcher in the area of child psychology at McGill University, and I believe these children offer a unique opportunity to generate an active lab for the study of children and the attendant child development theories. They will allow for the testing of child rearing methods to assess the necessity of "a family environment."

Healthy psychological development is often undermined, not promoted, by parents and teachers. Consider how these girls might thrive when surrounded by people who are skilled in different methods of child development. The average lower income Canadian parent is not aware of the remarkable advances made in child rearing techniques.

My colleagues in the zoology department at the University of Toronto concurs that this is a unique opportunity for study.

We will monitor, track and closely watch all of their behaviors.

This method of child rearing will encourage play while rejecting bribery and violent punishment. Its fixedness to routine should be reassuring. The children will be protected from the outside influence of family and will function as perfect specimens for our work in the field of child psychology....

ANTHONY RHYS OSBORNE

ANYONE WHO MET THEM marveled at the steadiness with which all five babies gazed at adults. It was odd. He hated being alone with them. He felt like they could see his thoughts. It was wholly unsettling.

Once, peering into their nursery in the early morning hours, he'd felt the focus of all five sets of eyes locked on him. They should have been sleeping, but there they, all five, were sitting bolt upright in their cribs. Their eyes were on him and he tried to match their gaze. They didn't smile or laugh. They just looked at him, unblinking. And finally, one opened her mouth and clearly said, "No."

He had never heard them speak before, and it frightened him. He wasn't even sure why. But he'd slammed the door as quickly as he could and called for one of the nurses. It was one of the few times he felt guilt in those twenty years. But the moment, as is typical of guilt, was fleeting.

He was in the office every morning by nine o'clock. Tea and a scone, and then right down to it. He didn't see many of the other staff during the day, and he hardly ever saw the babies. It was easier this way, not to think about them, when they were on the other side of the house and he could pretend that they were an idea instead of people. It was easier to broker deals for ideas. It was easier to forget the way babies might not like some things. Many things. It was easier to forget that these were her children he was talking about. He managed. And most days, he barely thought about them.

The marketing appeal of those girls was broad. And as they grew, so did the opportunities to use them to sell nearly anything. He created a byzantine maze of licensing agreements and fees. And with vigor, he went after anyone who tried to use my sisters' names or likenesses without express written consent. For example, Osborne filed cases in Canadian High Court against Quaker Oates, Hershey's Chocolate, and even the Canadian International Paper Company, who founded and funded the town of their birth, for trying to lay claim to the babies in any way.

At the end of their first year in January, 1941, he hired more staff. The children were alive. Alive and well. He had never expected it. They had been so frail looking when he initially saw them. He had imagined this might all be over more quickly than he had initially anticipated.

And in their life, in their continued existence, he saw potential. The kind of potential that, he hoped, would leave him wealthy.

He hired a full-time photographer and lured a nurse trained in the Pablum regimen away from the hospital. He laid the ground-work for a birthday party on the grandest scale, the kind every child in Canada would want to be invited to. And while the babies weren't actually to attend, he managed to get the *Toronto Star* to devote an entire issue to them on the anniversary of their birth. But this was only the beginning of the publicity blitz.

He cajoled the editors at *The Canadian Ladies Home Journal* to do an article on how to throw a Quint-themed birthday party to cele-brate the day in January. Next, he went to *Life Magazine* and offered to create an elaborate set-up in the mansion kitchen. He would have the babies placed in highchairs, identical in all ways except color, with five identical cakes for each of them to tear into, all of which was photographed for a four-page spread. When he pitched it at the New York offices, he could see the way the editors' faces lit up, the way they were dazzled by him. He set up interviews with Dr.

LeFevre for newsreels in French and English, and he went so far as to escort a crew to that damned pit of a town Témiscaming to photograph a nearby lake where packs of childless young, married couples clamored to drink from its cool, clear waters, hoping to gain some of its powers of fertility.

As their birthday approached, he supervised as an influx of gifts came from all over the world. Five baby-sized diamond tennis bracelets from South Africa, monogrammed wool booties from New Zealand, hair ribbons from the Dutch, prams from the English, and on and on and on. Things from all over the world. And to be sure, Canadians celebrated the children's birth, too—sending clothing, blankets knitted in their signature colors, maple leaf toques and miniature hockey jerseys. And books, and toys, and games, and dresses. Quint-mania seemed to take the whole world by storm, and he offered the children up as Canada's newest export, better even than maple syrup. Something about which the country, on a global scale, could finally be proud.

And he was most proud of all as he watched the sums moving into his personal account, his piece of an empire built on those Quints.

ARCHIVES

PHALENE QUINTUPLETS
For Bee Brand Golden Corn Syrup

The Phalene Quints get a tablespoon each of
Bee Brand Golden Corn Syrup every day to keep
them healthy and strong.
Bee Brand Golden Corn Syrup, the latest inde-
pendent manufacturer of corn syrup and starch
products in the British Empire. To be sure
of getting the Products of this all-Cana-
dian Company, ask for them by name. Bee Brand
Golden Corn Syrup.

MOTHER

THE CAR CAME OUT of nowhere that morning. She'd been in the kitchen, halfheartedly listening to the wireless radio from the drawing room. Her husband had just brought it into the home the week before, and he'd insisted it remain on all the time. The broadcast was in English, and she listened distractedly as she watched the darkening piles of snow in the yard, hoping that it would soon snow again to cover all the ugliness.

Having the wireless on all day made it feel like someone was in the house with her, watching her, and she couldn't stand it, so she avoided that room during the day. She was terrified that if she actually did turn it off, he would—somehow—catch her. That he would come home and it would be quiet and he would know how much she hated the thing, and he would be angry.

And she only cared about that because it was easier when he wasn't angry. Easier to keep the house quiet and do what she wanted.

She was waiting. She knew that. But she wasn't sure for what. It was different now than the waiting she'd done before the babies. Different too from the waiting that happened after they'd been taken. It seemed now like she wanted it all to end, like what had happened to her was all that was ever going to happen to her. What was she good for now?

The Christmas holiday had been a sad affair. Every Phalene she'd ever met, and many more she hadn't, crammed into the house, everyone pestering her with questions about the children. Did they think she knew any more than they did? She'd seen their pictures in the magazines and newspapers. She could hardly recognize them as her own children, and when she searched the smudged newsprint for some reminder that they were hers, she felt a kind of mounting hopelessness that they were the best that she could ever do, and that now, it didn't mean much for her or to her.

Her husband had been furious when he'd seen that everything she had so carefully ordered from the Sears Catalogue had been deducted from his paycheck. The accountant at the paper company told August that this was the way it worked, that nothing was simply given. And in response to this news, he'd yelled at his wife that he wanted to break every dish, to rip every sheet in half. But he knew that it was his money he'd be wasting, and he couldn't bear the thought of it. Instead, he made her pack up everything they hadn't used. And so she cried and begged and even screamed over crates of dishes and vases made of delicate glass.

She'd started to worry, too, that she was pregnant again. There was that same horrible feeling she'd recognized. Her period wasn't late yet, but she felt with certainty that it would be. Staring out the window, her breath clouding the glass, she felt that same anxiety all over again. What if it were six babies this time, or seven? What would she do? What would become of her?

She saw the car pull up—black with wood paneling on the side and shiny chrome tires. The man who came out of the driver's seat was tall and handsome. He had forgotten his gloves, and he rubbed his hands together before taking three swift steps up the walk. She rushed to pull off the apron that, out of habit, she had taken to wearing around the house.

The knock on the door was three swift taps, and she was there before the last of them had landed.

"Madame Phalene?" His hat was in his hand now.

"Mais, oui."

"Je suis ici pour le compte de Monsieur Osbourne. Je suis ici pour vous emmener à la fête d'anniversaire quintuplées."

How had she forgotten? It was their birthday! How had it only been a year? Or maybe, how had it already been a year? On different days, both feelings competed with one another. What was certain was that their whole lives had changed. But what about her husband? He was already in the car. Arrangements had already been made. She was only to get her coat and hat.

She did as she was told.

In the car to Toronto, her husband barely spoke to her. Instead, he read the paper, something he never did at home. And she watched through the window as they went south through thickets of trees and then past a vast expanse of water.

She'd never seen anything like it, stretching out as far as she could see toward the horizon.

"That is Lake Ontario, Madame," the driver told her. Everywhere there were people, and cars.

"August, look!"

He pushed the paper down for a moment and glanced out the window, but he didn't say a word.

Toronto was a blur, and loud, nothing like Montreal as she remembered it. Had she loved her husband then? She could hardly remember. The driver left her in the care of three women inside a beauty salon painted the most obscene shade of pink she had ever seen. Three English-speaking women buzzing around her, cutting and setting her hair. She was brought new clothing, things that would hide the weight that still lingered from the pregnancy, or perhaps was returning from the child to come. She hardly recognized herself when they were done. In spite of their hard work, she still looked unkempt. The curls they'd set dropped and the shoes they'd brought her pinched her toes and made her hobble as she walked. The dress that was too tight in the bust, which they'd tried to cover with a jacket. But even that didn't fit quite right. The three women smiled at her, adjusted her blouse and her stockings, clucked at her in English, and then as if by magic, the car with her husband and Mr. Osborne's driver had reappeared.

Her husband was clean shaven and wore what looked to be a new suit.

They drove through the city and she craned her head up at buildings so tall she couldn't believe there were people in them. Eventually, the driver took them down an alleyway to a back drive with a large garage. Ten young women in crisp nurses' uniforms stood at attention. It seemed they were all blonde and shapely, and they welcomed her and her husband in the best French they could. She still didn't know where they were, or what to expect from this birthday party. Wherever they were going, everyone seemed to be in a hurry. Shuffling down a long corridor done in dark wood, her husband held her by the elbow to steady her, but also to hurry her up.

They pushed open the door at the end of the hall and an explosion of light radiated out of the space, blinding her. It took her a moment to realize the light came from camera flashbulbs, seemingly hundreds of them popping and bursting, the heat of spent bulbs warming her cheeks. She squinted into the room trying to make out a person, or the babies, when she realized all at once that she would never be able to see anything.

A gentle tug on the elbow took her to a small divan in the corner of the room where she and her husband were enveloped by photographers and reporters. Again and again, she shielded her eyes from the glare of the cameras. She sank far too deeply into the velveteen divan. She let him do the talking; she cast her eyes down and avoided questions as much as she could.

It took her a few minutes before she noticed that the children were practically right in front of them, seemingly unbothered by the ruckus as they played on a bear skin rug. Up close, they looked even more foreign. She could not remember which one had wet herself constantly, or which one had occasionally rolled onto her sister. Why couldn't she tell one from the other?

She did her best to avoid seeming awkward in spite of the too-small jacket and the too-tight shoes and the feeling that, at a moment's notice, her clothing would become completely undone, would pop and expose her girdle, her garter, and her dimpled thighs.

She leaned over twice, each time whispering hoarsely, "*mon petit chou*." The babies smiled at her, turning their heads to look, and she wondered if they remembered her voice, or her touch. But when she tried to reach for them, they recoiled from her. She felt—for the first time, perhaps—those pangs of motherhood, that desire for these girls to know her, to love her.

They weren't hers, if they ever had been. The transaction was complete.

ARCHIVES

Radio-Canada's News – January 5th, 1941 – Radio Transcript

"And how are the children doing, Mr. Phalene?"

"Oh, just fine, just fine. Precious, precious little girls."

"And how different is your life today than this time last year?"

"Oh, very different. I have a new job, and a new house. Many new opportunities."

"And do you worry that this is due to your daughters' fame, sir?"

"No, no. Not at all. I am hard working man, and I am only now seeing the reward of that work, I suppose."

"And you don't think that has anything to do with exploiting your children's name?"

"Well, it is my name, was the name of my father, and my grandfather, and my great grandfather."

"And how often do you see your children?"

Silence.

"As often as any father sees his children, I suppose."

"And how often is that?"

No response.

"And is it true that you actually have no legal rights in relation to your children? That in fact you are not permitted to see them without permission?"

No response.

SISTER

AND AT THE END of it all, Edward R. Murrow, already stationed in London as a war correspondent, interviewed my parents and Rhys Osborne on the wireless. My sisters were so captivating, so transfiguring, in their ability to just live that the Washington Post reported that even Hitler took notice of the Quints.

It would be years before my sisters understood the idea of parents, and who they were and what they were to mean in a child's life. They didn't understand—didn't have a context to understand—the way that parents should love, protect and cherish their children. They didn't understand what it meant to be taken care of not out of obligation but out of something far more primal. I wanted to do all of that for them. But I am just a dead baby— an observer and, occasionally, a teller of stories, but without any power to act. My sisters learned of the reciprocal experiences of teaching and learning with parents exclusively through depictions of such scenes in books and television.

By the time my sisters turned two, my parents wouldn't even be invited to the spectacle.

SISTER

Report from child psychologist Dr. Matthew Stroz, "Quint Hospital" Log:

"... the Phalene quintuplet sisters are below average mentally as shown by the Gesell, Merrill-Palmer, and Kuhlmann-Binet tests. The retardation is greatest in language and least in motor functions. The children are growing more rapidly than average, and predicted that they will have caught up to the norm by the age of five years..."

PART TWO

ANTHONY RHYS OSBORNE

HE WAS BORN IN London in 1900 to George Osborne, the 9th Duke of Leeds, his second son and his first disappointment. As he'd heard it told, he'd been delivered with a caul on his face. His father was a superstitious man and on to his third Duchess of Leeds, the two earlier women suffering the ills of childbirth and lack of care. So the Duke was sixty by the time Anthony made his arrival in the world.

His oldest half-sibling, a brother (who was to be the 10th Duke of Leeds, and the kind of man who quietly preferred bedding soldiers to fighting alongside them), was twelve years his senior and their father's pride and joy. There was a half-sister, too, but he hadn't met her. Someone dragged her up on the first day of his trial in 1961. By then she was a tiny and frail old woman, her hair still done in pin curls. She spent the day grousing that she had come to see the damned babies and sat smoking Benson and Hedges in the lobby any time there was a break.

His childhood was neither remarkable nor happy. The family house was old and cold and there were no other playmates. His father insisted that maths should make a good hobby and his mother spent most of the day in the bath, having their maid constantly refresh the water. His mother, naturally, was much younger than his father, and she hated the heavy-handed feeling of what was later called Victorianism. Life had oppressed her into a marriage, corsets, and the company of older men, all of which she despised. She joined the suffragette movement in 1912 and spent as little time as she could at the manor house from then on, staying with friends in London and eventually renting a small house of her own.

He was without a mother's love, he supposed, and that had hardened something in him. But in truth, he couldn't remember either of his parents well. What he did remember was the house and its cavernous rooms, its musty smelling kitchen in the basement. The warmth of the cook's bosom when she hugged him, the jellied side dishes that were served at formal functions and the way his father enjoyed shutting the door to his study, or to his smoking lounge, or to any other place with a door that Anthony might be kept out of.

He remembered rattling around the house, aimless and lonely. He remembered the thrill of starting prep school if only so he could be around other people all the time. Still, he was the one boy who had to stay there during the holiday season, alone in the dormitories, eating Christmas puddings with the school's headmaster.

He took his courses at Oxford in economics, but his father died midway through his study. And the brother, the 10th and last Duke of Leeds, who had never liked him much, cut him off almost entirely. A small inheritance from his mother allowed him to finish his courses. And as soon as the war ended, he left for America where a job at a bank came somewhat suddenly. He hadn't remembered applying for it, but he took it anyway, desperately wanting to move away from England. And what could be more English than that? Wasn't it the duty of any good citizen of the Empire, to make a name or life for yourself in the furthest reaches of its borders? To make a name and a life for yourself in a place where you weren't just the younger brother of that Duke who threw crashing good parties?

In England, Anthony had thought that America would be some kind of paradise. Instead, he found New York City dirty and clotted with bodies. His bank job had him dealing with figures on international finance. He took a room in a men's hotel that gave him a small bed and a desk and a WC down the hall.

But there wasn't a decent drink to be had, and at twenty-five, to his shame, he was still a virgin. He couldn't talk about women like the other men in the bank. Most had wives, or girlfriends. And some had both. And there was something so vulgar, so American in the way they carved up a women's anatomy. Like a roast chicken. There had been talk like this at prep school, but he had never been invited to participate, and uninvited, he didn't know how to begin.

He found himself a couple of hobbies. Languages mostly. He read the classics in Latin at the New York Public Library. There he saw things he could barely imagine: men playing with themselves in public, couples in study carrels locked in passionate embrace, and once, while in the loo, a crush of Italian public school children had slammed their hands against the door until he opened it. Everything about the city felt wrong, and unfamiliar, and like it needed to be fixed.

He had seen the woman on the corner near his office on Wall Street for months. She always wore an elaborate hat, generally with a peacock feather or two and was always fashionably dressed, her curls hung loosely around her face. She looked like she was waiting for someone. From a distance, he had noticed how beautiful she was. But when she got close to him that day and leaned in, he caught a whiff of her perfume and the garish colors of the cosmetics smeared on her face and he knew then he'd been wrong. He understood then what kind of woman she was. He'd paid her, let her take him to the clapboard house near the Bowery.

He had thought about it before, of course. Walking up and down Broadway in the late hours of the evening. A lot of times avoiding the acts of pleasure going on behind the doors of the other rooms in his boarding house. In Times Square, he watched women open their coats to reveal peignoirs or lacy stockings. There were women who winked at him in the half-darkness under the glow to the electric advertisements. But that place didn't feel real and he couldn't imagine approaching those women, or offering them money, or worse still, haggling, like a common north London fishwife.

But now he followed this woman, down side streets and through alleyways, until they got to a house. The front hall was dark and covered in cobwebs. It didn't look like anyone lived there.

"In the parlor," the woman with the hat grunted.

He pushed through two double doors on a hinge into a threadbare parlor. The curtains were drawn and just the tiniest bit of light was visible on the floor.

Two sofas sat at opposite ends of the room, each with a giant slash down the center, stuffing pulled out from the middle. The place smelled musty, as though it had been shut up during many wet months, and the air felt damp and heavy. Although it was July, no breeze passed through, and in the light that dappled the room, he saw heavy dust particles hanging in the air. The bookshelves were completely empty and the ornate ashtrays next to the doors overflowed, stubbed-out cigarettes littering the bare wooden floor. Everything in this room was covered with a heavy coat of dust.

At the window stood a woman dressed in something he hadn't seen since childhood: a dress with a bustle and collar buttoned up tight.

"You need a woman?" she asked softly.

"Yes…yes, I believe so."

She laughed a little in a way that sounded like she was choking.

"What kind of woman?"

He tried to remember if he had enough money and couldn't recall. He tried to think about what he remembered from every changing room and midnight prep school whispering.

"Kind?"

"Old? Young? Colored? Blonde? You name it, I have it."

The question surprised him. He hadn't realized that he might be able to choose. He'd imagined instead that he would be pushed at random into some room and that she as a professional would know what to do.

"Young, I guess."

There was that same odd, laughing cough and she made a gesture and the woman with the hat reappeared.

"Take him to Petunia," she said.

Up the creaky stairs behind that giant feather. It felt like he was going to his death. Down a tight corridor and then she rapped three times on a dark door before opening it and ushering him in.

The room was thick with the scent of powder and a mentholated smell of something bought from a druggist to ease a chest cold. The girl—not a woman—sat in a corner blowing her nose into a hanky. She couldn't have been more than sixteen, and she looked nearly starved.

She raised her eyes up at him, and he noticed they were hard.

"So, whadyya want?"

He averted his eyes from her body, from the ribs that seemed to poke through the skin, her crossed legs like matchsticks.

He stared at the ceiling, thinking that he should leave, that he should go back to his room, to his book, to stay a virgin a little while longer. The longer he went without speaking, the more he was sure that was what he should do.

She sighed, frustrated.

"It's five," she said. He didn't know why. "Take off your clothes and lie down."

He turned away from her and undressed. Then he laid down on the small bed that creaked under his weight. There was little more than a sheet on the mattress, and like everything else in the room, it looked far from fresh. When he looked up and back over to the girl, he saw that she was bent over and peering into her own crotch. Finally, she looked up.

"Ready?" she said.

He nodded.

She climbed on top of him and he was relieved that she seemed to know what to do.

When it was over, she climbed off and picked up his trousers, while he lay there, unsure of what to do.

"I'm taking six dollars," she announced, "That was too much work. You have to tell a girl if you never been to the rodeo."

She had taken the money and hidden it away somewhere by the time he got up and got dressed. He wanted to say "thank you," but the breath was knocked out of him and so he nodded again and walked down the stairs and back out into the street as quickly as he could.

Years later, he would try to remember what the girl looked like, or sounded like, or smelled like, or even where the place was located. Perhaps it was a type of blessing that it felt like it had happened to someone else. Like it had been a dream.

He tried to stop thinking about it then, but he wasn't doing well at work either. The figures and maths he had studied so hard at Oxford were clearly not his strong suit, and he made one mistake and then another until his boss took a tone of voice with him that he had only ever heard before when his father addressed the hounds.

He was demoted and given a desk in the back where he spent most of the day reading his library books and doing the best he could to muddle through the statistical data they gave him, most of which was confusing to him. It seemed like painful little fictions.

When after two years he'd finished his list of classics and still no prospects had presented themselves, he enrolled in language school. He'd made no friends in the interim, had no close associates, had not been on a date. He hadn't returned to that girl in the dark room, either.

Later, it pleased him that when lawyers searched for witnesses from this time in Osborne's life, they'd found them extremely hard to come by. The librarian was long dead and the other people who lived at the hotel were nearly impossible to locate. The only people they could find were the other students at the language school, one of whose testimony noted a predilection for staring, even when the person in question would try to break his gaze.

He did have a gift for language, however. With Latin as a base, he mastered German in six months and then turned his attention to the romance languages, gaining Spanish, French, and Italian by the end of a year. Then he turned his attention to Slavic languages, and it was in his Hungarian class that he first met Elsa.

He sat behind her in class and watched as she took notes in handwriting faint, tiny, and neat. Everything about her was faint, tiny, and neat. Her hair was her only distinguishing feature. Dark brown and heavy, she wore it coiled in an unexpected twist on top of her head that he thought of as continental.

He fell in love with her before they had even exchanged a word, and by the time he had worked up enough nerve to ask her to join him for an ice cream, the class was nearly over. During their initial date they spoke in French, both for him to practice and for her to feel comfortable. They talked for nearly four hours about the oddities of American life, about a shared passion for the Chinese and Polish foods they had discovered, and about what it was like to live in a city with no family.

But she had plenty of friends and soon he found himself with invitations to bars, meeting other English expatriates. Because of Elsa, he was engaged, finally. Had engagements, that is. Fun. He had a social life that took him in and out of New York City's speakeasies. There wasn't ever much money among this group of friends, but it seemed as though Elsa's people, as he came to think of them, always planned picnics at the beach or dancing in some beautiful hotel or crashing a party where a friend of a friend had been invited. And he loved it all.

But he never managed to move things past friendship with Elsa. He knew there had been some sadness in her life—a husband who died young and, of course, like him she'd been a child in Europe during The Great War. Eventually he grew to feel content that that was the way things would be.

In the spring of 1928, while having lunch at a coffee shop, he invited her to a ball for an acquaintance of his, an English diplomat called Harry.

"I'll have to borrow a dress," she said. "But yes, I think I would like that very much."

The dress she borrowed was lilac colored and beaded. She had pinned a broach into her thick hair and she glowed almost, or so it seemed to him.

"I'm so excited," she said, skipping down the steps to meet him. She took his arm and, since it was a nice night, they decided to walk the three or four blocks to the party. He enjoyed the way the beads on her dress sounded as they clicked and clinked together beneath her thin coat. His tuxedo had seen better days. But he never felt as happy as he did that night with her on his arm.

The mansion on 5th Avenue had nearly two hundred rooms. Harry was a prep school chum and had been chosen as ambassador mostly due to his father being good friends with the President. He had been a widely unsuccessful student, but life stateside, with these big gaudy houses and big gaudy parties and big gaudy people, seemed to suit Harry just fine.

He could not remember the last time he had been in a place with so many people. The house was dark and smoky, and he and Elsa moved from room to room, watching people shimmy and shake. Women like snakes coiled around men in the haze of rooms filled with the threadbare furniture of the English elite that reminded him of his childhood but that seemed unfamiliar and disorienting in the smoke and the jazz and the noise.

"Do you know any of these people?" she called out over the roar of the band.

"Not a one!" he said.

But he wished he did. He wished that he had the kind of life where he could throw parties like this.

Of course, Harry had liquor, Canadian Club Whisky and gin smuggled over from England, not like the ghastly stuff that they sold at the speakeasies. They had two drinks, maybe three, before

Elsa went off to find the powder room. And when he tried to go find another drink, he found himself in another part of the house, entirely lost and completely disoriented.

His stomach turned and he went through a doorway that turned out to be a stairway to the basement. It was quieter down there, even though countless people were mashed into the small space. Someone pressed a drink into his hand, which he downed immediately. He quickly gained another.

"I like a man who can keep up with me," said the woman who was suddenly pressed against his side.

She had one of those husky voices that he'd always thought of as distinctly American. Her short blonde hair was cropped close to her head and she wore a lavaliere with a huge stone at the bottom. She touched his arm in a way that made him spill his second drink on her, something which made her laugh. He couldn't have expected this laughter. She had a kind of cheap and fast look to her that he was starting to like.

It wasn't love exactly, but he was dazzled. Stunned even. This Beatrice Underwood Townsend pulled him into her orbit in the same way she pulled him to her mouth for a kiss that night: rough, forceful, and without any regret. She was as terrifying as she would be pliable.

But she wasn't American after all. She was out colonizing too. An English heiress, she was living the high life in what she called "gay old New York." Her family wasn't peered as his was, and try as she might, as her parents hoped, it didn't seem as though there was any chance she or any of her siblings would be made Lord or Lady any time soon. Beatrice, or Bea as she was known to her friends and eventually to him, had lost a brother and then a childhood paramour in the Great War. She compensated for this by drinking as much as she could and spending her parents' fortune with the same abandon.

He quit his bank job the following spring after they were married. She gave him control of her finances, and he invested and bought them lovely things to furnish the Upper East Side penthouse that had been a wedding present from her parents, who hoped that the things they'd been hearing about his brother, the 10th Duke of Leeds, were true and that, soon enough, Anthony would have access to that title.

Beatrice was never what might be called happy. She was prone to fits of sadness, to raging, to cutting herself, to aborting the children they created together. In general, Mrs. Rhys Osborne worked to make his life as miserable as possible. She spent a lot of time fantasizing about her brother-in-law's death and the picture of herself as a Duchess. She went to many parties; she drank until she couldn't stand in public and made him hate her inside of a few months.

And in the spring before the market crashed, in what he thought she imagined as a final act of punishment, Bea threw herself off the balcony of their penthouse.

He hadn't been home when it happened. He was down drinking in one of those speakeasies in the Bowery, trying to steel himself for the night ahead. For the fights had grown increasingly long, increasingly loud.

By the time he came home in a liquor-softened haze, the police had already gone and it was the doorman who was left to share the tragic news.

Money does wonders for some people. It gave him a new sense of self-worth. He stood taller, he dressed better, he even put on a few pounds. As a widowed man with money, even if it was his wife's money, he felt more masculine than he ever had in his life.

And then the crash came. The penthouse mortgage couldn't be met, and what cash was on hand wasn't enough to keep the bank from taking it back. It seemed to him that this was the way things were supposed to happen. It wasn't sadness that he felt, exactly. It was a feeling more akin to relief that he could start over. The Islands and Canada had a way, he remembered, for disappearing his countrymen. His predilection to sunburn steered him away from Jamaica, and so he took what little he had left and went North.

And so he found himself in Toronto, where he experienced

the familiar and the unfamiliar all at once. He purchased a town-house in a fashionable part of the city. He took a job at the Trans-lation Bureau. He helped people coming from Quebec and from the northern territories to fill out forms in the King's English, to try and make sure they could navigate the world in what he had secretly started to consider the planet's most efficient language.

He wasn't unhappy, but he wasn't happy either.

Soon enough, his mind turned again to Elsa, and he resolved to be back in touch with her. At first, they'd reconnected mostly through letters. Then, occasionally, he would travel to New York to visit. They'd lost touch after his wedding; his wife had been jealous. And while Elsa hadn't married and didn't make much money, she seemed contented in a way that he never understood, and he admired that. It made him love her more. So much so that, after a dinner once, he asked her if she would marry him. He'd noticed a rip in her stockings and the way she looked a little thin. But she demurred and acted as if the proposal were a joke.

They hadn't spoken in three years, so he was surprised when she telephoned him one evening (from Témiscaming of all places!) to tell him about a miracle. She didn't pray much anymore, but what she'd seen was remarkable, and they were indeed miracles, from Jesus Himself, she believed. And they were going to be exploited.

She started crying when she spoke of the mother, of her abject sadness, and of the way the father looked, the way he smelled boozy, and she suspected he was mean and so she'd begged Anthony to do something, to do anything for those baby girls. And he was suspi-cious because he didn't believe in her God, or in her Jesus, or even in human biology as miraculous. He believed in numbers, he believed in his own two eyes. And when he ventured to the farmhouse himself only a few weeks later, he envisioned the way his two passions—noto-riety and money—could be realized. At first sight, with a single glance, he imagined how the Quints could make him a fortune grander than that of any Duke, would make his Osborne name noteworthy even without a title. And he would do it, even if those babies were the ones who were going to facilitate that process at their own great expense.

PART THREE

SISTER

THE HISTORY OF THE freak show and multiple births certainly doesn't begin or end with my sisters. In the 19th century Chang and Eng Bunker, joined at the sternum, toured the country getting a nickel a pop to have the masses gaze at their interconnectivity. The Keys Quadruplets, our nearest predecessors, were displayed each year at the Oklahoma State Fair in the early twentieth century. By the time my sisters were born, the Keys were at the tail end of a career performing music as a quartet. So it seemed natural, didn't it? That my sisters would be next as they were larger, more spectacular, more wondrous even than those Keys girls. But they weren't going to be freaks; they were going to be tiny, cute royalty. They were going to give Canada the kind of monarchy it yearned for—and through a miraculous act of divination.

This is the part of the story where you shouldn't feel bad for me anymore. I wallow in pity, but truly, I take pleasure in life. And it is a story that I like so much, both its telling and retelling. I like having the absolute knowledge, the purview of a god, a glance around the edge of all things.

Here is where it changes, where my sisters begin to glimpse, begin to experience, begin to know the things that will lead them toward their end. And its sadness eclipses mine, so deeply, so profoundly. Because they lived.

TÈMISCAMING

By 1942 International Paper was happy to unload forty acres near Témiscaming. With the taxes they were paying on the land they'd cleared of trees, it was worth their while to sell that piece of property. The government, under the direction and guidance of Mr. Rhys Osborne, broke ground almost immediately.

SISTER

IN HIS PLANNING OF the place, Rhys Osborne saw *Quintland!* as a structure that was to be both byzantine and functional. Caught up in the zeitgeist and the folly of the present, the grounds were designed to look like a Bavarian village (nearly everyone saw the folly of this—later.) The forty acres were a network of intersecting cobblestone pathways leading visitors to a petting zoo with ponies and goats. Another led to an Olympic-sized swimming pool, filled with water from North Bay, which was available for swimming in the summer and for ice skating in the winter. A small seven-room stone cottage would showcase my sisters' miraculous beginnings and the story of their births. Rhys Osborne imagined the walls lined with every framed newspaper and magazine article that he could find. He would place the story in chronological order, unfolding as he saw it, clearly exorcised of himself, Elsa, and the long-forgotten Mr. Harvey Gibson.

He planned for a photo studio and a gift shop to round out the *Quintland!* complex. But, of course, at the center of the park was the gaudy showpiece. The building—dubbed "The Famous Five Nursery" by Osborne—was a cross between the monkey house at the zoo and a museum exhibit. He oversaw the design of a circular public viewing gallery, complete with one-way glass like that used in psychological observation room. Behind this glass, feeling a manufactured sense of voyeurism, visitors could watch my sisters eat, dress, and play. And weather permitting, in their outdoor recreation area behind layers and layers of chicken wire, they could see my sisters "at recreation" in a tiny enclosed yard. So cute, so vulnerable, each baby an exact replica of the other. Like a show, like life, growing right in front of a customer's eyes.

Osborne decided that "The Famous Five Nursery" would be free to all Canadian citizens. The plan was a wartime boondoggle to pacify Canada in a way that would allow the government to stealthily (and steadily) take money from schools and healthcare and funnel it to the war, while charging our neighbors to the south for entrance to the park. There would of course be a charge for any corporate sponsorship and for the hot dogs, sodas, popcorn and commemorative pictures. They charged for the Quint-emblazoned serving trays and spoons and tiny identical plastic baby dolls. For all these things, the government made a profit and then some. The government built highways to make the trip north more convenient. They set up petrol stations and gave small business loans to country people in order to facilitate the growth of motels and restaurants along the highway running north from Toronto to Témiscaming.

My sisters were a $500 million asset to the country.

FATHER

THE PRIEST HAD BECOME his greatest confidant. He confessed to him that, in truth, he did not understand the work he had been given at the mill. All day he sat in this office and did nothing. He looked out the window, he sharpened pencils, he asked his secretary to bring him coffee. And for all this he got a paycheck? He worried all the time that he would do something wrong, and what would happen then?

"Ask for something else," the priest told him. "Ask for something to do. They are building that monstrosity just outside of town. There must be something for the father of the world-famous Phalene Quintuplets to do."

The government came back, via Rhys Osborne. That Osborne, a snake in the grass if he'd ever seen one. They offered August a plot of land near the property's gates to set up a souvenir stand. All he had to do was to sign another paper saying he wasn't able to care for the children himself. At least that is what he thought it said. Everything was in English. But he just needed to do something. And he signed.

He left his job at International Paper. He left all the furniture and the suits in the house too. They left the crates and crates of things his wife had purchased, some of which she hadn't even opened yet. But he took the wireless. And back in the farmhouse, he set the thing up right outside the bedroom door.

The new place where his children would live was just a mile up the road from the old farmhouse. Sitting on the front stoop, he could see men trooping up to hammer nails and saw wood. He's never seen so many people in Témiscaming in all his life!

The government bought them a little clapboard shack and he spent long hours figuring out how to label it.

AUGUST + CATHERINE "MAMA AND PAPA" PHALENE: PARENTS OF THE WORLD'S MOST FAMOUS BABIES." And beneath those words, in smaller letters, "REFRESHMENTS AND SOUVENIRS."

They would sell his wife's terrible pies and he would serve up pints of beer to thirsty customers. According to Osborne, they were also allowed to sell pins with the children's faces on them as well as flat rocks gathered from the shore of the Bay, which they would mark as fertility stones. He could sell his autograph even. He would sign them, "*It ain't luck, it's technique.*" That one was sure to keep them rolling. He was the father, after all.

He'd painted the thing himself using glittery red paint and installed shelves inside where they would keep the cooling pies and pint jugs of cold milk and whatever else he could think to sell. He was excited. Physically excited. The night before, he'd rolled over and climbed on top of her, and she'd let him, even though he couldn't remember the last time she'd let him. The possibility of money coursing through him—the world's strongest aphrodisiac.

TÈMISCAMING

ON JULY 15TH, 1943, *Quintland!* opened its gates for opening cere-
monies and my sisters were caravanned in a succession of sleek
black cars from Toronto to northern Ontario where there was a
ribbon cutting.

Songs written in their honor were performed by the Andrews
Sisters, and the Prime Minister went into the nursery where he was
photographed with each of them in succession.

The next day the gates were opened to the first crush of visitors.
By 9 a.m. there were cars backed up and wending down the road
for three miles or more. Many people pulled over, leaving their
cars on the side of the dusty road, loading themselves down with
parasols and picnic lunches. Young couples, families, old husbands
helping their wives get down the lane.

Thousands poured in. Thousands.... In the midst of a war,
and coming off a depression, visitors came from all over the world
to see those babies. Grown women wept at their first glimpse of
them, children stood up on their toes. Hushed whispers like wind
through trees passed around rumors that the babies got meals that
day lightly laced with amphetamines—to keep them up through
naps and alert for the first, second, third, fourth, and fifth meals
they got that day, which became a part of the show. The spectacle.

ARCHIVES

Quint Pie

½ cup melted butter

½ cup brown sugar

16 graham wafers

Mix all ingredients good, pat in 8x8 inch pan, keeping a little for top

Filling:

2 cups milk

3 eggs yolks

½ cup white sugar

2 ½ tbsp cornstarch

Pinch of salt

Mix the milk, egg yolks, sugar, cornstarch and cook in double boiler, stirring until mixture thickens, stirring constantly so it won't lump. Pie over cracker crumbs. Beat 3 egg whites until very stiff and 2 tbsp. sugar and beat a little more, spread over put and then sprinkle remaining crumbs on top. Bake a short time, until top browns.

MOTHER

It LOOKED LIKE IT might rain that morning, and as she pulled the drapes shut and ran the last crease out of her new dress, she hoped it would. The plan for that afternoon was to have both the mayor of the town and Lieutenant Governor of Quebec speak as crowds gathered at the gate to watch the ribbon cutting. But when she reopened the windows an hour later, the sun had come out and was beating down on the still-empty road in front of their house.

Less than a half hour later, she heard the rumblings of cars coming up the rutted dirt road—and she knew. She heard August stirring in the bedroom, and, when he came out, he hadn't yet put on his pants.

"It's hot," he complained. "Already so hot."

He bent at the hip and turned on the faucet, greedily scooping water into his mouth.

"It's the oven," she said. "I'm just finishing up the pies."

She'd made three different kinds: sugar pie, blueberry and apple. August thought this stand would be a good opportunity. A way, he pointed out, for them to profit from what was legally theirs and a way, he hoped, to help the girls. At least that was what he told her. What he said.

They hadn't seen the girls in nearly a year. Monthly updates came in the form of letters, but she was glad in some way that they would be closer now. Maybe there would be a chance, a chance to know them better.

He pulled aside the curtain and watched as the cars came down the road.

"Business is going to be good today. I can feel it." His comment hung in the air, pointlessly. And then, "Are the pies almost done?"

"Almost."

The tops of the last two pies were still browning in the oven. She opened the door and peered in at the crust, shiny with brushed egg white like her Mama had taught her, once upon a time, when she'd still been a stupid little thing. That was how she again thought of herself these days—as a stupid little thing—and the happier he got about the whole venture the more deflated she felt.

She went into the bedroom and undid the rag curls she'd set so painstakingly the night before, undoing each piece of cloth to reveal a misshapen and frizzy ringlet, not quite a curl, each one making it look as though she was wearing a halo. The dress the she'd pressed that morning felt uncomfortable the moment she put it on. Her body still wasn't quite right. It still always felt like she was wearing the body of a larger, fatter woman, one that she thought she could step out of. But no—she couldn't. The body was hers. She was reminded of the girls each time she tried to squeeze into the still-too-tight dresses and undergarments. Her breasts overflowed from her brasserie, hinting at a motherhood she didn't remember. She had begun taping her breasts down after the girls were taken, mostly as a measure to stop what seemed to be the tide of milk coming from her. And now, nearly eighteen months later, although she had long ago stopped producing any kind of sustenance for those babies, her breasts ached at the thought of them, at their being so near. She could feel them in this town again, in her space, breathing the same air, and it made her feel wild and young and pretty.

He was loading up the pies when she came back out. He had taken them out of the oven without even asking her.

"Put these in the truck," he said, handing her a crate loaded with pies.

"You have to let them cool," she shrieked, "or they'll be ruined!" She lifted one crate and saw that the liquid hot contents of one of the sugar pies had already slid from the crust.

"They'll be fine," he said. "Stop worrying."

The bed of the truck was already loaded with crates of soda, popcorn, and tins of hard candies and gumdrops.

"Where did you get all this?"

She took the crate from his arms, the smells from the pies wafting up, their heat warming her face.

"Don't you worry about it."

On the street the crowds were already six people deep and opening time wasn't slated for another three hours. How would they even get their truck through all these people?

"Why are you just standing there?" he shouted, coming out on the porch, his arms straining under the weight of two more crates. "We need to get started. We must go. Now."

She looked across at the people, feeling helpless and panicked. Would she have to talk to them? Have to answer questions about the girls? She felt her neck get hot and she made her way across the yard on uncertain feet to the garage.

His family had farmed this land for over forty years. He never failed to remind her of the French Huguenots from whom he was descended. It was their bloodline, their commitment to the land, their work ethic that made it possible for her to eat. The depression has wiped away much of the family's majesty, and the 150 acres that had all been Phalene property had now shrunk to this hard-scrabble plot of dirt, a mere ten acres, a rhetoric of loss.

He started the truck and he eased into the already-crowded road and inched along at a snail's pace up the one-mile distance between their home and the stand. He cursed the entire way, hardly stopping to draw breath. At the entrance he turned pleasant again, tipping his hat to the guard who raised the gate and let them onto the grounds of *Quintland!*, the same land that had once been his family's. He recalled this with bitter spite as they drove up the newly paved drive. The stand was about a hundred yards from the compound in which the girls had been newly installed. She hadn't seen them in months.

She helped him carry the crates from the car, unloading the food into the stand that August had already outfitted with paper fans, with handkerchiefs embroidered with the Quints names, with bonnets in each baby's signature color, with hand mirrors decked out with maple leaves, the girls' names etched onto the surface of the glass. In the corner of the booth, he had placed a glossy stack of pictures of the girls, the first that had appeared in the newspaper with her own face peering up sheepishly next to five tiny, half-opened mouths. She hardly recognized the woman in the photograph. The face was bloated and distended and peered up over the edge of a coverlet with the babies nestled around her head like a wreath. The eyes looked wild, like an animal cornered but not yet caged.

Was that really what she looked like then?

She set the crate down on the counter and picked up one of the pictures from the stack.

"And these?" she asked. "Are you selling these?"

He was already at work arranging the goods in what he imagined was a pleasing manner.

"If it's in here, we are selling them," he said without looking at her.

But how could he sell these pictures? She was already so ashamed—of the way she looked in those moments, stunned and scared. That picture had been her undoing; it was the one that made people think of her as a Catholic cow good for nothing but birthing and suckling. And she wasn't even that, because she hadn't been a mother at all.

"You can't," she said quietly. "You just can't."

He turned to face her and saw the stack of pictures in her hands, the tears streaming down her face, and he lowered his voice.

"Of course, we will sell them. You are the mama. The one who gave birth to them. To all of them." He jerked his thumb in the direction of the observatory. "People will want to meet you, to have you sign the picture, to have their picture taken with you."

"But I can't!" she wailed. She slammed the pictures down on the countertop, scattering them over the freshly-wiped surface.

"I can, and you can, and we will." He gripped her by the arm tightly to reinforce his point.

"I don't want to talk to people. I'm afraid," she whimpered. He let her go in disgust.

"Go and wash your face," he snapped. "There's a lot to do before anyone gets here."

SISTER

THE NIGHT OF THE opening, after my sisters were put to bed in five identical cribs, the gates of *Quintland!* stayed open and giant floodlights illuminated each cobblestone path as more and more people streamed up to the nursery to watch their chests move up and down almost in succession, each of them in a light, drug-induced sleep.

The drugging did not continue because Rhys Osborne knew above all else that it was important that my sisters appear like everyone else's children. The walls that comprised the boundaries of my sisters' lives were the walls of *Quintland!* And while the nursery cum observation gallery was outfitted with thick carpets and five matching beds with each of my sisters' names carved into the headboards (genuine Canadian maple), it wasn't home in the way one thinks of home.

ARCHIVES

Welcome to *Quintland!*

If this is your first visit to *Quintland!* Welcome! And for those returning guests, Welcome Back! We are the only officially licensed theme park devoted to and featuring the Famous Phalene Five—the world's first identical Quintuplets!

Enjoy the sprawling forty acres of the best Canada has to offer!

Stop by the **Plus Five!** Petting Zoo, where the animals are so calm they can eat right from your hand and there are pony rides for the kids. And when you get overheated, take the family for a dip in the **Nature's Wonders** Olympic-sized swimming pool filled with water from North Bay. Enjoy the cool beauty on a hot day or just lay out in the sun. But watch the wife, fellas! It was those powerful currents that gave Mrs. Phalene five bundles of joy all at once!

When you get hungry stop by the newly constructed **Five Little Ladies** snack bar run by the Phalene's uncle Leon. Enjoy authentic French Canadian delicacies from Mama and Papa Phalene's native Quebec as well as hearty traditional Canadian fare. Or bring a lunch and picnic on the grounds. Be sure to get an ice cold pop from one of the concession stands.

In the **Museum of Marvels** see the phenomenal story of the Quints' birth, rendered in sculpture, oil, and watercolor by some of Canada's finest artists. See their early moments in the two-room cottage, and meet Madame Leduc, the midwife present at the time of the birth, who is also the curator of the museum. Look closely at some of the most famous newspaper and magazine articles about the Phalene Five and try to remember where you were when you first heard about these modern marvels.

Make sure you don't miss Mark Van Patten's **Five Smiles Photo Studio**, located in the park's southeast corner. Van Patten is the official photographer of the Phalene girls and has photographed the Quints nearly their entire lives! Explore a gallery of his work that spans the time from the Quints' earliest days in the Dr. LeFevre Hospital in Toronto to their most recent days in *Quintland!*

At **Mama and Papa Phalene's Souvenir Stand**, you'll find an array of Quint-themed merchandise. From tasteful serving trays to pictures of the mother with the newborn babies. And if you're lucky you might get to meet Mama Phalene in the flesh! Make sure you have a souvenir of your visit to *Quintland!* All merchandise is licensed and approved by the Canadian Government and His Majesty King George VI. And don't forget to do your part for the country and buy some Quint-themed Victory Bonds to support our boys overseas.

And make sure you find the time to visit our five lovely ladies in the **Famous Five Observation Complex**. Here, you can see the five girls in their natural habitats, either in their state of the art nursery (where you can see them dress, eat their meals, and play) or, weather permitting, in their outdoor recreation area where the Five Phalenes get a taste of the best brisk air and lush countryside that Canada has to offer. Meet Calendre with her charming smile; Fabienne, our own little tomboy; Eliane, or as we like to call her, our little mommy; watch Madeline—this little one is as shy as she can be—and Anglette, who with her tiny mole we like to call "nature's little oops!" Decide which Quint you like best and then test yourself by picking her out from her sisters by using her corresponding color and shape. (Be sure to check signage in the nursery that indicates which shape belongs to which girl.)

Whatever your pleasure, there is something for the whole family at *Quintland!* Join us again soon and see how the girls have grown!

SISTER

THERE WAS NO WARMTH, no evidence even that small children lived at *Quintland!* It was sterile in all ways and as carefully constructed as a stage, an open canvas onto which my sisters were meant to perform, to dazzle.

And dazzle they did. They dazzled so well that during the first year of operation, the number of *Quintland!* employees nearly doubled to deal with what felt like a constant stream of visitors into the park. The gates opened at dawn and didn't close until my infant sisters were put to bed at seven. There was a barrage of nurses and nannies. There were grounds men, livery men, laundresses, and cooks. There were the girls who pulled the tickets at the gates and the young men, still too young for war, who took pictures and sold hotdogs and ran the chip wagons throughout the grounds. Even though the observation complex was made to look like a nursery, it was really more like television studio, with walls lined from floor to ceiling with double-sided glass and the skylights throughout that let in some glimpse of the outside world and its natural light. Something like a cage, something like a fish tank.

As babies my sisters would stick their faces up against the glass. They would peer at themselves with wonder, not understanding their own reflections, mistaking their own faces for another sister. Sometimes I like to think it was me they looked at. Looked for.

They pressed their noses to the mirrored glass, sometimes all at once, as they grew past the chair rail that cut the mirror in half. They peered into it, seeing all five iterations of themselves. My sisters stared at themselves with the same wonder with which the world looked back at them from the other side of the glass.

It was Madeline who heard *your* voices first. As she pressed the whole of herself onto the slick flat reflective surface, she heard you say:

"Well, isn't that one the little ham?"

She heard the chorus of laughter that followed your comment, and she jumped back from the mirror, both frightened and curious. Even though my sister couldn't use language to explain to the others what she'd heard, she pointed to the glass. And the other four understood, somehow. They didn't understand in that moment that people were there. But they understood enough to be wary, to be careful.

My sisters slept there, had their meals there, dressed there, and when the weather was bad, they played there as well. In the morning, a nurse roused them, they brushed their teeth (so much the better if they could do this in unison), they had their hair brushed and then were dressed by the army of nurses and nannies who oversaw their care.

As my sisters grew they remained perfectly identical except for Anglette and her mole, which she was made to show off once in a great while to prove the fickleness of Mother Nature. It was on display when they were made to change in the nursery in front of the mirrors. Nothing indecent of course, but they were daily marched in wearing, initially, diapers and then baby bloomers and then panties and little girl undershirts to be patted and dressed in five identical outfits. They were positioned in front of those mirrors day after day, year after year, in order to have their hair brushed with one hundred theatrical strokes.

Quintland! is where my sisters shared their earliest memory: a murmuring crowd of people gathered outside of the high fence that contained their playground. A group that gasped as they watched them run around, watched them take turns as they pulled each other in a wagon. My sisters made mud pies in the spring. Later, when the snows came, they made their best attempt at a snowman. Early on they played games to drown out the mutters and whispers, and sang "Fais Dodo" at naptime in an effort to lull themselves to sleep. Eventually, they would just pretend to sleep. Who can sleep under hot, bright lights and with the cacophony made by the endless shuffle of bodies in the observation gallery?

My sisters imagined you individually, and then together, as the throng you were, as you watched them. They knew that, fascinated, you watched them playing, making their beds, and eating pancakes slathered with the Bee Brand Golden Corn Syrup that Rhys Osborne wanted you to buy (even though everyone knows real Canadian babies only eat maple syrup). One of his lesser sins.

As my sisters grew, they peered into that mirror more and more frequently, and intently. And if they stared hard enough, they could conjure your faces, could feel your gaze. The glass was two-sided but wasn't well sound-proofed. They heard the coughs, the squeak of new patent leather shoes on tile, and you disciplining children on the other side of the glass. My sisters heard you every day, nearly all day. The disgusting hacks of those cold-ridden in the wintertime, the wet sneezes of those visitors not accustomed to the northern Ontario wildflowers in the summer. And the whispers. You always seemed to be whispering.

Those hushed voices would haunt my sisters. They could hear you when they were awake, when they were asleep. All of it, even the gasps of "My God" and "sweet Jesus," became white noise, and then became nothing at all. My sisters heard when you were there, and when you weren't. In some ways, the latter was worse.

TÈMISCAMING

BEHIND THE TWO-WAY MIRROR, Shirley Clarkson gazed at the babies with regret, sad and perhaps spiteful because she couldn't have babies of her own.

Velma Fisher, riddled with jealousy for those sisters she wanted so badly, because she was often alone at home, not even a goldfish to keep her company.

Jacques Lac suffering for all the things he wanted to do to those girls, and not just them, but to all children, a dark hallow inside him pulsing, compulsory.

Everyone looked at them…wanting.

ARCHIVES

VISITORS! ATTENTION!

Our Expert Photographer has just taken a series of Photographs of you while you were walking about the Grounds of *Quintland!* A Valuable Souvenir of your Visit to the WORLD'S MOST FAMOUS BABIES.

Before You Leave Take This Card to
the MAIN PAVIILLION
and SEE FINISHED PICTURES.
Pictures Mailed in 4 Days to Your Address, Postage Paid,
Wherever It May Be.

5 DIFFERENT PHOTOGRAPHS FOR 35 cents.

SISTER

MY SISTERS WERE NOT shy, and they did not ask why there were people watching them. They didn't know that it was in any way unusual. These days were all they knew, and soon enough, they paid no mind to the crowds, who faded like the colors of a sunset until they were gone completely. Absent. How *didn't* they notice? My sisters were made to understand that this was part of the glamour, that pretending they didn't know you were there was a conceit that added to the appeal.

Dr. LeFevre and Mr. Rhys Osborne explained to my sisters over and over again how important it was that they smiled, crossed their legs just so, said things like, "I know if I do my sums just right, Canada will win the war." All their actions, my sisters were told, were meant to make the country and their parents proud (our elusive parents, what odd creatures, who my sisters saw only every six months and who were made to wear paper smocks and rubber gloves when they visited).

As they grew, and as the staff swelled, the number of people in and out of the nursery was always in flux. Of course, my sisters always remembered Rhys Osborne and Dr. LeFevre. But everyone else was such a blur for them. Regardless of which two RCMP officers happened to be at the gate, they were nicknamed Pierre and Renee by my sisters, even though ten or more men rotated in and out of the post. Two Mounties in bright red coats were always stationed at the gate, sentinels atop their horses, making sure no one got in without identification or a ticket. My sisters gave names to everyone and everything. Their nurses became Prudence, Mary, or Hilda. Or if they liked a particular nanny, she might earn a fantastical name like Rapunzel, the nurses locked up with them just as Rapunzel was in her tower. At other times, they would sometimes simplify things and simply call them *Fat, Stupid,* or *Lazy,* because who was there to tell them to do any differently? If they started to favor one in particular, Rhys Osborne would have that nurse removed.

Quintland! was open seven days a week, eight hours a day, and closed only on Christmas and Easter. It was even open when my sisters weren't there. But when they were there, my sisters were aware that they had to be "on" at all times. They learned to communicate with each other through looks and with subtle gestures. They saved any important discussions for the latrine, the only place where, as time went by, they found a little privacy.

Mostly, my sisters were totally professional. By the time they were six they knew the ways to pose that were most flattering. Heads cocked to the side in unison. *Click.* Slightly crooked smiles courtesy of generations of poor Quebecois nutrition. *Click.* Hands propped on chins and eyes starring dolefully into the camera. *Click.*

On the days they weren't photographed, my sisters ate lunch in the nursery, alternating between the products they were selling and the things that the Canadian Food Council advised all children to eat during wartime: boiled vegetables, stews made of the toughest cuts of meat, potpies made barely edible with the addition of brown gravy. My sisters complained bitterly each lunch hour, and the nurses told them to hush, that it was good for them, that eating these meals would make my sisters grow up big and strong. The nurses said this warmly—visitors might always be watching—and then leaned in close and whispered to each of my sisters that if they did not eat, they would be locked in Dr. LeFevre's office closet at lunch, that there would be no dessert, no outside recreation, no anything. And there was barely anything anyway. Barely any books, barely any toys, barely any time when my sisters weren't meant to perform or smile or posture.

When my sisters got older there was a pretense of lessons before lunch. A petit young blond (who appeared years later in a Hollywood film) was brought in. She was, of course, an actress and not a real teacher and most of the lessons were a performance. The books they gave my sisters were empty, and the answers to the questions she asked them were practiced in the latrine with their nannies before they were ushered into the nursery.

---*What is the Capital of Saskatchewan?*
Regina.

---*What is the sum of 320 and 213?*
533.

My sisters would even get a couple wrong now and then, to show they were just like anyone else. And they were just like everyone else. They were all of Canada's modesty and all its grandeur. They were taught to speak both French and English perfectly. They sang and sewed. Their manners (at least in the nursery) were impeccable, their appearance flawless. They were the best possible measure to show a unified Canada during wartime. They sang "God Save the King" in French and then again in English. Learned the Lord's prayer, were taken to Anglican and Catholic mass on alternating Sundays. My sisters were sensationally confirmed in both churches (the Catholic ceremony was false, of course, as even my sisters couldn't belong to both the Church of England and the Vatican). Five tiny brides of Christ posed on the steps of two different churches, photographed both times by Mr. Van Patten for *Life Magazine*.

My sisters were worked until they were beyond simply tired, unsure of why they were made to go to church, made to dress up in confirmation gowns, made to pretend all day, every day. And they hated it.

And in perfect French and English, my sisters learned how to whisper, "Shut up, bitch."

They were employees of the government, of the crown, of the King himself—long did he reign over them. They were not Calendre, Fabienne, Anglette, Madeleine, and Eliane. Never individuals. Even among themselves it was hard to tell where each of them started or ended. A singular entity created so that the world saw *not* the several little girls they were, unexceptional in all but one spectacular way. The Phalene Five, the Quints, produced entirely for the world's pleasure; spectacular, miraculous, profitable.

With the power of Canada's imagination, aided by Anthony Rhys Osborne's stage direction, he showed the world the best that Canada had to offer. Canada saw in my sisters what it was meant to see. In my sisters, Canada saw what it hoped it was and what it hoped to be. Canada saw not what was directly in front of it. Instead, Canada—and the rest of the world—saw only what it wanted.

ARCHIVES

**Win a $10,000 Dream Home or the Cash!
A total of $15,501 in 3,114 Cash Awards.**

Just for supposing an answer to this simple question....

Which of the Phalene Quints would I adopt?

A $10,000 Dream Home FREE! Think of it! We make this remarkable offer to celebrate the spectacular example set for us all by the specialist charged with caring for the Phalene Quints.

Today and every day, the Phalene Quints have a dose of Quaker Quick Oats. Rich in Vitamin B, good for keeping everyone fit, from the young to the old. No matter what age, this amazingly important Vitamin is good for nervousness, poor appetite, and constipation. For just a few cents a day everyone in your family can benefit from the Oats that nutritional specialists have handpick for the Phalene Quintuplets.

Luckily, the government has already adopted the Quints and guaranteed for them a wonderful future. But just for the fun of it, suppose for a moment that you were asked to take one of them into your home. Study their pictures and read the descriptions of their personalities and traits. Make up your mind, and decide which of the five would fit into your surroundings ideally. Then send a short statement of 100 words explaining your choice and why. The best letters in the opinion of judges will win one of the 3,114 awards named above.

Everyone who enters before May 1st will receive a free beautiful 7x9 picture of your favorite Phalene Quint.

When you get hungry stop by the newly constructed **Five Little Ladies** snack bar run by the Phalene's uncle Leon. Enjoy authentic French Canadian delicacies from Mama and Papa Phalene's native Quebec as well as hearty traditional Canadian fare. Or bring a lunch and picnic on the grounds. Be sure to get an ice cold pop.

SISTER

Wʜɪʟᴇ ᴛʜᴇ ᴡᴀʀ ʀᴀɢᴇᴅ on, my sisters stayed safely ensconced at *Quintland!* Gifts came from all over the world. From the Allies *and* from the Axis. The Fuhrer himself sent our parents more than one telegram (thankfully, each had been intercepted by the RCMP) entreating them to come to Germany where he hoped to have his scientists run tests on our mother. The thought of building the Third Reich five at a time dazzled him. He was wise enough to know that he wouldn't be able to get a crack at my sisters, for by then the world was coming to understand what had already been fact for several years: my sisters were no better than orphans. Better off, perhaps, but orphans nonetheless.

So it was not without irony that I noted that my sisters fell in love with each other, and at times fell in (and out) of love with some of those who held them captive. A type of Stockholm Syndrome, perhaps. They played games entirely of their own invention—"test laboratory" being a favorite, where they poked and prodded each other as they were poked and prodded daily. I watched my sisters' childhood with fascination. Watched them talk amongst themselves. I tried to identify with the things they were interested in. I tried to collect memories that we would share when we were together again someday.

By the time they were five, my sisters had already had far more exposure to the outside world than our own mother ever had. They spent their days interacting with reporters and photographers, meeting diplomats and prime ministers, smiling and preening and posing. They were a war effort like none other. Their nurses often noted their odd maturity in their charts, their adult sensibilities and their distinct lack of childlike imagination. But my sisters did imagine *me*, did include a sixth sister that would complete their symmetry. And I longed for them too. The watching was sometimes as bad as being there. The sense of loss I felt for the sisters I'd never met was acute.

It was in truth profoundly boring at *Quintland!* My sisters found ways to pass time through the intricate and subtle torture of their nurses at every turn. They took turns piddling on the floor, kicking the nurses, and throwing things on the ground. My sisters' favorite game was Double Dare. Fabienne always won; she just didn't care. Calendre often dared her to find a way to scare the visitors they all knew were peering at them. Fabienne spent nearly an hour facing the mirror while mouthing the name of the Duchess of Windsor over and over again, five hundred silent "Wallis Simpsons" reflecting back to her while simultaneously startling the anonymous faces on the other side of the glass. And the nannies couldn't get her to stop. On and on it went through the afternoon, the course of the abdication to taunt their guests.

On May 7, 1945, Germany announced its unconditional surrender and my sisters, an imagined possibility of eugenics in Hitler's fantasy, were dressed quickly in the colors of the flag and photographed in front of a huge tableful of bonbons. They were photographed pretending to eat them, flashing the victory sign while hugging each other with fat baby arms.

They hated these photo shoots. For hours, my sisters were arranged under hot, glaring lights while a photographer snapped endless images of them that were used to sell church shoes, soap, or syrup. And in this case, my sisters were used to sell a victory that had resulted in nationwide food shortages, rationing, and a *Quintland!*-style set of barracks (minus any cold comforts) for the Japanese in Western Canada.

ARCHIVES

Karo finds the "keynote" to Madeline's personality

This is the first portrait of Madeline ever painted from life! It is the first in a series of individual studies of the happy, healthy Phalene Quints. Madeline is the first and her portrait will be followed by paintings of Calendre, Fabienne, Eliane, and Anglette. Watch for them! They're exquisite!

Madeline is straightforward, honest and adorable. A good girl, a good organizer, and a lot of fun.

Wise Madeline says:

"I like Karo because it makes my milk so good!" As Madeline and thousands of other children have discovered, Karo does flavor milk deliciously! Just two teaspoons of Karo in a glass of milk greatly increases its energy value.

Dr. P.F Le Fevere says:

"Karo is the only syrup served to the Phalene
Quintuplets. Its Dextrose and Maltose are ideal
carbohydrates for growing children."

MADELINE

THEY SAID THEY WERE identical, but she thought that she was the most attractive. She thought her eyes sparkled a little more brightly. Maybe it was because she was blessed with the best set of teeth, the shiniest hair, and a way of looking simultaneously innocent and mischievous, a peculiar articulation of lovely.

Being the pretty one let her get away with a lot. The photographers always wanted her in the middle of the picture and she got first choice when it came to choosing cookies, or toys, or (eventually) men.

On V.E. Day they were brought into a large room, dressed from head to toe in red and white and sat in front of a huge tableful of bonbons. She and her sisters were photographed pretending to eat them and flashing the victory sign. She secreted some of the candy in her pockets. She liked to steal. Not to get the things she collected. No, it was the stealing she liked, and she stole her sisters' toys, or pocketed things from the nurses who worked for them. Her hands fit easily into pockets and pocketbooks.

Fabienne, who was always misbehaving, was the perfect distraction. She stuck out her tongue out and kicked the nurses in the shins. And it gave Madeline the opportunity to go into pocketbooks for pound notes and candies, to pop open briefcase and snatch lozenges and candy bars.

When she was done she made faces at the camera. She screamed hysterically that she didn't care about the war, another distraction to keep anyone from noticing her crimes.

At night when the staff was out of the nursery, Madeline shared the candy and trinkets with her sisters and they each ate a sweet as they lay in their beds, imagining what lives were like for other children. For real children.

Real children were what they called those who were not one of them. Because they had started to understand that their life wasn't like the *Luc et Martine* reader. There was no loving Mama, no doting Papa. No house with a warm kitchen and a full pantry. She and her sisters understood that their lives weren't like those of the people who watched them in the observation playground or through the glass in the nursery. And by then they understood it was those people on the other side of the mirror who were normal and not them.

ARCHIVES

RIOTS LEAVE HALIFAX $1,000,000 HANGOVER
1,500 Plate-Glass Windows Smashed as All Stores
Looted Floor by Floor--- Liquor, Beer, Stocks
Stolen--- Three Men Reported Dead

By Eric Dennis
Special to *The Star*

Halifax, May 8--- I have just walked, crawled and
climbed through the ruins of Halifax business
districts. There is devastation everywhere. The
business areas look like London after a blitz.
Streets are littered with broken plate glass,
with paper, shoes, whiskey and beer bottles.
The jails are jammed with civilians and service
personnel--- men and women alike. The hospitals
are overflowing with injured, some of them dying.
Three navy men are dead, one killed in the rioting
and another, an 18-year-old Vancouver youth, who
succumbed to over-intoxication.

A body identified as that of Lieut. Commander
John George Smith, R.C.N.V.R., of Halifax and
England was found this morning on the campus

of Dalhousie University. An investigation is in progress to determine cause of death.

Fire was the only thing left for the drinking, reeling, shouting crowds to completely lay the city in ruins. Thousands of panes of plate glass windows have been smashed. Stores have been emptied to the last shoelace. Dozens of merchants have been financially ruined. Few, if any, had carried riot insurance.

STORE AFTER STORE WRECKED

From the ocean terminals in the south-end to the colored settlement of Africville in the extreme north, from the waterfront to northwest Halifax, store after store lies in wreckage. Their stocks which were not carried away to caches by organized looters or "souvenir hunters," have been trampled into the street slimy with rain and debris. This is the final scene in Halifax's VE-Day riots which raged unchecked for hours on end and cost city merchants over $1,000,000.

Ambulance and police sirens are shrieking in the streets this morning, as new casualties were being found in the dawn cleanup. Police and services provost corps are still chasing solders, sailors, airmen and civilians over the streets, fences and rooftops.

Two downtown buildings stand charred in fire ruins. They were torched by incendiarists early last evening as a last fling before a curfew was clamped on Halifax and all service personnel were ordered back to barracks by Rear Admiral L.W. Murray, C.B.E. commander-in-chief of the Canadian Northwest Atlantic.

ANTHONY RHYS OSBORNE

THE NEXT MORNING AT dawn the lights were flipped on in the nursery, which was well before the usual 7 a.m. wake-up and hours before any visitors would have been permitted to observe them. He stormed in, his arms full of newspapers.

The Halifax riots pushed my sisters off the front page. Servicemen and civilians had taken to the streets, looting the shops of Halifax. A city pushed to its limits by the war displaced what was meant to be a picture of the Quints on the front page. For the first time, something had eclipsed their spectacle.

They had not made the features section or even the local papers. They had not made the papers at all. In spite of the way that the Allied victory might have made for good news, five brightly scrubbed Canadian faces had ruined it.

"You made a fool of us all yesterday!" he said.

He set the papers in the center of the room and pulled back each of their bedclothes.

"I'm sorry," Madeline sobbed, and a moment later the other sisters echoed her tearful apology.

"So very sorry, Mr. Rhys Osborne. So very sorry."

All five little faces crumpled simultaneously. How could he yell at children? His mind reached for that question just as Fabienne laughed, and he then saw that they were not, in fact, sorry. They were bored by him and his blustering. And even worse, their faces were covered in remnants of pilfered chocolates. Were these children both liars and thieves?

He threatened to have them all beaten. No longer performing sorrow, the girls laughed and laughed.

"But who will pay you then, Monsieur?" Fabienne asked.

He felt first his cheeks get hot, and then his hands, his scalp, and even his ears—because they were right. He couldn't do a thing.

Walking into his office, he slammed the door with all the energy he could muster. He wondered what he could do beyond punishing them. He wanted to hurt them, although he felt guilty about it right away. But that was what he wanted to do; he wanted them to feel ashamed. In that moment—as he'd done before—he questioned why he had put his fate in the hands of five children.

To remind himself, he checked the ledger again, something he usually did in the evening, and he called for his secretary to being him a cup of tea.

He flipped through the sheets of numbers, calming himself and calculating the 25% he was owed from their returns.

And as much as he wanted to hurt them, their profitability was undeniable. Each month, sales of snack stand drinks brought in thousands, and the ticket sales to visitors from as far away as Belgium and China brought nearly a million dollars each year. A million dollars.

Near the front gate, there was even a donation box, an innovation of his making, where tourists could drop coins, some even stuffed dollars, as a way to contribute to my sisters' future. This box alone put $700 a day into the coffers.

He closed the books and started his day. No, the Halifax riots wouldn't deter him, wouldn't keep him out of the papers. Narrowing his eyes, he decided that he just had to work harder, to find new sources of revenue and income. To show how worthy he was.

The next day at *Quintland!*, two Mounties lowered the flag to half-mast and he gave orders for the girls to be kept inside. He said that he was concerned that the combination of joy and terror the sisters' appearance would illicit in the visitors might cause them to act out. In truth, he wanted to show them that he was still in charge.

He read more in the papers about the riots and understood then how important it was to keep the children within the collective Canadian consciousness as viable and important and something to preserve. It frightened him how easily they could be replaced. How fast they might become irrelevant. And worse, without the weight of patriotism or war to keep them in the national eye, would Canada even care any longer about its best export, its greatest raw material? He thought about these things all day before bathing and putting on a clean suit and having a drink in advance of going to see the children.

They came into the nursery scrubbed free of any trace of candy, and they were smiling in their way, practiced, perfect, each chin pointing subtly down and to the right. Facing each other, they waited for him to talk, and he hoped in vain they would apologize. And when, after a few moments of clearing his throat and adjusting his tie, he realized it wasn't coming, he told them to remain strong. He told them their surrogate Papa—the King—and their real Mama and Papa, the Phalenes who lived across the street, needed that from them. He told them to be the best little girls they could be in this difficult time. And they listened to him, their eyes round and knowing. They didn't blink all that often as they made promises to behave, to do whatever they could, to make things better. And he believed them. He told them that they were to say their prayers and he hugged each of them stiffly before leaving.

MADELINE

WHEN HE BENT TO hug her, she took Osborne's pocket watch, because she could.

ARCHIVES

—Newspaper fragments—

"Approximately 6,000 people per day enter through the turnstiles at *Quintland!* to visit the observation gallery that surrounds the outdoor playground to view the Phalene sisters."

"They saved an entire region from bankruptcy. They launched Northern Ontario's flourishing tourist industry… Between 1941 and 1948, nearly three million people made the journey to Témiscaming, to see those five little girls…"

PART FOUR

FATHER

When Rhys Osborne set the money down on his table, for the first time in eight years, August thought of that sixth baby. It was only the briefest flicker across his brain, nothing like shame or guilt, but a remembrance and an image nonetheless. He saw himself placing the body into the ground all those years ago.

"But what about the party?" he asked. He'd read about it in the newspaper that morning. And when he'd seen Rhys Osborne on their doorstep, he assumed he was there to extend an invitation. But instead he'd offered money, which had thrown him, left him unsteady. And in that moment of recollecting the death of what would have been his sixth child, he felt indignant. He had planned on dressing up, on being congratulated.

Rhys Osborne took a handkerchief and wiped his hands carefully. His nails were perfectly manicured, his cuff links studded with small diamonds.

"That won't be possible, I'm afraid. You have a newborn child and God know what kinds of germs you might be harboring."

The new child, the one mewling in the next room, was the boy he had always wanted. A son to carry on his name. He looked around the farmhouse, trying to see what Rhys Osborne saw. Yes, he could understand that it wasn't as nice as where the Quints lived, but this was good enough, wasn't it? It would have to be for the boy.

SISTER

It rained on my sisters' eighth birthday. That January was uncharacteristically warm in Témiscaming, and what started off as morning flurries became a wide sheet of heavy rain that afternoon. My sisters were bathed and brushed. They had their hair washed and their eyelids oiled with petroleum jelly to make them look luminous, to help them radiate diffuse light.

My sisters were instructed under threat of severe penalty not to get dirty. They waited for the party to begin by lying on their backs on the recently updated and refreshed nursery carpet (green that year), the stiff crinolines tucked up around their waists acting as a voluminous itchy blanket on which they were able to recline. The nursery had just undergone its yearly refurbishment, and a host of magazine covers and advertisements had been framed and hung around the observation gallery chronicling specific moments from their lives. Framed images of my sisters looked down on them just as their present selves reflected back at them from the mirrored glass. To pass more time, my sisters took turns reciting what they wanted, what they hoped for.

"A bicycle."

"Boxes of bonbons."

"A book of paper dolls with replaceable outfits."

"A pair of pink-handled scissors."

"Pierced ears."

"A vacation."

I could see inside, and what they wanted more than anything else was to spend hour after hour just as they were at that moment, alone and together.

The party was to be broadcast on the CBC for all of Canada to hear. There would be music and games. And seven preselected children (who had been vetted by Rhys Osborne and subjected to disinfectant and round after round of antibiotics—as if in preparation to travel to Kathmandu or Nairobi) were going to attend. Five were children of executives from International Paper with whom Rhys Osborne had become chummy, and the remaining two were from the Catholic Church whose families had made rather large donations to the church coffers that year.

As my sisters reclined in the nursery and the staff decorated the *Quintland!* complex library, all of the other children stood outside in the rain. Little girls in knee socks stitched with pink pansies, the boys outfitted in their Sunday best, their hair Brylcreemed into submission. They didn't speak to each other, but the girls took turns curtseying while the boys punched each other in the shoulders and pushed each other with the assortment of brightly wrapped packages they'd been handed by their mothers. The RCMP officers on duty held umbrellas over their heads in an effort to at least keep the shivering children's party dresses and miniature suits dry. Behind them, a cluster of reporters stood smoking as they drew their raincoats up over their heads in an attempt to shield themselves from the unexpected downpour.

As the rain began to let up, one of the nannies came to fetch them into the library. My sisters wore identical navy-blue velveteen dresses, their hair tied back with large pink bows. They stood there quietly, hardly moving, hands folded in front of them, their faces set in five identical smiles. The photographers' flashbulbs sounded like thunder. My sisters turned to the left in unison a beat before they were requested to do so. They blew out the candles on five identically frosted pink birthday cakes and were introduced to five matching corgis, a present from King George VI. Finally, Rhys Osborne read a message of birthday greetings from the Canadian Prime Minister William Lyon Mackenzie King.

"Thank you so much, Prime Minister," they chirped. They opened the baby dolls, roller skates, and sets of Chinese checkers brought to them by the children Rhys Osborne had invited. My sisters were already so practiced by that point that they'd pause in the midst of pulling open a bow to turn and smile for the camera, exclaiming, "Oh goody!" at nearly everything they opened. And the reporters laughed each and every time as though my sisters had said something clever.

The seven invited children stood in the back and watched. Not knowing what to do, they sat stiffly on divans and when the cakes were cut, they ate rhythmically, careful not to spill a crumb, and watched as my sisters continued to open gifts. In the pictures from that day, the guests look frightened. My sisters barely looked at them. They didn't even have a chance to look at each other. My sisters kept their focus on the camera, on the click of the shutter. Like every other day, this wasn't celebration—this was work.

The other children whispered to each other between slow bites of cake.

"They don't look anything like they do in the magazines."

"My mother said she doesn't think they can speak."

"Well, my mother said that it's cruel to make them live behind a fence."

"I don't care what either of your mothers says. They scare me."

Another seven sets of eyes on them that day were no different than the usual collection of gazes, and so my sisters hardly took notice. These little boys and girls would grow up to recount this peculiar story time after time to, first, their own children and then their grandchildren. They would haul out scrapbooks and with shaking hands point to the grainy photos of themselves clipped from the newspaper that showed them sitting in the background staring at those five girls.

ARCHIVES

Father Phalene Claims Party Wash-Out

TÉMISCAMING, Ont, Jan 30--- The Phalene Quintuplets' eighth birthday party may have brought a rain of presents—including a $250,000 cash movie contract for the world's most famous little girls— but the day was a wash-out for their parents, Papa August Phalene made clear today.

Phalene denied that the girls, through their guardian Anthony Rhys Osborne, had given their parents $1,000 to mark the day, and he denied that he and Mrs. Phalene had been invited to the party at *Quintland!*

And what is more, he concluded, he and his wife were obliged to listen to the birthday festivities over the radio, just like thousands of Canadians across the country.

ANTHONY RHYS OSBORNE

THE EIGHTH BIRTHDAY PARTY had been an unmitigated disaster. While most of the country's major newspapers featured full-page print advertisements, there was still the problem of the parents not having been invited. Still, it was not a choice he regretted. When he showed up on their doorstep, they looked as though they had been shoveling dirt all day and now, on top of it all, they had a screaming—and no doubt filthy—brat.

That useless August Phalene, looking for another handout, had contacted the papers a week after the party and given a story that he and his wife had been presented with cash to celebrate the Quints' birthday but *not* an invitation to the festivities. Phalene told reporters that when they'd asked to see the children, they were told "no." It was reading that line over his morning tea that left Anthony completely gobsmacked. Yes, those people has asked for money and a house and clothes, but he couldn't once remembering them asking to see the Quints.

He'd had to go on the defensive almost immediately, issuing denials and doing all but calling the people liars. He touted the risk of infection that might come to the Quints should they end up in their parents' home. He warned of dysentery, cholera, and even polio, frightening the country by suggesting the girls' potential ruin. He encouraged mothers across Canada to worry about the cleanliness of their own households. He cautioned them to disinfectant with vigor, scrubbing their houses and even their bodies with Lysol, doing whatever they could to eliminate festering germs. Because if illness could hurt those million-dollar babies, they could hurt their babies just as well. In the process, he had secured a lucrative deal with Lysol.

But most of what August said was, in fact, true. He had come to the door of the farmhouse a week earlier bearing stacks of neat bills— a thousand dollars, counted, sorted, and noosed tightly in the official paper of the Royal Bank of Canada.

"What is this for?" August asked.

"For the girls' birthday," he said.

He looked around the two-room house, the birthplace of his good fortune, and he couldn't imagine how anyplace so bleak and so uninviting could have been the genesis of such a profit. In the next room, the new child yelped and then let out a cry. He unconsciously shivered.

The mother excused herself.

"I don't understand." August looked down at the money, away from his eyes.

"It's what you want, isn't it? A birthday gift, Mr. Phalene. August. But it's from the girls. To you and your wife." He hesitated a moment. "The Quints —your daughters —want you both to know how much they appreciate your gift to them. Your gift of their spectacular lives."

SISTER

THE DISCOVERY OF CALENDRE'S epilepsy came only four days after my sisters' eighth birthday. Her first seizure was mild. In the bathroom, brushing their teeth, Calendre felt light-headed at first and then saw her face receding from the image in the mirror. It was the last thing she remembered before waking up in the doctor's suite.

My sisters remembered seeing her knees buckle and watching as the toothbrush slipped from her hand, all of them watching, not sure if she was joking or not. Her head hit the tile with a sickening thud. My sisters were momentarily silent before rushing to Calendre, sprawled awkwardly on the floor. It was only then that the nurse who had opened the window to smoke a cigarette turned. (She was, of course, fired later, for the cigarette, not the seizure). Calendre's eyes had rolled back into her head, but there was no foam, only the gentle seizing of her chest and her gasps for air. My sisters weren't scared in the way children often are. Instead, they crowded around my sisters, trying to shield her from anyone's prying eyes or indelicate hands. But when the doctor arrived, the nurses forcibly pulled them away from Calendre's damp little body on the bathroom floor so that Dr. LeFevre was able to reach her side.

The curtains were drawn in the observation gallery and a small cardboard placard indicated that my sisters had a "tummy ache." Visitors complained at the front gates and many were given refunds, even though it pained Rhys Osborne to part with a cent. My four sisters lay around the nursery, their bodies so still even though their minds raced, unable to find any distraction, any game or toy or book to occupy them as they nervously waited for Calendre to come back.

I was fortunate in that I was able to stay with her, to telegraph whatever comfort I could, to watch as she was subjected to a full day of tests as Dr. LeFevre came to his diagnosis. All of the nurses had been forced to sign non-disclosure agreements upon beginning to work at *Quintland!* and they were threatened, explicitly, that should knowledge get out, not only would they be fired, but they would be sued as well, with his Majesty King George VI as a plaintiff.

At twilight when Calendre was returned to the nursery, my sisters swarmed her with bisous and hugs. Anglette took charge and led the inspection of every part of Calendre, like a mother might do, making sure no harm had come to her. They shook and fingered Calendre's hair, studied her fingernails, and implored her to remove her shoes and socks so that they could see that she was all there, so that they could see that she was still one of them. They did their best to pile into one bed together that night. I thought it a mercy that the nurses didn't separate them immediately. But they were never told the truth. No one ever told Calendre, never told my sisters, that she was ill.

ANTHONY RHYS OSBORNE

THEN TO TOP IT all off, one of the children was ill. In the days following the diagnosis, he and LeFevre spent days in his executive office sketching out plans to adjust the Quints' diet, to include medication in Calendre's food to control her seizures, and to do everything they could to cover the fact that the children weren't perfect. Because if they lost even one Quint, if even one fell ill or perished, they both knew they were going to be lost as well.

It was time to start considering new revenue sources and, in the evening, after the other staff has left for the day, he would make a précis of his ideas in his office. In the wake of Hitler's defeat, the Quints were no longer needed to rally the troops or to raise morale. And by then, selling syrup, oats, and soap had become old hat. There wasn't much left that he hadn't put their likeness or their name on, everything from blankets, to toothpaste, to life insurance policies. Over forty household products bore their likeness.

But their English, it was quite good. He couldn't quite remember when he alighted on the idea of a film. He'd never really been one to go himself. But he knew that if the parents were any kind of indication, they weren't going to get better looking or more attractive. Their mother was slovenly. He had never seen the woman when her hair didn't look anything but unkempt, and the crawling ruddiness of her skin repulsed him. The father's teeth were haphazard and his skin rutted and pockmarked. And oh, how he smelled. Even when he had managed to get the ingrate a job, the people at International Paper had complained to him about the smell of the man, his odor like a wall. And the horrid, ill-fitting suits he wore. Where the woman was too fat, he was far too thin. He reminded Osborne of the unspeakable pictures beginning to come from the continent. People who looked like ghosts, people who did not look like people at all.

His brother had been in Germany before the war, spending time with the Duke of Wales and Wallis Simpson. He'd gone missing for a time before turning up again in Southern Italy. His brother had written to him about the things he'd seen, about the way he had felt abandoned by the Duke and Duchess, about how, when he returned to London, it seemed a broken shell of its former self. He asked to come to Canada, to stay awhile, to recuperate. It was with some pleasure that Anthony burned the letter, and with some satisfaction that he catalogued his brother's suffering. This insolent man who had never cared anything for or about him now wanted something, when it was Anthony who had suffered the most, who had pains and scars deeper than anyone. How rich. No, there would be no tearful reunion, no coming together of kith and kin. His brother had made his bed and he could lie in it.

The idea for the movie came to him as he was watching the images of a bombed out and gutted London on the newsreels. He recognized the places he had been, a street where an aunt lived and a shop where he liked to buy books. Nothing more than rubble, now. Familiar places made strange. And wasn't that those girls, too? Their faces as familiar to any Canadian as their own. But in the pictures, they could talk. He hadn't considered the Quints for a picture, but the sense that they were perfect woke him like a cold wind. He would write it and they would be the stars. And he could get out of this miserable, blustery mess of Toronto and go to California where it was always warm.

And he did write the film treatment himself, calling it *The Country Doctor*. The movie was the fictional account of the life of a doctor very much like LeFevre. The script detailed the story of a kind and humble country doctor who practices in a sleepy Oregon lumber town. After delivering the miraculous quintuplets—to be played on screen by the actual Quints—the doctor rockets to fame and celebrity. In the script, he changed the children's and the doctor's names, hoping to Anglicize the details in an effort to realize more profit. In the film they were the Wyatt Quintuplets and LeFevre became Dr. Ogden.

He had no trouble pitching the film. He didn't know why he hadn't thought of it sooner. Hollywood had become big business since the end of the war. Money and projects were being funneled into Hollywood, and he wanted a piece of it.

He spent a few weeks establishing the details. The picture would film in Los Angeles, and although there had been editorials denouncing him in the *Toronto Star*, and nationalists made a point of saying that like everything good that was Canadian, my sisters would be commoditized by the United States, he knew (much like Mr. Gibson—that profit-minded visionary of the World's Fair — had known all those years earlier) that those children could make a lot of money south of the border.

ELIANE

SHE KNEW SHE WAS destined to be a star. Although she could admit she wasn't the cutest, she liked to think she had the most personality. She was the one who drew the largest crowds at the nursery, and she was most often chosen as favorite Quint in a variety of contests. And, so, she was excited about this trip. She wondered if she would be discovered, if this would be her big break.

The day she flew with her sisters to Hollywood from Toronto, the city was blanketed with a thick snow. The airport always stank like stale cigarettes, and she felt like the smell coated her lungs and her skin like syrup.

The nurses had already washed their hair twice that morning— just to be sure she and her sister were polished and presentable. And she was worried that if they got dirty, there would be a third bath.

In the airport, they waited, and then they waited more. She first passed the time by playing gin with two of her sisters, and then by trying to find ways to scuff her patent leather shoes. Because of another of Rhys Osborne's peculiar mandates, none of the nurses spoke to them in public settings and she grew impatient and bored.

She walked up and down the rows of seats making sure she stayed in Rhys Osborne's or the doctor's line of sight, which was the rule when in public spaces. Never more than twenty paces away from either of them.

When she'd gone as far as she was allowed, she climbed into a chair next to a man reading a magazine, on the cover of which a short, square man sat smiling as he stared directly at the camera. He wore short, tight pants, and he held the wrist of his left hand in his right. She didn't understand the pose, but she wondered at the tan arm bulging with bright blue veins.

"It stinks in here, doesn't it?" she asked him.

He looked up from his magazine and nodded. She pulled the little purse she'd been given that morning tightly to her chest and smiled at him.

"So where are you going?" she asked before the man could start reading again.

"St. Louis," he mumbled.

"Why?"

He set the magazine on his lap. "I'm going to compete in a weightlifting competition."

She smiled and looked right at him. As if this interested her.

The man gave her a too-long and -complicated explanation about the things he could lift, after which he even flexed his biceps, rolling up his shirt sleeves to show her the veins in his forearms and biceps that stood up rigid and blue, nearly bursting as though they wanted to be let out of the trappings of skin.

"So where are you going?" he finally asked her.

"Los Angeles," she said. "My sisters and I are making a movie."

The man laughed, and so she pointed to her sisters who were sitting composedly just up the row. They were, as always, wearing nearly identical outfits. Looking at her sisters and then back at her, the man recoiled. And got up quickly.

"Oh my God," he said. "You're those little girls, the ones who all look alike."

He swallowed hard.

She smiled up at him like she'd been taught to do. He gazed back at her, looking frightened and then just walked away. It was odd, she supposed, the way people reacted. And, also, not so odd.

When she and her sisters got on the plane, they sat separately from the other passengers and slept nearly the entire way.

Los Angeles was nothing like she had imagined. They'd left Toronto nearly snow blind and landed in a warm and sunny world lined with spiking palm trees. She and her sisters peeled off their sweaters as soon as they left the terminal, handing them to the cadre of nurses who accompanied them before climbing into the back of the biggest car any of them had ever seen.

They were taken to lunch at the Brown Derby, and they brought her and her sisters turkey sandwiches ladled with brown gravy. They all smiled as they had been told to do for the reporters from *Movie Town* and *Variety*. Or at least that's what she thought they'd been told to do. It was all going too quickly, the plane ride, the heavy lunch, and now they needed to perform. Although she thought her smile was the best, under the table she held hands with Madeline, to whom she was closest, with whom she shared everything.

A long, oil-slick black car took them from the restaurant to the rented house that had a pool and a yard, one that seemed nearly as big as the yard at *Quintland!* At night, she and her sisters slept in a smaller room with five identical beds. But she slept soundly; they all did, perhaps because they knew in the morning they would wake up without anyone watching them. The house was large and roomy with doors that seemed to let the outside in. The tall hedgerows around the back garden made her feel safe, as if no one could see them here. She swam in the pool with her sisters and ate avocados from the trees in the backyard. She felt free. Her sisters felt free.

They had two days like this, relaxed—joyous—before the same black car turned up to take them to the studio, depositing them at the stage door where Mr. Osborne met them and reminded them how to behave. Though she'd been an actress of sorts her entire life, she didn't know anything at all about the movies or performing in them. According to the rules, she and her sisters were only to film for forty-five minutes a day, always under the supervision of Dr. LeFevre and Anthony Rhys Osborne.

If there was a script, she never saw it. She was split up from her sisters. Some went to learn lines, and others to have their hair washed. But she alone was sent to the makeup room. It was in a dark corner of the studio and one of the nurses walked her there.

"Will you be okay in here on you own?" the nurse asked her. She had never seen this kind of thing, this type of room—fake, different—and so many people and such bright lights. But she took a deep breath and nodded.

"Oh good," the nurse said. "Thank you." The nurse bent at the waist and whispered in her ear, "There's a cute guy over there that I'm dying to talk to."

The nurse adjusted her brassiere and smoothed out the skirt of the starched white uniform that Osborne made them wear.

"How do I look?"

"You look okay," she said.

They got to the door of the makeup room.

"I'll be back for you soon."

She opened the door without knocking and found two men smoking cigarettes and looking though cartons of powders and creams.

"You must be Eliane," the older of the two men said.

They both stopped what they were doing and came over to peer at her.

"And your sisters? They look just like you?" the younger one asked.

"Of course," she said. "Of course. Only...I'm a little bit cuter."

They laughed at this and the younger man lifted her into the makeup chair and turned on a set of light bulbs ringing a mirror that seemed to make her face look larger than it was. Then there they were again, closer now, peering at her face. She smelled stale smoke on their breath.

"She looks too ethnic," the older man said. He grabbed her chin roughly and jerked her face upward. "What then? Maybe it's her eyebrows that are doing it?"

The other leaned in close. She could feel his hot breath on her
face and she smelled onions behind the smoke as he peered at her
and jabbed his fingers into the space over her eyes.

"Just tweeze these. She'll be fine."

And then, as if he just remembered she was there, he ruffled
her hair and asked, "Why you so hairy, kid?"

She wanted to cry, but instead she composed her face into a
practiced smile.

The first makeup artist let go of her face and shook his head.

"Nah," he said. "We need to wax them. But whatcha gonna
do? You know what they say about those French girls and their
hair anyway...."

He stopped himself. The men exchanged a glance and laughed.
She watched them without saying anything. She was French, and
she wondered how it was that she didn't yet know another thing
about herself.

"Come on, Gus. I'll show you how to use the wax."

They opened a door at the far end of the room, walked through
and shut it behind them. She was alone. She heard low muttering
and then dueling bursts of laughter. Almost immediately the door
opened and the older man came back to the chair holding a small
silver pot of something that looked like honey. He walked toward
her, stirring quickly.

"This is very hot, so I'm just trying to cool it down before I
put it on your skin." He was quiet for a moment. "I'm Ennis, by
the way."

She nodded but didn't look him in the eye.

"Tilt your head back."

She hadn't been away from her sisters often. Certainly never
for any real length of time, and certainly never to endure any
humiliation that they didn't share, too. She couldn't comprehend
what it meant, this first time, to be completely on her own.

"Will it hurt?" she asked.

"Yes," he said. "But you'll get used to it."

ARCHIVES

COMING THIS SPRING...

"EVERY WOMAN IN THE WORLD WILL WANT TO SEE THEM" —Daily Variety

THE *Phalene* QUINTS

in

THE COUNTRY DOCTOR
with FRITZ FELD

Maura Houser	Buddy Jones
Michael Lemon	Judy Devere

Photographed with the approval of DR. PIERRE LEFEVRE, the Quints' personal physician.

A FOX PICTURE

SISTER

THE MOVIE WAS A rousing success. *The Country Doctor* made back
the entire cost of production within the first two days of its run,
and my sisters spent weeks in Hollywood promoting the film.
Rhys Osborne's plan had worked, and the Quints were a hit in the
States now, too. With the film came a slew of new endorsement
deals. Their lessons, such as they were, were all but abandoned at
that point, and more than once I saw Rhys Osborne snatch a book
away from one sister or another in order to keep her focused on the
task at hand. Instead, they were taught a perfect curtsey, sewing,
subtle flirting, coy smiles. More and more, I watched my sisters
being trained like dogs. Rhys Osborne had grand designs for them,
imagining that they would be heads of state and function as the
face of Canada and all that the country had to offer. Rhys Osborne
understood the inherent dollar value associated with monarchy and
the lengths to which people would go to ensure its continuation.
She walked up and down the rows of seats making sure she stayed
in Rhys Osborne's or the doctor's line of sight, which was the rule
when in public spaces. Never more than twenty paces away from
either of them.

ARCHIVES

Get Our 9th Birthday SOUVENIER "QUINT" TEASPOONS!
EACH SPOON ONLY 10c WITH THE INCLUSION
OF BLACK BANDS FROM 2 CAKES OF PALMOLIVE SOAP

Try new improved Palmolive, the beauty soap the
Quints use, and get beautiful Quints Birthday
Teaspoons.

Take this grand opportunity to get as many of
these lovely valuable Quint Birthday Teaspoons
as you desire! You're sure to want a complete
set — for each attractive spoon is different in
design and crafted by one of the world's leading
silversmith.

And they're almost a gift. You get each spoon for
only 10c in coin when you include the black band
from just 2 cakes of Palmolive Soap. Send for
yours today.

Dr. LeFevre chose Palmolive for the Phalene Quints because Palmolive is made with *Olive Oil* and for that reason is gentler, more soothing to the tender skin of the Quints. Since their first bath, these lovely little girls have used no soap except Palmolive.

Why don't you try this gentler, more effective soap made from Olive and Palm Oils? Buy the new improved Palmolive today, and send for your Quint spoons.

Remember they cannot be bought at any store!

CALENDRE

SHE HAD BEEN DREADING this next trip. After the whirlwind of the movie production, she felt so tired all the time. Trying to be cheerful and chipper (as they had been instructed) was difficult, particularly when she would have preferred to lie in bed all day long. Business as usual had resumed at *Quintland!* upon their return, as though all of Hollywood had been a dream.

The movie was released to glowing reviews and big box office numbers, and then in January, she and her sisters turned nine, at which point, plans were underway concerning their second big trip, a goodwill tour of England. Rhys Osborne told them the trip would provide the time necessary to renovate the nursery, but in truth, she and her sisters suspected he wanted to go home.

They left from Halifax, outfitted to spend two long weeks on a ship before docking in Southampton, England. She hoped that something might happen, that someone would fall overboard, or perhaps there might be a chance to meet some other children on the ship. Instead they were made to sit for interviews with the CBC, the *Toronto Star* and *Life Magazine*.

---*Oh yes, we love traveling.* (She'd only ever been to Los Angeles and Toronto.)

---*I can't wait to see the King.* (She couldn't pick him out of a lineup if she'd tried.)

---*We look forward to meeting all the lovely ladies and gentlemen of England.* (She was especially tired of the crowds!)

By that time, she and her sisters had learned their answers so well. They always talked of how they missed their parents, though they hadn't seen them in months and had no expectation or concern about a next visit. They talked about how much they loved Canada, and ice cream, and school. They had said these things many times, both one at a time and together. She didn't like talking nearly as much as her sisters did, and she hated these inter-views more than anything.

The trip was long and dreary. The water off the side of the ship was gray and rough and they weren't allowed to talk to anyone but the reporters or their nurses. She and her sisters tried their hardest to make the best of the time. Her sisters found excuses to misbehave. Fabienne and Anglette spat over the balconies at the other passengers. Madeline tore through three dresses in a single day, which meant they all had to be changed. And one afternoon while they swam in the pool on the ships lower deck, Eliane announced loudly that she was peeing.

She was quiet most of the time. Even though the travel was boring, she found things to love about the ship and being on it. She loved running up and down the wide corridors. She loved trying all the new foods, the cold soups and the hot buttered fish. She loved the French pastries and the sugary sweet English teas that the nurses let them drop huge globs of cream into. And there were moments when, because the ship was so cramped, it was just the five of them and she and her sisters whispered to each other and giggled and made up stories about all the people they'd seen that day. Nowhere else had they had that luxury.

These moments, of course, were spoiled when they went to dinner and passengers stared and leaned into each other to whisper their astonishment. But back in their stateroom, she was grateful for the privacy that they didn't get at home, nurses in another room and Rhys Osborne tucked out of site. Privacy was somehow more delicious than all those sweet treats.

The cozy intimacy ended as soon as they docked in Southampton. Osborne had picked the most awful outfits for the occasion, dresses starched to an uncomfortable stiffness with crinoline and giant bows on their backs, all identical except for their signature colors. They wore genuine Canadian fur hats and muffs made of beaver pelts that scratched their skin terribly. The town had organized a parade in their honor and, almost immediately, she felt exposed to a new set of English eyes. As they got off the boat, she tried to crowd in behind Fabienne, who snapped at her without turning her head.

"Christ, Calendre, you're too close."

She blinked rapidly and sniffed to stave of the heavy tears she felt gathering behind her eyes. Feeling exposed, she buried her face in the beaver-pelt muff. Almost immediately, she felt something like a burn on the skin at the back of her neck. Two thick fingers pinched, lifted, then twisted her flesh, and the tears she had somehow managed to hold in sprang back to her eyes. Osborne hissed into her ear, "Move that muff and smile, goddammit. Smile!" His jaw hardly moved as he muttered under his breath, "There are photographers here from all over the world."

She smiled as best she could, her vision still blurry with tears. She caught her breath and focused in on the back of Fabienne's neck, a neck she supposed was identical to her own save for the welt that she could feel raising under her hair.

They took the train from city to city through England and Wales. They made appearances and they sang their well-practiced Canadian folk songs to the delight of the English hordes—even though she just mouthed along, too afraid to sing out, too scared that someone would hear the truth, that she couldn't even carry a tune.

England felt exactly the same to her, everyone wanting to touch her, to peer at her. They ended the trip in London. It looked to her like nothing she'd ever seen—chunks of everything missing, as if a petulant giant had smashed the city with sledgehammer fists, and it terrified her. They were only going to be in the city a few days and their nurses kept them in the hotel as much as possible. The night before their last, they were to recite a poem at Royal Albert Hall.

In the back of the car, as they made their way to their engagement, she threw up. She leaned back into the seats, imagining that she was anywhere else, even back at *Quintland!* Her shoes would smell like vomit, and she would get yelled at. Just thinking about it made her nervous all over again, and she vomited again backstage as they waited to perform. This time the vomit splattered up on her sisters' outfits and several nurses were dispatched to make her, and all of them, look presentable again.

She heard the swell of an orchestra and followed her sisters out on stage beckoned by a smiling, older gentleman with glasses. She couldn't see a thing. The lights obscured everything beyond the edge of the stage and she took Eliane's hand without realizing it. Her sister squeezed her palm tightly as Anglette lead the way to the mark at the center of the stage that they'd been shown earlier. She was at the end of the line, the youngest of her sisters, the last to be born, ever-so-slightly smaller than the others, a detail invisible to all but the nurses and Dr. LeFevre. Everyone seemed to see all of them at once, as though they were in fact one person, not five. Looking out into that crowd then, she was glad. People wouldn't remember that she was the one who stood stock still while her sisters repeated the breathy words they'd all learned:

> *"April is the cruelest month, breeding*
> *Lilacs out of the dead land, mixing*
> *Memory and desire, stirring*
> *Dull roots with spring rain.*
> *Winter kept us warm, covering*
> *Earth in forgetful snow, feeding*
> *A little life with dried tubers."*

She had no idea what the words meant. Or why they'd been made to say them. In that moment she couldn't remember why she was there, only that she felt paralyzed on the stage, unable to see anything, any movement out in the audience, but she could feel them there, waiting, breathing. As her sisters transitioned to singing rounds of the songs they'd learned on the boat over, she was surprised to realize that pee had begun to trickle down her leg. She had begun to urinate. Eliane shot her a look that told her it was okay. That she only needed to stand there a little bit longer.

When they came to the end of the song, the crowd roared. She had never been so grateful to have her sister take her hand, to guide her off of that stage, behind the curtains, into the arms of a waiting nurse where, cold and wet, she burst into tears.

She was lucky—no one mentioned her accident to Osborne. Two nurses helped her get cleaned up and it was never spoken of again.

The next day she and her sisters were taken for a private reception with the King and Queen in a sitting room at Windsor Castle. The royal daughters, the princesses, peered at her and her sisters but wouldn't come close enough to shake their hands. She stared back at them, even after her sisters had curtsied and averted their eyes, even after Madeline told them how very lucky we felt to meet them. She couldn't imagine what those girls, those princesses, must have thought of them. She imagined that it was the same as everyone else. That they were odd, and queer. That they deserved to be stared at.

Two days later they crossed the Atlantic in reverse. Something in or about their time in England had bothered Osborne, worried him, and for no articulated reason, a nurse was put in their room all the time. It was one of the more rigid nurses, not one who might occasionally give Calendre the extra hug she needed. There was no more running around the ship's corridors, no more meals in the dining room. They ate alone, in their room, with a rotating cast of nurses. Perhaps he had noted her accident after all, or had grown suspicious of her sister's misbehavior. She wasn't sure and neither were her sisters. But whatever the reason, they just felt more trapped.

ANTHONY RHYS OSBORNE

IN ENGLAND HE'D FELT simultaneously nostalgic and resigned. London had been ruined by the Blitzkrieg, and nothing of his life as a young man remained. There'd been friends to see as he travelled around. But their lives now were so very pathetic. Threadbare suits, and most living in flats in the city. The boys he'd grown up with had lost their country estates or had let them out for tourists on holiday.

His own ancestral home was in no better condition. His brother had all but abandoned it, and when he found an open door, he went in. The place had been ransacked. With both sadness and satisfaction, he saw that most of the furniture had been taken and that there were mice dropping everywhere. He went from room to room, looking for some memento, waiting to feel something at seeing his childhood home ravaged.

In his father's study, a place he had never been permitted to enter, papers were strewn around the room. Everything was damp from an untended hole in the ceiling, and while it was dry on the day of his visit, he could see the spots on the well-worn carpet where water had pooled, leaving seafoam colored patches of mold.

There was his parents' divorce decree, a deed to some land in Hertfordshire, notes and letters and bank statements, photographs of his brother, his arms wrapped around a man in one and another of him in dark sunglasses standing on the back veranda looking toward the horizon. All of these things, scattered around the room, as if a tornado had torn through his past, devastating the things he himself had wanted to ruin.

In the end, he did take one portrait. It was a small painting of some distant relation that the banks and looters from the village had overlooked. It was one of his lesser ancestors, not particularly well painted, but someone who at one time had also been in charge of this once-great house. He thought he recognized his own overly large ears and a distinctively English nose that seemed to have made its way down the Osborne line. The man's eyes had a softness to them. Not anything he recognized from any of his relations. This forbearer had taken care of peasants, had built the Osborne name around this piece of land and these stones. He wasn't sure if he took it for sentimentality or as a reminder that he too had built something. Something to be proud of, something that would make a name for him in the world. He wasn't sure. But he had the picture wrapped up and shipped back to Canada where it was placed in his office in Témiscaming.

The children only made the travel more difficult. He watched as they pouted through dinners and lunches. They were sullen and moody when he tried to address them. In the papers there were picture of them pouting in Essex, frowning in Wales, rolling their eyes in Piccadilly Circus. And during their audience with the King and Queen, the ladies in waiting had told him that the whole family found the children "ghastly" and "frightening."

One evening during the few days they spent in London, he would attend his father's old gentlemen's club in the city, where with the name Osborne he was still welcome. The place had grown unbelievable shabby, and the head captain told him that, sadly, they may have to close. The world had gotten the best of this particular private club. The war had left it without gentlemen to attend it or individuals who might afford to buy what was offered. He drank brandy and tried to think about what his life would be, would have been, back in England. But there was no life for him here. He knew that.

He increased his control over the Quints. He hired additional English nurses, and any kind of woman who would have perhaps frightened him as a child found her way into his temporary London offices for a job meeting. So many of them were ready to escape England. They all wanted to see what life in North America had to offer, and Canada, they figured, was about as close to home as they might imagine, and also so close to the glamour of America.

Recalling his own misfortune there, he laughed bitterly when they talked about America. These moronic women didn't seem to realize that from Témiscaming, it was nearly an entire day's trip to the outer edges of New York. Canada had made him the man he was. But so many of them had met an American soldier and liked the jazzy way they talked and the cigarettes they smoked. These were not the women he hired. He hired women whom he would have never described as nurturing or matronly. He hired the kind of women that he knew would keep those girls in line. These were the people he knew would help him ensure that his own legacy didn't end up a pile of damp papers, discolored and dusty with mold.

When he returned a few days before the children, *Quintland!* looked so cold. And admission to the park was down. The day before the park was to open again, he explained this to the children over a dinner of boiled meat, which they ate in the nursery. He had not been pleased, he told them, with their performance abroad and they needed to learn how to transfer their new skills as performers to the nursery. They were to learn new songs to sing, poems to recite, and narratives to retain the public's engagement.

While they were away, he had had the nursery painted pink and stretched thick, plush white carpet from wall to wall. One of them provoked him thoroughly, by pushing a wet hunk of the boiled beef off her plate and onto the floor. He couldn't tell which one it was. And he also couldn't tell if she had done it intentionally. He reminded them that Canada, that the *world*, was already less interested in them. They were no longer "hope." They were the government's property and so the country paid for them, another tithe to make after the one they sent to the King. The Quints needed to do better for Canada in order to continue paying for their pretty dresses, for their care, even for the renovations to the nursery where they lived. And where they lived, he took a private pleasure in reminding them, was much nicer than most any home of boys and girls their age.

He pulled back the curtains then, pointed to the small light far off in the distance. Their parents, he said, the ones whose blood flowed through their veins, lived in a house with no insulation, with no fireplace, with none of the delicious, fatty beef with which they filled their bellies.

ARCHIVES

Bumper stickers

"We Have Seen The Phalene Quintuplets!"

"The whole family will be happy in *Quintland!* this summer."

SISTER

A GROWING NUMBER OF people across the country had started to question the ethical implications of the park. When my sisters were small, barely breathing, barely life, it had seemed right to keep them confined. But as they continued to live, to act out, to perform, everything about keeping them locked away felt wrong.

Watching babies behind glass was less troubling than looking at a group of sullen young girls suffering their days.

At least three articles in various newspapers decried Anthony Rhys Osborne's behavior after he had been caught coming back from a splashy holiday in the south of France. A year earlier, two reporters had written stories after Fabienne discovered a pair of scissors and had gleefully given herself an impromptu haircut.

But the real outcry began in 1949 when our mother was elected "Mother of the Year" by the Catholic League of Young Mothers after the birth of their youngest son, Claude. The other two children—August Jr. and Ingrid—had never met our famous five sisters. Even August Jr., the sibling closest to us in age, had only ever seen their pictures in the newspapers. His potential for being a carrier of any number of childhood diseases was the primary excuse Rhys Osborne used to keep him far away.

The League sent for our mother by train and she went to Toronto with my youngest brother and was given a new dress and had her hair curled. Following a mass at Holy Rosary, there was a banquet in her honor. Afterwards, while being interviewed by a young reporter from *The Catholic Register*, my mother was asked how often she saw the Quints.

"Every six months or so."

The reporter was incredulous. He knew—as most people did—that it was only a mile from my parents' farmhouse to the gates of *Quintland!* Though he wanted to, the reporter refrained from asking her how it was possible that she only saw her children every six months. Or so.

ARCHIVES

Administering Angels of the Phalene Quintuplets

A true story of the birth of Phalene Quintuplets from two country midwives in whose care the final three babies were born and who did so much to preserve and sustain the babies and their mother during the most critical moments of their lives.

The true story told by Madame Cartier and Madame Leduc will be of particular interest to the millions of mothers who reside in towns and cities where medical assistance is so readily available, and who have no awful conception of what the country midwives mean to their less fortunate sister-mothers, living in pioneering and back-country settlements, during their distressing and most critical moments of their lives. No wonder these women call the country midwives the Administering Angels.

SISTER

WHEN *THE CATHOLIC REGISTER* published the article, her husband was livid. He slapped her face so hard he left a handprint. He'd hit her before, certainly, but this, this signaled the end of their marriage in any meaningful sense. But in the same way, at that same moment, his hand across her face also announced the beginning of her motherhood, because even before her cheek stopped stinging, she felt a sense of maternal guilt she'd never before experienced. And she felt some kind of connection, some desire to protect and guide those children she didn't know—and the ones she did know. It was something she'd never felt before.

She'd registered his disappointment well before he vocalized it. Palpable as an oncoming cold, she felt it drip down the back of her throat and into her lungs and her stomach. It seemed like it was eating her from the inside out. As the babies kept coming, she felt herself wasting away, unable to find that part of her that once had been Catherine.

When the criticisms finally did come, they came in a hurry and pointed in every direction; it was her weight, her appearance, his knowing that she could never, would never, be able to do what she had done again. "It" was bearing five babies, was being a woman, was being a French Canadian woman.

Everything she did, the meals she cooked, the way she kept house, each of the three subsequent children, none of it was remarkable or spectacular. None of it was profitable.

She ate disappointment, breathed it in, felt it seep through her like a cancer. It was sickening her, sickening him, sickening all of them in that ramshackle farmhouse. Finally, he told her outright that he hated her. Hated everything she had done, become, was. Hated those three little brats and their desires, hated the five that came before them. Wished she were dead. Prayed she would die. Fucked other women in hopes that the shame and the sadness and the disappointment would kill her dead.

And she hoped it would, too.

When the campaign to have the children returned to them began, he went straight to the press and told any newsman who would listen that he was willing to give up the souvenir stand, willing to adjust to any way of life that his children knew. None of this was true.

But even so, she stood by his side—dutifully—and nodded in agreement, determined to appear as a good wife. The truth, however, was that she was indeed excited to live with the girls again, excited to see the ways their lives might intertwine. Excited that there might be another story for their family, or for her.

ARCHIVES

PHALENE ASKS FOR HOME WITH THE QUINTUPLETS

TORONTO, Aug 15 — The *Toronto Globe and Mail* says today that August Phalene, father of the quintuplets, would be willing to give up his business of selling souvenirs and submit himself and the rest of his family (now grown to include three more children) to the same restrictions imposed on the five daughters if he were allowed to live with them.

The Quints' guardian, Anthony Rhys Osborne, will meet with Phalene in nearby North Bay tomorrow to decide whether Eliane, Madeline, Calendre, Fabienne, and Anglette will be allowed within the next year to leave their present home, *Quintland!*

Dr. LeFevre, physician to the quintuplets since their birth, has argued that the farmhouse is not adequate for such a large family. When told of the doctor's comment by the reporter, Papa Phalene responded, "Then build us a bigger one."

FATHER

IT WAS SHORTLY AFTER their return to *Quintland!* that the story ran. He'd read other stories in the papers about the children's travel, and at the movie house in Nippissing, he'd seen a newsreel detailing their meeting with the Royal Family. The whole things had bothered him. He saw Rhys Osborne in the background of every picture. He'd begun to wonder why it wasn't him.

He'd had to shut up the souvenir stand while the five of them were away, the trickle of tourists coming was nowhere near what he needed in order to turn a profit for the day. Instead of working, he waited and he drank. He wondered how he might change his story, or at least alter it to include himself in his daughters' story in a way that might earn him a bit more money. He had enough, certainly. He wasn't starving. But he'd been worrying the idea that he should have more. Weren't those girls alive because of him? Why was he scraping by selling trinkets while Osborne was wearing suits and travelling to England?

To the reporter at the *Globe and Mail*, he said that he wouldn't mind living at *Quintland!* Said that he wouldn't mind not being a farmer in the winter, not suffering for five months each year with a dripping nose.

The reporter who interviewed him seemed to offer a solution to his problems when he wondered aloud whether there might be a place for the girls at the Phalene homestead, a place where the entire family could live without chicken wire and RCMP officers.

He told the reporter to call Dr. LeFevre, to check with the man who had birthed those babies in the very same farmhouse, to ask him why he was arguing that the place was inadequate. And when the reporter came back with a detailed quotation about the size needed to accommodate and rear a family of ten, he'd had his answer ready.

ANTHONY RHYS OSBORNE

HE RIPPED THE *GLOBE and Mail* into the tiniest bits of paper he could. He did it methodically, and then he burned the scraps when he was done.

FABIENNE

THEY HEARD THE TALK—THE talk that they would have to go back home with their parents. They hadn't seen them in nearly a year. They knew they had other brothers and a sister, but the thought of other children always made her sad. She could not really imagine talking with them or playing with them. How did the rest of the world do it? She knew her sisters as well as she knew herself, and she sometimes had trouble distinguishing her thoughts from theirs, had difficulty understanding that any differences between them extended beyond their assigned colors. They were a group, The Phalene Five. Each of them a Quint, they were together the Quints.

Her sense of sameness and shared identity among the five made the idea of other children—children unique and distinct from one another, separate, unburdened by the puzzle of multiplicity—confusing for her.

She always did the best she could. She didn't complain about the crinoline that chafed her thighs. She let them curl her hair and didn't scream even when the hot metal plate singed the back of her ears. She did her best to sing the adaptations of show tunes as she was taught. She always tried so hard to make the world love her, to make it love her sisters.

But, in the end, she just gave up because it felt like so much sweaty desperation. And she got older and she cared less. And she got older and she got less pretty. And she got older and she learned secrets.

And for a time, it didn't even seem like her sisters noticed.

SISTER

THEY HAD BEEN LATE to bloom, looking like little girls much longer than they imagined they would. They were all a bit small for their age. But shortly after they turned ten, puberty came to my sisters, it seemed, almost overnight. Madeline was first. She woke up one day with a dark patch of hair under her armpits, and my sisters followed in quick succession.

The nursery (or the prison, as my sisters began calling it) became cramped and overwhelming in new ways. Rhys Osborne ordered that the curtains of the observatory remain shut. Their faces were steamed once a week and then scrubbed with a hard cake of lye-based soap, their scalps scoured with medicinal shampoo to prevent dandruff.

They each developed a set of tiny breasts around which Rhys Osborne instructed the nurses to wrap bandages every morning before they got dressed. Some days they felt like they could barely breathe. Puberty made my sisters less pretty too. The roughness in their features came to the surface. Their cheeks became ruddy, and each of them put on five or six pounds. They lost the dewy sweet scent of childhood and started wearing both deodorant and perfume. None of this was remarkable except that my sisters were always looked at, always photographed, always examined, so their inevitable movement toward adulthood became scary for everyone involved in their care.

Their constant physical upkeep meant my sisters needed to stay close to *Quintland!* at all times. The number of nurses was decreased, but three more aestheticians were brought in to make my sisters presentable. The promotional tours stopped. A planned goodwill train trip across Canada was cancelled and a trip to New York City to appear for a week on Broadway never panned out. Their small world got even smaller. And the crowds of tourists who came to *Quintland!* to see my sisters laughing and playing more often than not found them lying in their beds or on the floor. They looked through movie magazines, they blew bubbles with their gum, and they decided never to speak to each other when those curtains were open.

That fall a Canadian oil man from out west sent them a set of five ponies. Rhys Osborne had them photographed in jodhpurs and riding hats. They slouched and pouted through the photo session. They stuck out their tongues and sighed every single time Rhys Osborne asked them to do anything at all.

It was a combination, perhaps, of the visitors and the Alliance of Franco-Canadian Mothers that started to make a case that my sisters should interact with other children. And while Dr. LeFevre gave his usual weak arguments about germs and bacteria, it had been ten years and my sisters continued to thrive.

ANTHONY RHYS OSBORNE

THE *PHALENE QUINTUPLET GUARDIANSHIP* Act expired in only eight years, but they were still there. In the two years since the act had expired, he had quietly waited for the other shoe to drop, but no one said anything and so he continued his work, shuffling money into his account every so often and making himself crazy with worry. He woke up at night from fitful sleep. He took to smoking. He stopped eating.

It was LeFevre who proposed the idea of a school. The Phalenes were already winning waves of support for the case that the girls should come live with them, and he had to staunch the money that was hemorrhaging out of *Quintland!* each day.

Their snack bar was quickly converted into a one-room schoolhouse, and although they couldn't see it from the observation nursery, it was reported back to him that the children peppered everyone who came in with questions about the size of the room and its dimensions.

He wanted to make sure he hired someone he could trust during this new chapter of my sisters' lives, and it was Elsa who came to mind immediately. He called her in New York late one night, and when she answered the telephone, her voice was muffled as though she'd been sleeping.

"It's Anthony, darling," he said quietly. "Did I wake you?"

ELSA

HE HAD, AND SHE asked him to give her just a moment. She hadn't heard from him in years. She went into her small kitchen and drank a glass of water, hoping secretly that his patience would wear thin and that he would just hang up. But he was still there when she picked up the receiver.

"A school?" she said incredulously when he had explained the scheme to her. "You want me to run a school?"

"Not a school, exactly," he said. "Just a couple hours of lessons each day for the Quints and some other local girls."

"And what would I teach?"

"Some language skills, and perhaps some basic household accounting skills. Have them write a few themes and you should be fine."

Elsa thought about those little girls, remembered them wedged inside that farmhouse basket, and she felt drawn to them and to the opportunity. But to leave her life in New York and to give it over to Rhys Osborne's desires felt wrong somehow.

"Can we do it on a trial basis?" she asked.

"Certainly," he said. "I'll expect you in two weeks' time."

She was there in a week. Leaving New York had happened more quickly than she anticipated, and she soon found herself back to Témiscaming.

She was drawn to the farmhouse before she even made her way to *Quintland!* She asked her driver to stop the car so she could look at the place, which looked even worse than she remembered, if that was possible. She could still smell the woman's body, feel her warm tears, and she wondered if she got out of the car now and knocked on the door, would the woman embrace her? Or would she think this was all her fault?

"Drive on," she said.

And he did, a mile up the road through the wrought iron gates and the sign announcing: Welcome to *Quintland!* And she was stunned, because in her head she had imagined something akin to a boarding school, less like an attraction at a traveling show. She was to live with the other staff at the back of the property and she spent the week before she began getting to know them. While she wasn't permitted to see the Quints, their nurses—Elsa's housemates—told them of the girl's strange peccadillos, a penchant for hoarding sanitary napkins, and another who refused to eat anything but beets. They warned her not to get too close, that Osbourne had a habit of firing staff who were too friendly with the children.

On the morning of her first day, she was in the classroom early. The room smelled of disinfectant and on the far left side of the room was a map of the world, big enough to cover much of the wall. Elsa flagged it with pushpins, marking all the places the children had visited. At the front of the room, a large chalk board and the ten pupils' desks were clustered around what was to be Elsa's own sturdy wood desk.

The other children arrived not long after she did.

"Mr. Osborne warned our parents that we had better be on time," one finally admitted, "or we weren't going to get our picture in the paper."

The five girls Rhys Osborne had selected as the Quints' classmates were not only attractive but, she quickly learned as she tried to chat with them, also extremely docile. They spoke of sewing circles, their brother's sports teams, and their favorite hairstyles.

She found herself getting frustrated and hoped that somehow the Quints would be more challenging.

They waited nearly an hour before there was some motion over at the nursery. All five emerged all at once surrounded by a phalanx of RCMP officers. She stood at the window, watching as they made their short walk from the nursery to the schoolhouse door. She would learn from them later that, although it was only a distance of five hundred yards, they had never before walked it in all their years at *Quintland!* Behind them was a gaggle of photographers, snapping away as one of the sisters bent over to straighten a strap on her shoe and another pulled at a pigtail fastened too tightly. For the first time she was horrified by the reality of their lives.

The Quints stopped when they entered the room, posing as if on cue, as if the flash bulbs were second nature. Elsa hadn't seen the photographers come in, but they were here now, so palpably. The smell of their tobacco, the pop of their chewing gum. The other students stared at the girls. They'd told her earlier that they had all been to see the Quints in the nursery at one time or another. Some had been several times and others only once or twice. They knew them by name and by color. They had grown up with the Quints all of their lives. They had all seen *The Country Doctor* and each of their homes had Quint tea sets, thimbles, paper dolls, all decorated with the same five faces in front of them. All they could do was stare.

"Welcome, girls," Elsa said. "We are so very glad to have you in class!"

All ten of the students settled into their desks as the photographers tried to capture both the Quints and their classmates from every angle possible. Each time she paused to gather a thought, to examine a student's work, a flashbulb went off. She watched Eliane turn to catch the photographers' eyes as she went over a geography lesson. And during arithmetic, Fabienne simply stood and walked out of the room, trailed by five or six grown men.

And when she could not take it anymore, she slammed her heaviest book on the desk and bellowed, "Out! Everyone but my girls, get out now!" She paused briefly before adding, "Please."

"Ma'am, we're here at the request of Mr. Rhys Osborne."

"I don't care," she said. "I can't get anything done with you people around."

She shooed them out the door and locked it behind them.

And then she started over. She had everyone reintroduce themselves. She sang them a French folk song and gave everyone a candy from the tin she kept in her handbag.

It was like that day after day. The photographers shuffled in with the students and took pictures until she asked them to leave. Or shouted at them to leave. She took to bolting the door behind each student as she came in, once forcibly resting her palms against a man's chest as he tried to use his weight to press himself into the schoolhouse.

And no one offered her any help; not Osborne, not the RCMP officer. She was the only one who seemed bothered by their presence. The Quints were woefully under-educated and so she did the best she could. She fought almost daily with Rhys Osborne about the presence of the photographers in the classroom, but he insisted that he needed photographic proof of kindness and care to combat the low but growing grumblings throughout Canada and the world. He couldn't help, he argued, if he didn't stop the swelling murmurs that *Quintland!* was cruel. But, she held her ground and threatened to quit each time he became too obstinate and adamant in his demands.

Rather than lose her, again, he relented.

SISTER

THEY WERE LEARNING THINGS for what felt like the first time. They learned to conjugate verbs in French and English. They took to writing in their journals, which Elsa encouraged them to do. And she touched them, lovingly, with gentle hands. Her touch was electric and kind. While my sisters had been coldly measured and weighed their whole lives, had their scalps brushed and their nails painted, Elsa's small hugs and gentle pats on the head made their hearts race.

One of the girls, Sophie, had a brother named Paul, and Elsa suggested to Rhys Osbourne that he be hired to tend the horses. Money had been tight in Sophie's family as they came out of the war, and a job for her brother would help.

Anglette liked him right away. He singled her out, I suppose, because he had heard about the mole. That May, once it had warmed enough to ride outside, to take them up to a full canter, my sisters were outfitted in riding clothes and brought back to the stables.

They started riding once a week. They took the horses out into the pastures behind the swimming pool when the gates of *Quintland!* would close for the day. They smiled. They laughed. I was jealous of them, and happy for them, and so very worried that it wouldn't last.

ANGLETTE

THE FIRST PAUL, THE one who worked at *Quintland!* stable, was three years her senior, an eighth grader at the local public school.

His sister was Sophie with the long, blonde braids, which is how she and her sisters refered to her. Sometimes, they would invite her into the nursey and they would make her uncoil her hair while they ran their hands through it.

Sophie had cried once, when Fabienne had pulled her hair a little too hard and called her a Nazi for all that fine golden blonde hair. Because they all hated their hair, which was becoming curlier, coarser with each passing year.

Rhys Osborne made them keep their hair short. And she hated it so much. After each of Sophie's visits, she would joke about wanting to cut the braid off and divide it among the five of them so that they could each have a little piece.

The other girls in their class were mostly dumb, but they were useful. They could bring her lipsticks and magazines, things they weren't ever allowed to have but always wanted.

The ponies they'd been given for their tenth birthday went unused until they hired Paul the next year, after they'd turned eleven, when spring came around again and they could be outside after spending long months behind glass in the nursery and the schoolroom.

She liked him right away. That May, once it had warmed enough, they were permitted to ride on their own through the space that extended from the only home they had ever known, space that somehow was as strange and unfamiliar to her as anywhere else in the world.

In the stables, alone for only the second time, the first Paul helped her gain her stirrup, and whispered in her ear, "Can I see it?"

She knew right away what he meant, and it excited her. She told him to stay after the park had closed and to tell a particular nurse—she told him which one—that his sister had left her sweater in the latrine. She would meet him there. How did she come up with a lie so quickly? She surprised herself.

He came with a friend, the second Paul. She could only imagine how they managed it. She pulled him into a stall and bolted the door. She could hear the other Paul pacing outside of the door, and she pulled at the neck of her nightgown so that he could peer in and see it, the mole on her left shoulder, her one distinctive identifier, that thing that made her different from the other four.

"Can I?" he asked.

She thought he meant touch it.

"Yes," she said.

Instead of reaching toward her with his hand, he leaned in and pressed his entire mouth over the mole, his tongue licking it slowly. The pressure of his tongue dropped her stomach, and she loved it. When he pulled his mouth away, her mole was wet and sticky.

Before she could figure out what had happened, the second Paul was also in the stall, grabbing her elbow and pulling her close. He must have been chewing mint leaves, because his breath was tinged with peppermint. And when he released her, his saliva tingled and felt cool on her shoulder.

And then they were gone.

In the morning when she told her sisters, they didn't believe that the boys had been there at all. They said she'd imagined it. But when the second Paul's note came a few days later, they believed. They had to.

The second Paul's father worked at *Quintland!* Maybe as a guard or janitor? It seemed unimportant. Two nights later she asked Eliane to watch the door when she snuck out to see the boy.

She met him in the wooded area near the private playground. It was wrong, and she knew it was wrong. Not just the being there, but being there without her sisters, creating moments that were hers alone. But knowing this did not stop her from asking Paul to show her how to load his gun. It was for hunting, he told her. It was how they got some of their food in the winter. Squirrels mostly. But when she asked "what else?" he rolled his eyes at her and laughed, and she felt stupid for asking at all.

The bullets made a pleasing sound when they clicked and dropped into the chamber; there was something hypnotic about the ritual. When it was loaded, the second Paul performed a demonstration for her.

First, he stood like a cowboy from the pictures—legs bowed, gun at his hip—and he tipped an imaginary hat in her direction. Although he was serious with her, she giggled. She couldn't help it. Her heart quickened in that moment. The second Paul pointed the gun directly at a tree and tried to look tough, tried to look like a man. He dropped to his knees and gestured for her to come over to him. She kneeled down to his level and imagined that she could see their faces reflected in the barrel, his features and her own—so familiar to her that she was bored by them. He cupped her hands around the trigger and they pointed it together.

"Now we always treat guns with a certain respect," he said, trying to sound like an adult. "They aren't toys, and this isn't the movies."

It was her turn to laugh at his corny line, but he gave her a sharp look. The gun was wobbly in her hands, and Paul steadied them and told her to focus on a target. He told her that the gun would kick a little when she fired. He explained to her that she needed to squeeze the trigger, not pull it like they did in the movies. She didn't understand the difference. So wrapped up in his words and the moment, she forgot where she was, where they were, until together, they gently squeezed the trigger.

The gun kicked more than just a little.

CALENDRE

SHE'D SUFFERED THROUGH ANOTHER episode that afternoon. This one had been scarier than most. They'd been eating lunch in the classroom and she'd had the sensation of falling, as if from a great, great height. Her head had jerked back and, as she went down, it caught the end of the table. She'd woken on the floor, looking up at four mirror images of herself. When the doctor asked if she was seeing double she said, "I don't know."

She ended up with a large bump on her head but not an open wound. More than anything, she was frightened. After her sisters had gone to sleep, she climbed out of bed and sat with her back against the mirrored surface of the observatory, trying to gather her feelings but still feeling shaken and nervous. Her other sisters slept fitfully, fighting their way through troubled dreams.

She tried to imagine what it would mean to live beyond and outside of *Quintland!* She fantasized, believing that she wouldn't be sick on the other side of the gates.

She imagined that, out in the world, they would need and get to be together. All day and all the time, together and alone. She wanted it even more than the others. She wanted it the most.

She started it almost without thinking. It was like her body's muscle memory knew what to do. She gathered all her sisters' books and magazines. She tore handfuls of pages from the nurses' scrapbooks. She took hair ribbons and crinolines, letters and the journals that they each kept, and she made a pile of it all in the middle of the bathroom floor, heaping every bit of ephemera she could find, every tangible record she could uncover.

She lit the fire just at the moment she heard the pistol's report. Eliane ran from the door where she'd been waiting on Anglette and got back into bed.

To light the fire, she'd used a set of matches made to commemorate their birthday earlier that year. She watched the name "Phalene" curl and darken before becoming subsumed in the growing and glowering blaze.

Easy as that.

She felt like it had needed to be done and that she had needed to be the one to do it.

By dawn, most of the place was in flames. She couldn't stop smiling.

QUINT

THE TRUTH WAS, WE hated you. All along we hated you. Perhaps the reason for that hate changed, but we could always hear you coughing and snorting behind that glass. We saw the movement of your shadows like eclipses and heard the things you said as if we didn't understand language, as if we were animals in a zoo.

We hated the way we had to suffer through piles of thank-you notes because we could barely read or write. We hated the pictures we had to pose for, and we hated the man who took them, Mr. Van Patten, who unsettled us with his lazy eye and the way his hand would linger on us a beat too long.

We hated having to sell peas, and plates, toothpaste and Laurentien colored pencils. We hated the Mountie promotional posters, and the slickers we wore to advertise kosher salt, and the film reels and eventually the spots for television that pictured us done up in cowboy duds in front of a panoramic picture of the Canadian prairies. We hated the way you loved us so hard, so recklessly, so selfishly, and then—later—how you didn't seem to love us at all.

The more we changed, the less interested you seemed, and the less interested you seemed, the angrier Mr. Rhys Osborne got.

And when we tried to pull away from him, tried to explore new things, to have other interests, he attempted to yank the reigns even tighter. He gave each of us a potential career to which we could aspire, although they were all variations on the theme of "wife" and "mother." He picked for each of us a "favorite" song and forced us to take lessons in dance and voice and piano. He tried to make us and remake us so that you would love us again. The harder he pulled, the more we hated him.

But we kept singing for you until our throats were hoarse, kept smiling for you until our jaws ached, kept waving in pictures, and kept pretending you weren't on the other side of that glass. All of that, until they shut the gates of the place for good, and off we went to somewhere new.

PART FIVE

SISTER

SHAME IN ALL ITS incarnations surrounds the story of my sisters.

A peculiar business, this idea of shame. Performing an illicit act and not getting caught might leave some feeling tinged with guilt.

But not everyone.

That same shameful action, on a larger scale, brings guilt, sure. But something else, too. Sorrow, and contrition. A feeling that, had you done something differently, that action might not have been quite so illicit, might not appear seamy in hindsight. This feeling is the sister of regret and the cousin of remorse.

Those who should feel ashamed, I think, are my parents. But they never seemed to. Rhys Osborne felt none either. But it is bigger than that. It is the country's shame, Canada's shame.

Unraveling who should be most ashamed? That is a difficult question—but perhaps it is Canada, the entire nation, that's most at fault. Not just my parents, not just the town of Témiscaming, not the bureaucrats (not even Rhys Osborne), but the nation itself, for its love of spectacle, the freak show, in all its twisted glory. Canada, that sold my sisters to countries and people all over the world. They knew the name Phalene in Istanbul, in Rio, in Botswana.

Canada liked to judge those neighbors to the south. They were slick and crassly commercial. They were brash, they were loud, and they were lawless. They were morally decrepit and slovenly and everything Canada was not. Or so Canada believed. They thumbed their noses at our sovereign and thought they would come out differently. But Canada invited them in with tax breaks and vacation credit, revenue-generating packages to explore the Great White North.

Canada is not a country of apologists. Or religious zealots. It is absent the historical shackles of slavery. But they are guilty of the internment of the Japanese during World War Two, the slaughter of the native Iroquois of Ontario, and the decimation of the Prairie Provinces' buffalo. Canadians don't believe in faith, or providence. They believe in nature.

For Canada, it felt natural, as though the world had simply taken its course. While Canada is responsible for the exploitation and ruination of my sisters' lives, the decimation of their childhood falls squarely on the head of Mr. Rhys Osborne.

And regarding the sentiment that he would echo again and again: "Have you done enough today for Canada?"

My sisters had.

Osborne would often tell my sisters, "Just embrace your misery, girls. Happy isn't fun or interesting. Happy is an idea. It isn't real. You can't accomplish much by being happy anyhow." He almost always paused for effect before concluding, "Just be good girls and wait to be delivered to the Lord."

The Lord? What this meant exactly, and why he said it, they never were sure. They knew only that they were supposed to listen to and obey him without question. It was only in the name of capitalism and profit that Rhys Osborne chose to invoke religion.

I had the benefit of seeing everything. Without country, claim, or even a name, my loyalty was only to my sisters. Those sisters whose lives I watched, who I waited for, knowing that I would see them again at some point. I held out the hope that they would know me as one of them, as the part of them that they had missed.

All I wanted was that they feel my absence.

QUINT

It felt like the blaze burned all night. The sound of the popping glass and the heat of the fire warmed our faces. We found each other, right outside the observation gallery, in the patch of grass where we'd romped as children. We held each other tightly as the flames pushed back the insulation, the wood, as it licked the glass on the outside of the observation gallery, a place we'd never been.

We joined hands and walked out of the u-shaped playground surrounded by the gallery onto the cobbled path. The bushes lining the path between our nursery and our schoolhouse meant that it would probably go next. Without speaking, we stumbled down the path, all of us coughing from the thick smoke before we realized that we needed to pull up our nightgowns to act as a mask.

Down the path on the side of the hill, a place we rarely came, we stopped for a moment at our parents' souvenir stand, their pictures and ours pasted to the walls and the front. The sign, recently painted in a metallic silver paint, reflected the flames behind us and we kicked the thing as hard as we could, heard things scatter inside and ran.

We ran as fast as we could, further and further down the path. It was hard to see in the dark. We didn't see our nurses, didn't care if they'd made it out of the nursery alive. We went past the pool and the photography studio. We all knew where we were headed, holding hands and running in not nearly warm enough nightgowns.

Running and running, until we could hear our hearts beating in our ears and our lungs burning, until we reached the stables and threw open the door. We liked the way it smelled in there, the way it felt warm and cozy, so different than the antiseptic smell in our nursery. We would be safe here.

The horses were terrified and smelled the smoke on us. They whinnied and bucked. We patted their manes, whispering *calm, calm,* like Paul had taught us to do. We clung to each other and sat in a pile of hay and waited.

We waited for someone to find us; we waited for someone to notice we were gone. We waited for what would happen next. We waited for the person who was meant to take care of us. No one would save us and we waited.

We didn't need to talk, we all knew who had done it. And we were all grateful.

ANTHONY RHYS OSBORNE

HE'D BEEN DEAD ASLEEP when the alarm sounded. His office was nearly a half mile from the nursery but he hadn't heard a thing. He'd fallen asleep listening to jazz records and drinking gin, something that happened more often than not at the end of his day. The divan in his office was the perfect spot to nod off. He slept there a lot of nights, bathing early in the morning in the staff quarters and changing his shirt.

He had a house off the main street in Témiscaming, but he hated going there. It had the staid air of his childhood home. The place was furnished when he moved in and he always felt as though he was staying at someone else's house, not living in his own home. His office offered him a comfort better suited to him. The wood paneled room smelling of cigarette smoke and his ancestor's portrait over his desk looking down at him all made him feel cozy. It wasn't a feeling he'd ever really had. He talked to the chap, some nights, when the gin wouldn't work, when he couldn't drift off. It was only after he'd done it a few times that he realized it was because he didn't have anyone else to talk to. There was sex, enough of it when he wanted it, from nurses or local women wanting to work at *Quintland!* That part was easy, but Elsa, she was the only one he ever really remembered talking to. And now she hardly ever spoke to him at all. She was always trying instead to push him to do things for the girls that she saw as best.

He thought it was a gin-soaked dream in which he heard his wife, wailing the way she used to. He only realized that it was not her protracted screams, but a siren when someone on the security force came into the room and he sat up, realizing the way he looked, shirt tails out, rumpled hair and his shoes tucked under the divan.

He had to come right away. The nursery was on fire and no one could find the Quints. The panic gripped his stomach right away and he raced to tuck in his shirt and tie his shoes. The officer transported him as close to the nursery as he could, but by that time, the air was filled with thick, black smoke. He held his shirtsleeve to his face, trying to make out the observation gallery or the playground, but he couldn't tell if there was anything left at all.

The fire brigade had already arrived and pumped gallons of the Témiscaming water onto the blaze; and the nurses who'd been inside treated each other by placing cold, dripping clothes over their noses and mouths, hoping to pull the smoke out of their lungs.

He and the security officer who'd awoken him doubled back and turned toward the staff quarters, still far enough away that the thickest of the smoke had not yet reached the dormitories.

All of the staff were seated on the lawn in front of their residences. Some, still in their once-white uniforms—already smoke stained—looked like ashy members of a dilapidated army, their tears streaking clean, white lines down their soot-smudged faces. Others in various states of undress and evening clothes cried while leaning into friends, stretching their arms around necks and waists. Everyone asked, what of the girls?

"Have you seen them?" He went from nurse to nurse demanding the same thing, pausing occasionally to berate some of them for not keeping better watch over the girls. And where the hell was Elsa? In all the confusion he couldn't find her, and he figured that she would know.

Finally someone hiccupped out, "Have you checked the rest of the grounds? Maybe they were running from the fire, too."

He looked dazed by the question. Yes, why hadn't he thought of that? He wondered if he was a little bit drunk. He set out at once and organized teams of searchers, sending one group to the pool, another to the gift shop. He gathered a team of nurses with him and stomped down to the stables.

He knew one of them had set the fire, but he didn't know which. When he found them huddled together in the stables, all of them hacking and smoke-streaked, they didn't seem overly surprised that the only home they'd known lay smoldering behind them.

He gazed down at them, seeing now for the first time the ways in which their faces were different. Seeing the way one held her mouth lax while another clenched her jaw, noticing how Fabienne held her chin a little higher than the others, how Eliane's eyes turned down ever so slightly at the corners. While he had seen their faces a thousand times, it was in this moment that he saw them more clearly, and he couldn't say a word.

He noticed Calendre panting and moved towards them. He was grateful all at once that they were alive.

He helped each girl to her feet and into the arms of a waiting nurse.

Did he know them? Had he ever known them?

They took them all to the hospital in North Bay to treat them for smoke inhalation, and he went back to his house. He hadn't been there in nearly a week and it had the smell of a musty place left too-long unattended. It felt haunted too, by the previous owners, by his wife, perhaps even by those children who had nearly died. He fell asleep in the living room that night, fully dressed, sitting upright, his head lolling down and to the left awkwardly.

Later, in yet another of his ingenious cover-ups, he blamed faulty wiring. A French Canadian electrician who'd worked at *Quintland!* named Parnasse spent nearly three months in Ottawa testifying with the aid of a translator before a High Court, never exactly sure what he'd done wrong.

TÈMISCAMING

Sirens blared all night long. Fire brigades came in from Hailey-berg and Cobalt. From North Bay and Nippising. The blaze was enormous. It chewed up their school and their parents' souvenir stand. It ate up the photography studio and that little museum.

Sorry to see it go? Not exactly.

The next morning when some of us women took our coffee in Madame Grenier's farmhouse kitchen, we spoke again of those moments in the beginning. The way that mother had been ungrate-ful for all the help we'd offered. Hadn't we been good Catholics? Hadn't we worked to help the weakest among them? Madame Grenier made a sound that was a laugh crossed with a harrumph when she talked about all the junk that must have gone up in smoke. She didn't mention all the lumber, all the food.

The Phalenes were nicknamed *La Famille de Cochon*. They were pigs. His family had moved away years ago. The building of *Quintland!* had brought tourist and photograph seekers to the doors of the other Phalenes. And even though they had been a part of the Témiscaming community for as long as anyone could remember, they were gone now, and no one really knew where to.

But August and Catherine, they feasted while the rest of the town was struck by famine. And they continued to have children, each one uglier than the last, when the women were still without sugar for their coffee. Things hadn't been good since the crash in '29, but it seemed that our positions, put simply, had never gotten any better. The war had taken some of our husbands and sons, many of whom never returned, and left them with no one to work the land. Farms were being sold at auction and any work the women had in International Paper went back to the men as soon as they came home. So here we were, at loose ends again.

Madame Grenier leaned back in her chair. She tipped her head back in the seat, and her eyes locked on a cobweb in the corner of the ceiling. In response to nothing whatsoever, she laughed that same laugh and got up to refill her friends' cups, because she couldn't offer them anything to eat.

"God knows an ungrateful soul when He sees one—and He will smite it," she said.

The Canadian International Paper Company began to move operations out of the town, so even though the Quints were the region's second most profitable industry, they were not beloved. The influx of tourists—diminished as they were—had kept some of these women afloat, however precariously.

But that particular autumn was the driest autumn we had ever known. No jobs left for anyone but the farmers and the lucky ones who worked at *Quintland!* And in that autumn absent rain, there were no real crops to speak. Fires had flashed up elsewhere, burning some of the lumber mills in the next town over, and cruel winds had blown fire onto their land, their dry brush and brittle crops. The local school had to close when the smoke from a mill fire became so thick that the students could barely see the blackboard. Boys wet handkerchiefs in the water fountain to tie around their mouths, and bigger children had given piggy-back rides to the smallest to try and escape the smoke that poured over everything.

But up on the hill, those Quints had been protected. Their school had been untouched from fire. Their plates were still filled with food. Their priest gave them a private mass when the rest of the town didn't even have enough to tithe. Our children got skinnier and skinnier and we quietly wished that someone would call the Pied Piper to come and take them all away. We didn't know where, exactly, we wished to be taken—but in our imaginings, it looked like *Quintland!* It smelled like *Quintland!* It tasted like *Quintland!* If the children heard the Piper's call, they would go, happily, and cast themselves into any mountainside portal he took them too, if only that lute promised a better life. A Phalene-like life.

> *The Pied piper...*
> *... As a rule*
> *I refrain from calling any man a fool.*
> *Heed me now.*
> *I'll wait until yon clock strikes the hour.*
> *Don't let me go away*
> *Without my pay.*

Sorry about the fire? No. We weren't sorry.

FATHER

HE'D WAITED NEARLY A year to hear back from a lawyer about the status of the case. The Quints were nearly twelve and he saw the window of their potential profitability winnowing away. They weren't exactly cute anymore. They'd seemed to have inherited some of the worst aspects of both his looks and their mother's.

He'd heard back from the man only two weeks before the fire, and he promised him that he would have his day in court. He found the simplest suit he could. The lawyer promised that the case would be easy. He was the Quints' legal and lawful parent. But his day in court never came.

The fire changed everything. The souvenir stand gone, *Quintland!* was reduced to a heap of ashes behind a wrought iron gate that had been warped in the heat of the blaze. He thought for some reason that this would solve the problem. With nowhere else to go, it stood to reason that the Quints would be returned to him without any fuss.

He imagined the cars lining up to the gate of his farmhouse and how he might gesture out over the horizon to the place where *Quintland!* used to be. He imagined telling tourists that fire was God's way to wipe out sin. He would quote the Bible, point to Noah as a cautionary tale. First water and now fire, and what next? He wouldn't be the one to test God.

Oh, what a sin *Quintland!* was.

But they never came. He didn't even know to call to ask where they were. The money he'd saved from the stand started to wear thin, and there were still bills to be paid for the boxes of paper fans printed with his daughters' likenesses and for the hundreds of pictures they'd had printed. All of it, up in smoke.

Without the steady income from the stand, life had come to a standstill. He hadn't worked the farm in years and the fields were fallow and the stables were empty—no animals. He'd sold them all the first time he left.

Fall turned into winter as he tried to stretch the dollars. He still had to feed the children, and he felt somehow that he was in a worse state. He took to buying ten or fifteen bottles of Detant's homemade wine all at once and storing them in the desolate barn. Throughout the day, he'd go in and take a swig to sustain him from the children's noise and to avoid having to look at his wife.

He took to reading the paper again, if only to find out what was going on with his other children. He had his wife write letter after letter to the lawyer in an attempt to figure out what was going on with the case for custody. The Quints were in the hospital briefly to get treatment from the injuries of the fire. Soon thereafter, they'd been shuttled out west on the Canada Rail to get fresh air and some of the ocean weather that Osborne claimed they needed.

Two months after the fire, his lawyer turned up on his front porch.

"Where have you been, you bastard? I've been writing you for months!"

The man wasn't French. A tourist up from Toronto that he'd met at the souvenir stand had put him in touch with a lawyer who'd come to see him about getting the children back, a man who had taken his money but whom he hadn't heard from since.

"Good afternoon, Monsieur Phalene," he said in perfect French. "That wasn't quite the reception I was expecting, but not a problem. Can we go inside? To talk?"

He could hear the children fighting inside as his wife crowed at them.

"No. Out here will do."

They sat together on the porch. If things had been different, he might have offered a glass of wine, but he could not extend himself for this man. He was no better than Osborne at this point.

The lawyer opened his satchel and took out several stacks of paper.

"So these are the facts, Phalene. Your case, quite frankly, is unwinnable."

"But you said it would be no problem." He paused briefly, and then he looked the man in the eyes for the first time and jabbed his square fingers towards his chest. "You said it was my right to have those girls." He wasn't shouting, but he wanted to.

"Christ, it's cold up here," the lawyer sighed and rubbed his hand together. "Phalene, you gave the girls up willingly. On several occasions you've signed documents that you didn't tell me about, documents that provided you the house you used to live in, giving you that job at International Paper and the souvenir stand. Each time, each step of the way, again and again, you've relinquished your parental rights for some kind of compensation from the government."

He didn't know what this word meant, *relinquished*, but he didn't like it and he knew none of the rest was any good either. He hadn't read anything when he signed. Is that really what he had been agreeing to? To lose his children forever?

"But you are lucky," the lawyer said, pushing the stack of papers towards him. "The government doesn't want to fight." In an effort to appear as if he were collecting his thoughts, he paused for a moment before continuing. "It is in everyone's best interest for you to stop demanding the children, and for the government to stop saying no. This doesn't look good for them, and each time you talk to the press, you aren't winning any friends."

"Explain," he said.

The lawyer described how it was unlikely that *Quintland!* could be rebuilt. Much of the cost would fall onto taxpayers and the Quints' reduced revenues over the past six years didn't justify the expense. Here was the compromise: the government would pay for the construction of a new home for the entire family, including the Quints. August would give them the farmhouse in exchange. The new house would be just outside of downtown Témiscaming—on a couple of acres of land. However. Rhys Osborne would remain their legal guardian, and to keep him close by, the government would also build him a house in Témiscaming, near the mill on Ottawa River.

Would this suit him?

It would.

ARCHIVES

"I simply beg of you to restore to me my five little babies as a 'coronation gift.' Can't your Majesty understand how I feel without them?"

FABIENNE

AFTER THE FIRE, THEY didn't know what was to become of them. They spent three weeks at the tiny hospital in Témiscaming. Although they'd barely been hurt, there seemed to be some concern about where they would go next. At night, she and her sisters planned their own escape route from their hospital beds.

Soon enough, they left the hospital and headed out west to Vancouver where they met crowds of people. Then, back on the train again, making their way south into California. Everywhere they went they talked about the fire. She was the best at making the blaze sound terrifying and amplifying their plight. Her stories, while not true, pleased Osborne—although she hated the way he tried to give her his approval, awkward winks and smarmy smiles. It was enough to make her throw up. She'd gotten an odd feeling about him. The way he stared at the five of them…. Maybe he always had? She couldn't remember or she hadn't noticed. But every time she looked up lately, there were his eyes. Something in his gaze, she realized, bothered her, containing an edge that shouldn't be there when adults look at children. She was familiar, had felt that gaze countless times from strange men nearly everywhere she went. But she'd never seen it on his face before. Or at least she didn't think she had.

They were hardly ever alone anymore. Osborne indicated that

they'd made themselves untrustworthy. The school, he conceded, had been a mistake. Those other girls, those little French girls, as fast as they were? Well, he hadn't thought it through. When she asked what had happened to Elsa or their schoolmates, he simply waved her away.

When they arrived in Los Angeles, back at the same odd house in the Hollywood Hills, there were no more reporters, but lots of lessons. Private tutors picked up where Elsa had left off. Voice teachers came to give them lessons on dictions, to stop their tongues from slipping into the "yeas" and "okays" like the other kids did. The voice instructor would hold their tongues, making them repeat inane nursery rhymes over and over again, telling them to stop being lazy with their glottal stops. An angular, severe-looking woman from Paris came twice a week to help give their French a precision that—as she often reminded them—the French Canadians were too lazy to learn. A makeup artist trained them to pluck their eyebrows and their widow's peaks. They were taught to shave their legs, their armpits, to put on stockings, to help each other fasten themselves into girdles and brasseries. They learned to sew on buttons, to mix cocktails and tie a man's tie.

She utterly hated all of it—the schoolwork, the lessons, the tutors. She would stay a little girl, if only she could. This "learning to be a woman" was not what she had imagined. Most of all, she hated the way each bright, sunny California day mocked their imprisonment. She and her sisters read the movie star magazines, read about the restaurants and the parties, but they weren't going anywhere themselves.

They were trapped in the house for months during their twelfth year—but at least they were together, they reminded each other. And in July, within days of each other, they each menstruated for the first time. Anglette was first, discovering three droplets of blood on a Tuesday morning. She rushed into the bedroom, holding her underwear aloft her head, tears streaming down her cheeks.

"It's happened," she sobbed. "It happened, it happened—it happened."

They gathered around Anglette, hugging her, and she felt a stabbing pain in her chest. She tried to hide her secret wish from her sisters—that she would be last, or that it wouldn't happen at all to her.

Wednesday afternoon, after a swim in the pool, Madeline and Eliane discovered they were next. Another round of tears, and she felt the mounting fear like a belly full of ice, and she hardly wanted to touch her sisters for fear that womanhood was catching.

She nearly screamed the next morning when, brushing her teeth, she felt something trickle down her leg. She pulled up the nightgown and saw the slow rivulet of blood against her white skin. She felt the hot tears on her cheeks and when she looked up, there was Madeline who held her tightly and said, "It's okay, okay? It's okay."

Madeline helped her into the menstrual belt and hooked the sanitary napkin to it. She helped her into panties and then a dress, all the while singing to her softly because she could not stop crying.

Later that afternoon during a geography lesson, Calendre was the final member. When she came back from the bathroom, she announced, "It's here. I'm last."

They gathered around each other, a fresh round of tears beginning anew. It meant some sadness to them. Even if they weren't sure why. The tutor stared as they piled on top of each other.

"Girls, girls, the lesson," she called out softly once or twice before leaving the make-shift classroom entirely, thinking it would be indecent to stay.

As they squeezed each other's arms and faces, as they pushed their hands into the depth of each other's hair, they realized finally that all the *stuff* they were learning meant that they would have to do these things one day, to have a husband, a house, a family, children. Would have to be apart from each other. She could feel the pain of that realization radiating off of each of her sisters and she realized that the older they got, the more distant they would become.

They moped around the next few days, wanting to spend their time huddled together in a pack. She felt panicky when she was more than arm's reach away from any of her sisters. She stole several cigarettes from a nurse's purse and Anglette and Eliane practiced smoking with her in the bathroom while they examined themselves in the mirror to see if they all looked more like women yet. Anglette and Eliane agreed that, although she'd been next to last, she was the one who looked the most grown up. Unlike her sisters who would just play at inhaling, she breathed the smoke into her lungs and blew it out of her mouth, movie star style. She looked at herself in the mirror and realized that she did look different now, had a hard edge to her face. She couldn't see the same little girl who, just a day or two earlier, gazed back at her from the mirror. She looked at her sisters' faces searching for it too, trying to see if they had changed as well. But she couldn't find it in their eyes, their cheeks, or their brows. They looked utterly the same to her. And she felt gutted.

When they got caught, they were sent to Rhys Osborne, who looked the three of them up and down.

"It isn't the smoking that hurts me," he told them while lighting his own cigarette. "But the theft."

They had new dresses made, longer ones that made them look less like little girls and more like young women. In a few month's time, she and her sisters would be thirteen. She could hardly imagine it.

Six months in Los Angeles and then they were back on trains and planes, crisscrossing the United Stated like a sideshow carnival. With a troop of nurses and Osborne leading the charge, they made stops at places whose names she could barely remember. She felt some days that she would simply close her eyes and die if she had to smile again, if she had to wave again, if she had to tell anyone how wonderful it was to see him or her.

In a coastal town somewhere, the weather still warm for January, they turned thirteen and spent the day eating pieces of crunchy fried fish and having their pictures taken hundreds of times while the new stockings and brasseries itched their young bodies in the damp heat. The light wool made her sweat, and she was relieved that night when they returned to their hotel, her belly aching from the lard-laden fish.

Osborne was waiting for them in their room, and the girls exchanged glances. He rarely met them at the end of the day unless it was to reprimand them for their behavior. But she thought that they had all been exceptionally charming that day, even Calendre had managed to eat her fair share of the fish though she was easily the smallest of the five—not that people ever noticed.

"Relax, girls. Get comfortable."

He lit a cigarette and sat down in the lounge in front of a big picture window. Their room was on the top floor of the hotel and afforded them a little glimpse of the ocean off in a distance. Rhys Osborne stared out at it as she and her sisters removed their shoes and sat in a semicircle at his feet like they had been trained to do when he came to them for one of his little talks.

"I have some news for you girls," he said quietly. "The government has decided to return you to your parents' home once we get back to Témiscaming." He paused before continuing. "They've built a house close to the river, and when we return, you'll live there with them. I will continue on as your guardian to make sure that you receive the best of care. I've already hired some of your favorite nurses to work in the house."

She felt the ice return to her belly and she exchanged looks with her sisters. They all looked as frightened as she felt. Who were their parents? Certainly, they had met those people before. They were always awkward and smelled a bit of outside or of a barn or something more foul, but they hadn't ever imagined their day-to-day life with people other than their nurses. What would this mean to live with a family? With their family, if it was in fact fair to call it theirs?

"And as another surprise, I'm having a television installed in the house."

He took a drag of the cigarette and stared out at the sun as it dropped in the sky.

"A little enthusiasm here, girls. You're going home."

And what was home? she wondered. What did it mean?

MOTHER

DURING THE INTERVENING YEAR and a half between the fire and the day that the house was ready to be inhabited, Rhys Osborne had given her only the briefest explanation regarding the Quints' location—they'd shot some new advertisements, attended the Academy Awards in Los Angeles, and had travelled around the United States making goodwill visits.

He mentioned much of this casually between the lists and directions he kept sending her. Money was transferred to the bank weekly and lists of things she needed to purchase came nearly every day from Osborne's office. She poured over the lists of things that Rhys Osborne had told her, the map of things that she did not know about her own children—Calendre was an epileptic, Madeline liked to steal, and Anglette would not eat anything green, not ever. Briefly, she thought of the reporter's face when she'd said, "Every six months or so."

But it felt like a chance to be a real mother for the girls, to be a real family. She hoped it was. It might offer her the "lasting happiness" that she kept reading about in *Ladies Home Journal*. It would fill that empty hole that just seemed to get bigger and bigger each year. There was a brief period, after they had taken the babies and before they had become the *cause célèbre*, that her life had felt like her own. Afterwards, everything felt like erasure. In some ways the erasure was who she was now, always Mrs. August Phalene. Or, Mother of the Quintuplets, without so much as a courtesy inclusion of her name.

Rhys Osborne supervised the entire move remotely through an army of secretaries and assistants. He didn't let them take much from the farmhouse. They left behind the Sears & Roebuck stove, the large family bed, and even the wicker basket that had been the Quint's first bed and then, after, the bed of each of their siblings. Of course, her husband insisted on taking the wireless. She prepared for the arrival—the return—of the girls as best she could.

She was happy to go, and she wasn't. Her destiny seemed guided entirely by them even though their connection to her own life seemed fleeting.

Men and more men moved things into the house. Large ornate beds for all five girls. More clothing than she'd seen in a lifetime. Identical sets of hairbrushes, nightgowns, shoes. A seemingly endless supply of objects was marshaled into the home.

The new house was sizable, with the largest of the bedrooms reserved for the Quints while the remaining four bedrooms were for the rest of the family. A small house at the back of the property would be reserved for the staff that Rhys Osborne had hired. He'd dictated the furnishing of the rest of the house—wall-to-wall carpeting and thick, heavy drapes printed with scenes of girls and boys riding bicycles through the countryside. There was indoor plumbing and a massive kitchen that frightened her with its appliances that hummed and sang. Machines to wash the dishes and the clothing. A hoover to pick up crumbs, and a pale blue icebox that didn't need ice.

Worst of all was the television. While her husband brought the wireless radio to the bedroom they shared, the television sat in the part of the house that Osborne's assistant kept calling a "rumpus room" And what did this mean? What kind of chaos were the children meant to make on the chintz sofas in front of the hulking, buzzing television? She hated the way it sounded—all the voices were high-pitched and nasal, as though someone was yelling from down the hall. The women with their tiny waists and perfect makeup. How in the world did they run a household? The other three children were fascinated by the thing and spent the first few days in the new house turning it off and on and begging to eat dinner in front of the giant box. She prayed each night to the Virgin that the thing would fall apart, that she would never have to hear it again, not ever.

The new staff helped her scrub and disinfect each of the rooms in the house, and the Quints' personal cook went with her to the market to help her purchase a selection of food that would be prepared only for the quintuplets. She fumbled through her purse trying to make do on the budget her husband had given her to feed the other five members of the family.

On the night before the Quints' arrival, she and her husband met with Rhys Osborne in the kitchen of the cavernous new house. They all spoke in French as Osborne laid out the specifics of his plan.

He instructed her not to give the girls chores, not to discipline or interfere with their daily routine, which would be overseen by himself and his stewards, a maid, cook, and governess, all of whom were to live in the small servants' quarters in the rear. Her husband, who had been unemployed since the fire, had resumed drinking with new vitality. He had come home only moments before and she steeled herself for what was bound to be anger amplified by drink.

"Who do you think you are?" he said, leaning across the table to look at Osborne.

She watched as Osborne's face wrinkled. He had smelled the drink on her husband. He looked at his watch, and then gave her a small tight smile as her husband continued to rage,

"They are my children," he said, slamming his square hand down hard onto the newly purchased table. "I will raise them how I wish."

"They are *not* yours, Mr. Phalene," Rhys Osborne said, gathering his papers and getting up from the table. "They are the children of the King, and they are under my care, and I will do what I wish. And if you interfere with that, Sir, I will make it so you never see those girls again."

The men looked at each other for a moment.

"You know I can do that, August."

He shrugged, and she felt her heart rise to her throat. She remained silent, knowing that saying anything would reveal just how important this was to her.

The next morning, waiting for the children to arrive, she was as nervous as she had been when, years ago, she waited on August to arrive for their first date. She'd gotten up early and scrubbed the other three children. As she tried to dress, she hardly recognized her face in the mirror. Were those her dark circles? And when had that collection of wiry grays appeared on each side of her parted hair? She saw her mother more than herself. She wasn't even forty. As she peered at her own face, she wondered if she would have looked this way had she chosen not to get married at all. She tried on her best three dresses before her husband called to her from the bed.

"You look fat in everything. It's no matter what you wear."

He pulled the covers back over his head. In spite of the fact that it was he who had insisted on how badly he wanted the Quints back in his home, he had no intention of greeting them.

There was still a chill in the air but with an indication that spring would be there any day. At 7:30, she bundled the children up in the heaviest coats they had and instructed them to sit quietly on the porch. They were not to touch each other or themselves. She had never beat them—could not bring herself to hit a child—but their father had and would, and that is what she promised them would happen should they mess themselves up before their sisters arrived. She went back in the house. Without the children or the television or the staff at work, she could hear the electric hum of the lamps, of the appliances. She'd never heard this kind of buzzing before, as though tiny bees had suddenly inhabited the house. She took some extra time to brush her hair and to put on what little makeup she had. She dressed herself warmly and looked out the window where she saw the children sitting stock-still. A small group of photographers had gathered outside the front gate and were doing their best to photograph the others, waiting for their siblings to come home.

At half past 8 o'clock, a glossy car pulled into the newly inlaid driveway that glistened with tiny pebbles from the shore. She waited with the three children as, one by one, the girls stepped from the car. Long limbed and quite pretty, she thought, they wore red wool coats in printed plaid and knee socks so blindingly white that the swath of cream-colored skin peeking out at the top of the fabric looked sallow by contrast.

She had anticipated coming to them warmly, scooping them up in her arms and covering them with kisses. But they hung back, interlocking their arms and then whispering to each other. When Rhys Osborne finally emerged from the car, he pushed them forward.

"*Dis bonjour,*" he said, his voice hushed but authoritative.

It embarrassed her that someone had to tell them to greet her. And it frightened her the way each set of five eyes focused on him—sharp and narrowed—but then their faces turned suddenly toward her, warm and lively.

She couldn't remember then when she'd seen them last. However long ago, the meeting had taken place in the confines of their nursery and she had been scrubbed up to her elbows and had her throat and hair sprayed with antiseptic. She and her husband had never been allowed to physically touch them. So during visits, they'd sometimes look at them—as any other visitor to *Quint-land!* might—through a glass partition. On rarer occasions, she and August took tea in Rhys Osborne's office—always chaperoned— the children sitting a short distance away and spending the majority of the time communicating only with each other in a rapid-paced

English that they could barely understand. Their French was just as good as their English, but they were not interested in their father's schemes for new products or in her laborious detailing of household chores. English was a border—a useful one—and using it maintained separation.

Once, as she recounted a story about their little sister Ingrid's christening, one of the girls had announced rather loudly in French so that she understood perfectly, "Are you done yet? Can you go? This is so boring."

Shocked, she dropped her teacup, which was still nearly full because anything ingested for hours after being doused with the antiseptic spray tasted strongly of chemicals.

That morning though, they came forward all at once, climbing the porch steps in unison before curtsying.

"*Bonjour, Mama.*"

They gave her *bisous* on both cheeks as they'd been instructed to do. She introduced them to their younger brothers and sister, each of whom stepped forward one at a time—shyly, almost begrudgingly—and shook hands with their older sisters. Of course, a special photographer hired by Osborne was present, and he captured the curtsies and the handshakes. He was there, too, when August finally stumbled out of the house, dressed only in slacks and a wrinkled dress shirt. That image didn't appear in the next day's papers, but a lovely picture of the family posed on the steps of their new brick house—each smiling broadly and brightly, all seemingly eager to plunge into their new adventure—made many front pages.

Even with the Quints in the house, she barely saw them. Staff brought breakfast to their oversized room at half past seven. Soon after, a maid cleaned their quarters while she was left on her own to clean and tend to the rest of the house, except the kitchen, which she was only permitted to enter during certain hours of the day. Their tutors came in every morning at about 8:30 while she bundled the three smaller children off to public school.

"Why do they get to stay home every day?" August Jr. whined one particularly cold morning as she double—and then triple—wrapped a new scarf about his face to protect him from the cold.

"They aren't like you," she told him.

The big house—as they all started calling it—was a beast to manage. Entirely on her own, she spent what seemed most of the day cleaning up after both the family and the parade of people who came in and out. There were tutors in the morning, and in the afternoon, a revolving schedule of psychologists, reporters, makeup artists, and photographers entered and left, seemingly of their own accord. After a while even Rhys Osborne stopped knocking and began letting himself in through the rear entrance in the kitchen as though he lived there, as if it were his right. And who was she to argue? Who was she to say anything at all?

SISTER

My sisters didn't bother to try and get to know the family. It was odd for them, living with these people who weren't their nurses. They were connected—always—to each other, but any other ties, such as DNA or love, seemed foreign and unfamiliar. Our father, they ignored almost entirely, and the little ones were warned by Rhys Osborne not to get too close to the Quints. They seemed only to like each other, to want to be only with each other, and this made our mother increasingly depressed.

The earlier promise of spring receded and remained a promise, and the bitter weather of March and April meant the youngest Phalenes brought home colds from the world outside the big house. All of my sisters got sick, one after the other, teetering like a row of dominos waiting to collapse.

"This will keep happening," Dr. LeFevre said, furrowing his eyebrows, after his fifth visit to the house in as many weeks. "You've got to keep them away from the other children."

Mother wanted to argue and explain to him that the Quints rarely saw their brothers or sister as it was. But instead, she just said, "Of course."

She had not seen Dr. LeFevre much since his prescription following our birth had sent her into the yard to chop wood. He always spoke to her like she was an idiot, and she resented most how he spoke to the press, as though *he* had given birth to the Quintuplets. As though she was not a real person, her body only a vessel to hold us prior to our birth. She hated the way advertisements and posters and even the silly movie had made it seem as though he was an authority on childrearing, this man who'd never been married and had no children of his own. What could he know?

But like our mother, LeFevre had also changed in the intervening thirteen years. There was a sizable paunch where his stomach had once been flat, and he drove a Packard Convertible Coupe that he paid to have simonized each week. While he maintained he still lived in Témiscaming, it was an open secret that he'd purchased a big house on Lakeshore Drive in Toronto. So while he was, in title, the Quintuplets' primary physician, LeFevre greatly preferred to perform his duties when the little girls traveled anywhere sunny and warm.

In response to their runny noses and phlegmy coughs, Dr. LeFevre prescribed heavy doses of penicillin for my sisters. And our mother tended to them—to all of her children—as best she could. Wanting so badly to mother, to feel that she was needed, or at least wanted, she had taken to sleeping with Ingrid—the youngest child— at night, crawling in bed next to the little girl after everyone else had drifted off. She wanted to be in any bed but her husband's.

My sisters were always to be somewhat sickly after they left *Quintland!* They'd grown up in an antiseptic and largely sterile environment and hadn't built up the defenses to germs that most children develop naturally. They were delicate in a way most people didn't understand, in a way I think they never understood. Because they had managed to stay alive in spite of war, polio, and the chickenpox, I think everyone believed them to be a little invincible. But they weren't. Not at all.

When my sisters had recovered, *Life Magazine* came to photograph the new house, to see how the girls were adjusting to life outside the gates of *Quintland!* Mother was surprised at how well they responded to questions. Almost without thinking, they rattled off answers about the warmth of family time and the love of their parents. They complimented their mother's cooking (which they had yet to taste) and their father's sense of humor, and soon even she was caught up in this idyllic (and patently false) vision of what their family must be like.

At night when visitors and staff had finally left, Mama would sometimes go to the wing of the house where their bedroom and bath were. She would stand in the doorway and watch them get ready for bed. She'd stand there hoping that they might stop reading or drawing or stitching—might stop whatever it was they were doing—and ask her to come in, to sit down, to talk. They never did. They would only pause momentarily at her voice when she might finally say, "Good night, my little ones."

"Good night, Mother," they would say, almost in unison, in a manner so stiff and formal they could have been addressing Rhys Osborne. It wasn't her fault. They just didn't know her, and my sisters had no idea how to be with a mother, and she had no idea how to mother them.

This went on for three long years, everyone living like a boarders in the big house. At times, when my sisters travelled, the house got even quieter. But things had slowed down for them considerably. As they turned fourteen and then fifteen, their allure waned and their popularity tapered off, but there was still a strong enough passing interest that they could always draw a crowd.

As my sisters continued to age, the ravages of our parents' poor genetics manifested itself in their features again and again. Without the insulation of *Quintland!* my sisters had to do more for themselves than ever before—though in truth, it still wasn't much. Rhys Osborne continued to exact control over all aspects of my sisters' public appearance. For example, Eliane's teeth desperately required braces, but Osborne refused to present her to the public with a face full of metal, so she was instructed to smile with her mouth shut. Madeline's breasts developed more quickly than my other sisters' had, and it pains me to think of the way they strapped her breasts down with bandages over an already tight brasserie to maintain the illusion of perfect childhood symmetry.

They were at best average. Average looking teenage girls with knobby knees and a look of preternatural excitement in their eyes. They wanted all the things that most teenage girls wanted, I supposed. Time on their own, friends and boyfriends, math class homework and an allowance. Normalcy. But instead, they worked, still using their image to push product, making public appearances before crowds of hundreds, sometimes thousands, and generally doing whatever Rhys Osborne expected of them. Even still, they managed to occupy most of our mother's time and energy. They demanded movie magazines, trips to the cinema on Main Street, and anything else they associated with being real girls. And Mama tried. Oh God, how she tried. So much that some days, she woke up feeling panicked as though she had forgotten a task, a request, or a wish, and as a result, the girls would be pulled away from her all over again. And when Mama vexed them, as she often did, they spoke over her to each other in English at a rapid pace in an effort to confuse her. Then she would be in tears. Not in front of them. No, never. But they saw the ways her eyes welled up, or became ribbed with red. They noticed how she'd dab at her face with a handkerchief to mask her sadness. That was the depth of their meanness and perhaps the only way they could exert a little control in this house, could find a little meaning in this strange space where they didn't belong and couldn't know anyone but each other.

FATHER

THE HOUSE HAD COST $140,000 to build and furnish, and it felt like a prison. For two years he walked up and down the halls, unsure of what to do with himself. He acted as a jailer of sorts to the Quints, making sure that no one left the house and spending time each day grinding Calendre's pills in a mortar and pestle to put in her food. But no one ever told him or his wife what the pills were for. It was like he was as trapped as they were. There was no work to be had for him. And besides, what use could he be to the world when he could hardly get up before 10 o'clock each day? In truth he thought he *should* be in jail. Here he was, a man with eight children and he did nothing to provide for them. His own parents hadn't spoken to him in years. They had changed their names even, not wanting to associate with the mess their lives had become. Everyone knew the Phalene name. But he couldn't hide from it any more than he could hide from himself. His children were the Empire's favorite citizens, and what was he? Nothing. The cabinets and cupboards were filled with more than forty products that the Quints endorsed. They had more toothpaste, and more linens, and more soap than he'd ever seen in his life.

He felt that the whole world was against him. Except for the church. His priest, always his council, came by the house each day and took his confession and said a rosary. It was the only time of the day that he felt safe. When the father's fingers made the sign of the cross on his forehead, for a moment, he felt whole again.

He started spying on the girls shortly after they turned fifteen. At first, he did it when they were sleeping, after the staff had left for the day. He waited until they were asleep. The house needed to be completely still before he crept across the upstairs corridor into their rooms. He would crack the door just slightly, imagining that he could see their chests move up and down. He didn't imagine how these could be his children, so different than the others. He didn't understand them, the way they spoke, or ate. He didn't understand what they did all day, or why they looked at him with such contempt. He didn't understand why he did it, or what it was that pushed him out of bed each night. But the more he saw, the more he wanted to see.

He started feeling like he needed to watch them when they were awake. At meal times, or in the evening, when they would deign to sit with the rest of the family around the television, he found himself staring at them. He analyzed the backs of their necks. He noted the moles on their faces and snuck glances at the faint shadow of hair across the tops of their lips. He registered the sounds of their laughter, the ways they tucked their feet underneath them, and marveled at how one bit her nails and another didn't. Everything from their eyelashes to their fingertips, he worked to commit to memory. He noticed how some of them scuffed their shoes, or when one or another had a loose string on her dress, or a hangnail, an ingrown hair. These little things haunted him into the night. He lay in bed, unable to sleep, cataloging their being in his head.

Finally, when the Quints were away on a day trip to Toronto and the rest of the household was quiet, he drilled a small hole in the wall of the adjoining room, hiding it in a dark seam between two wood panels. The hallway closet provided him the perfect opportunity to watch as long as he liked without being caught. He'd been so long and so often absent from the house that no one missed him, no one suspected him. Was he doing something wrong? Were these feelings wrong? He didn't want to know, didn't want to ask such questions, though they rattled around on lower frequencies in his mind. He found that watching the girls six or seven hours a day made him feel better. He watched their bodies, small and nubile, trying to remember if their mother had even looked like that.

He watched them laugh and talk when they thought they were alone. He watched as they stiffened themselves whenever any of the staff or their mother came in. He listened to them sing along with records, practice dance steps. They braided each other's hair, teased and fought in French and in English. They hugged and kissed. They talked endlessly to each other, gossiping about their mother and their siblings, and sometimes about him. They made fun of the nurses, and the staff, even Osborne. They revealed hidden stashes of chocolates, maple candies, bubble gum.

He told his priest to stop coming. He didn't need or want him anymore. When the priest would show up anyway, he'd hide in the root cellar after threatening his wife's life if she so much as looked out the window as the Father banged against the door. He'd often make a show of going down to the cellar, demanding that no one bother him or intrude. He wouldn't explain it—just make it known that he was not be disturbed. No one cared enough to wonder where he was or to suspect that he wasn't, in fact, down in the cellar. Other times, he'd leave the home, walking out the front door, saying he'd return when he wanted to. Out of sight from the house, he'd circle back and sneak in the back or even a side window. Though he was hiding indoors, no one waited for him, and no one pondered his absence. In their minds, if they thought of him at all, he was simply "away," and that sat comfortably with everyone and so the truth didn't occur to anyone.

Dedicated to watching, he started missing meals. And when circumstances allowed it, and when he kept his nerve up, he took to hiding in the armoire in their bedroom, a massive piece of furniture used only to store the Quints' out-of-season clothing. Among their light cotton summer dresses, parasols, bathing suits and sun hats, he made an oversized nest for himself. Poor craftsmanship meant the doors of the armoire never completely closed, and so through the hairline opening, he watched them. In the small, confined space he breathed in their scent on their clothing, the slightly powdery and acidic odor of teenage girls stung his nostril each time. And eventually he realized his own scent mingled with theirs to create a smoky, earthy combination, like something from a barn.

The few times his wife questioned him on where he'd been, he slapped her, hard, across the face and told her to mind her business. The weight of the watching took its toll, and he wasted away, becoming so thin that he had to cut extra holes into his belt. Eventually, he bought a pair of suspenders.

He stopped going to Detant's pasture, stopped drinking entirely. All he could think of was the girls. When he'd finally find an opportunity to sneak out of the closet or the armoire, his legs would ache so he'd do deep knee bends and lie on the bed for an hour or two, listening to the sounds of the bustling of the house and wishing that he could go back there. He wished that he could spend every hour of every day in that armoire. He wished he could touch them. He wanted to run his hands through their hair, down their faces, along their shoulders. He wanted to smell their breath and to feel the moisture under their arms. He imagined birthing them, kissing them, marrying them, killing them. He could not understand how he had spent so long away from their magic. It had cured him. It had restored him, and he thought now that he might be a better man, a better father, a better husband.

CALENDRE

SHE DIDN'T KNOW WHY or how, but she could feel him watching them. Terror. The very panic she felt seemed to induce her seizures, evermore violent, and her sisters, well-trained by this point, would stick spoons or sometimes, dangerously, even their flat palms into her mouth to keep her from choking on or biting off her tongue. When she would come out of it, vaguely looking around, the feeling would be gone.

The seizures always came on when she could sense him there. She would try and check under beds or in the bathroom to assuage her mounting panic, but before she knew it, she would enter the blackness of a fit and by the time she was out of it, the sensation of being watched was gone. How could she explain this feeling to her sisters? How could she make them understand that even in this house, even in the privacy of their room, there were eyes everywhere. Just as there always had been.

ANGLETTE

SHE FELT CHAFED IN the big house, squashed by the expectation that they would try to love these people, try to make nice with these strangers. Her father stared at her and her sisters like a freak. The other brothers and sister were the same. They never really talked to them, mostly just looked up at them with big eyes that blinked too infrequently. Their table manners were atrocious, and they had nothing to talk about. When they tired of them, she and her sisters switched into a rapid English, mocking the way they smelled, the way they ate.

She and her sisters wiped their mouths between bites like they'd been taught to do and exchanged looks and made faces at their father when he wasn't looking. Which was almost never. Anglette couldn't say for certain why they disliked him so deeply. But they did. For her, something about their father reminded her of someone else. Of many someone elses, perhaps. All those men's voices on the other side of the mirror. Or those photographers who always called them *baby doll* or *sweetheart*. They pushed the food around the plates making decorative formations. They always had their food specially made, even though they often ended up eating alongside their family at the big, formal dining room table.

"Eat, please," her mother would plead with them, and they would roll their eyes before, sometimes, taking a bite or two.

"So wasteful," their father said before leaving the room before anyone else, thus ending his participation in the family affairs and thereby ending theirs as well.

She started spending more and more time each day peering into the mirror, watching the ways in which her face was becoming different from her sisters' faces. She could see the way Madeline's nostrils flared ever so slightly, that Fabienne was more muscular, that Eliane weighed a few more pounds than Calendre, who was so slight. However, their match was still perfect enough that even her mother had trouble telling them apart. At this task, however, Rhys Osborne seemed particularly adept, being able to identify the difference between Fabienne and Madeline—or any other of her sisters—without a moment's hesitation.

She thought her face was the most unremarkable. But she had her mole, and she had her hair. It was long and thick, lustrously curly and less coarse than her sisters. She wore it in a braid that reached the middle of her back, longer hair than any of her sisters, all of whom suffered from what Dr. LeFevre called trichotillomania. It started slowly. A tic or affectation. Unnoticeable, mostly. Over time, the sisters began to be unable to stop themselves, finally pulling and tugging at strands and then fistfuls of their own hair, raw hunks of scalp peeking through, skin littering their shoulders. Other than her, they all had bald spots around the napes of their necks or at the crown. Hair stylists tried to cover the baldness with victory rolls or elaborate up-dos. She alone stayed away from the stress-induced pulling and tugging and instead let them undo the braid and brush it gently.

She wasn't docile in the way her other sisters could be. She fell asleep in appointments, purposely stared into the camera during television interviews. Sometimes she talked a lot and other times not at all. Sometimes she was worried she would have nothing to say, and other times she worried that if she did talk, everything would come out.

She had secrets, secrets from her sisters even. She believed in her happiness, which she was certain lived around her heart. She hid two lipsticks in her dresser drawer because she didn't want to share, and she kept a diary in the space between her mattress and box spring. And then there was her biggest secret: the way she felt about Rhys Osborne. There had been so little contact with any boys since that first tingle announced by the two Pauls, and since then, boys were all she thought about. She wondered about the way they looked and smelled. She imagined the way their hands might feel on her bare skin, and the boys in her mind became vague men, who then took the singular form of Osborne. She spent a long time in the bath each night playing out imagined evenings with Osborne. They would go to dinner, or to a film. He would put his hand on the small of her back as she got out of the car. She imagined the feel of her cheek against his, and eventually, she thought of his lips pressed firmly against hers.

She couldn't remember when she had started to feel that way, but she thought it may have begun in a dream she'd had a year of two earlier, when she'd woken up feeling panicked, breathing quickly, excited. When Fabienne had asked her what was wrong, she'd only mumbled "nothing" under her breath. But what she remembered about the underwater tension of her dream life was Rhys Osborne taking off her blouse, of her calling him Anthony. And after that, she didn't know what. She knew from the nurses that men and women slept together after they were married, and at least two of them had cautioned her and her sisters that they could get pregnant now, could become mothers. But she wasn't sure how. Not exactly.

Even though his ears were much too large for his head, perched perilously on each side, as if somehow ready to take flight in an attempt to find another body, one with a larger face, she liked him. But she fell in love—not with the man, but with his mole, a mole that matched her own in shape and diameter. The mole on the inside of his neck. She hadn't seen any other. His flesh was remarkably unblemished, as though he were new, as though he had just had the packaging pulled off of him. So she was happy to find the mole. The hidden imperfection, his mark was somehow proof to her that he was a good match for her. This blemish on his otherwise smooth surface made it all make sense.

"What do you think of Rhys Osborne?" she asked Eliane one night as they brushed their teeth.

"Think of him how?"

She spit into the sink and considered the question.

"Do you think he's…cute?"

Eliane stepped back for a moment and peered in her face. "Are you being silly, or are you just nuts?"

She rinsed her mouth. She knew that her sister could sense a lie and she felt her cheeks get hot. Eliane grabbed her by the wrist.

"What are you talking about? You know that he is the reason that we live like this. Like freaks."

She shook free of Eliane, who followed her back into the other room where her other sisters lounged around listening to records.

"Thank God you're *finally* done," Madeleine said, getting up off the rug. "Other people have to go, you know!"

"Wait," Eliane said. "Just wait until you hear this. Anglette had a crush on Rhys Osborne."

There was a chorus of *ewws*….

They prodded her, but she wouldn't answer. They teased her all night and well into the next day until she final broke down and denied it all. Said that she was making a joke, said that she was sorry and they hugged her and told her that it was all right, that they were lonely in the big house too.

But she was lying and she would find ways to spend time alone with him. She made excuses to visit him in the small office he kept down the road from their home. He always welcomed her warmly. She started by eating the toffees he kept in cut glass dishes in his office. She rolled the toffee around on her tongue. She would close her eyes, the sweetness filling every crevice of her mouth. And when she would open them again, Rhys Osborne would always be looking at her peculiarly.

They started meeting almost weekly. He sent a car for her and made tea. Her sisters always asked why she was going. But she didn't answer, feeling herself pulling further and further away from them.

She listened to him, but she didn't talk. Because what could she say? He told her that he could see the Quints with his eyes closed, could see the depressions and angles of their faces. He told her his degree had been a waste, that he was a dreamer, that he had a powerful imagination and so much energy flowing through him.

She knew it too. She could feel it; she wanted him to touch her. Wanted him to be close to her. Every time she let him talk, she couldn't look at him, knowing that if she did it would confirm that she was making a mistake. Instead, she bit the inside of her mouth and clutched at the sleeves of her dress and looked down at the expanse of fabric in her lap. She liked the sound of his voice, how he told a story in a way that felt like he was making it up, not repeating it.

He gave her the cakes and tarts they weren't allowed in the big house. He served her savory pâtés and rich creamy soups, and on occasion, a half glass of port. He saved her favorite for last, serving tart pickled beets right before the silky smooth *tartin de pomme*. He would press his fork onto the last crumbs of the tartlet, making sure he didn't miss anything. He would wipe his mouth, sigh contently and murmur, "Very nice, very nice." The pickling juice from the beets made the tart that much sweeter.

One afternoon he told her a story about his life. His wife who died, his time in New York. He said that he was just like them, a child who didn't know his parents. He only wished that he'd had someone like himself to look out for him. As she prepared to leave, gathering her pocketbook and dusting crumbs out of her lap, he touched her hand.

"I like our talks so much. You really seem to hear me, to understand me."

She nodded. She felt as though she were glowing. As though, if someone saw her in that moment, they'd think she'd been lit for a scene in a movie. He really saw her. Who knew her better, outside of her sisters? And who else did he have that he could trust?

"You can help me with your sisters, can't you?" he asked.

She nodded.

"I need someone who understands that I want the best for you. That I know what is best for you."

He didn't look as old in the light as she thought he was. She couldn't tell. She leaned down to him sitting in the chair and she kissed him. He stood then, wrapping his arms around her waist and it felt nice. Safe. Warm. She couldn't remember that kind of embrace from anyone. His hands felt smooth like she'd imagined they would be, and his vinegar breath was hot on her face as he pulled her closer than anyone ever had.

"Nice," he whispered. "Like the cake. Very nice."

She wished that he had told her she was beautiful, or that he had found something about her to call beautiful. He slid his hands down her legs and reached around and grabbed her braid, touching it to the tip of his nose.

It wasn't like what she'd expected. He undressed her without ceremony and was then on top of her. She liked feeling this close to him. She'd only ever been in such close contact with her sisters, and the weight of his body on hers made her blush suddenly, as if she were in a crowded room instead of a locked office. He shifted and pushed her leg so that it was perpendicular with her hips, and then he groaned deeply.

It hurt, felt almost like she was being ripped in half. His weight on top of her felt like she was being smashed onto the desk, again and again. She chewed the inside of her cheek to keep from crying out from the pain. She imagined that with each exhale of his breath, she understood something better about him and who he was. Finally, he climbed off of her and helped her to her feet. He pulled up his pants and dressed her. He fastened the zipper with sure and steady hands, making sure that he smoothed the skirts down against her crinoline, taking care to look her over from head to toe.

"Are you alright?"

She nodded.

She was shaking when she got back in the car. *Why was she shaking so much?* Her whole body felt raw from head to toe. On the way home to the big house, she felt odd, and when she got there, she went straight to her bed. Soon, she jumped up, ran to the bathroom and vomited once. Eliane had followed her and, in the bathroom, held back her hair.

"Are you not feeling well?" Madeline asked?

"Call the nurse," Fabienne said.

The nurse took her temperature, checked her throat and pressed on her stomach.

"You seem fine," the nurse said. "But take it easy if you aren't feeling well."

She stayed in bed for the rest of the night, willing herself awake as she listened to the house sounds, wondering what made her so special.

SISTER

IT WAS ANOTHER AFTERNOON when they ended up on his office divan, naked, that she became infatuated with him. I wanted to help my sister, to explain that the universe was not orderly and divined. I wanted to explain that if it were, I would be there with her. That if it were, she wouldn't be there, in an old man's arms. And I wanted to tell her that sometimes a mole was just a mole, an angry collection of cells. Nothing more.

MOTHER

SHE WANTED SO BADLY to teach them something, anything. She spent two years trying desperately to become a mother to the Quints, while she could barely mother the others. They would come each day and it physically pained her to have to kiss them, to have to pretend like she cared about the pettiness that occurred at the playground, or their games of "Mother May I?"

Nothing in the house felt like hers—not the husband, not the smaller children, and certainly not the Quints. She felt like a lodger nearly everywhere. The only part of the day she enjoyed was the early morning when the house was still quiet and she could sit staring out at the churning icy Ottawa River and imagine jumping into it. Winter never seemed to end in the big house and all the days blended together in an endless cycle—cleaning, laundry to be washed, food to be bought, dishes to be done, and three small and needy children to deal with. She tried hard not to snap at them, because even though *she* couldn't feel it, she wanted *them* to feel love.

Most days she tried to stay out of the way. She woke up early to have the solitude of the house before the Quints' staff arrived to begin their day. She tried to avoid her husband, who, although he had stopped drinking, had only seemed to get angrier and angrier with her. He pestered her with questions about the Quints and when she couldn't answer or didn't know, he threw things or broke things or stomped off to wherever he went to during the day. He made enough trouble, enough frustration, and enough weight on the other side of the bed. She questioned why she got married to a man she wasn't even sure she liked—certainly now, but perhaps ever. She had been in love, she thought. Or what she thought at the time was love. Now, she saw it as something quite different, as an attachment to the first man who had shown her some interest.

The television helped to pass the time. She would hide in the rumpus room when the house got glutted with people, glad to hear the TV voices that she at least recognized. Sometimes she would put on her boots and coat and slip out the back door, often forgetting that her other children, the ones she was obligated to care for, would arrive home shortly. She avoided walking into downtown Témiscaming and stayed along the river instead. She liked that it sounded so loud, the thundered rushing felt like it was beside her and over her and under her. She couldn't imagine being that free, raging that openly.

Sometimes she thought about her life before August, wondered what would have happened if she'd never been married. Other times she had fantasies that the house was totally empty and she would run through it in nothing but her skin, shouting out whatever came into her head—songs, poems, her favorite color. She would land out of breath in the kitchen, sweating and relieved. But the house was never empty. She was as trapped as those girls.

Those girls, she could hardly remember being their age. Who were they? What were they like. She remembered vaguely that she had liked to paint. She remembered at one time doing flowers and portraits of friends, but she couldn't remember what any of the pictures looked like. Her mind was crowded with other things now; she'd stopped dreaming at some point. When had that happened?

When she came back from these walks, she would lock herself in the downstairs bathroom—tiled entirely in pink—and stare at herself in the mirror. Where was she? She touched the mirror as though the image would evaporate. She smudged its surface and her reflection.

ARCHIVES

Catherine Lillian Phalene

Catherine Phalene, who gave birth to quintuplets in 1940, died yesterday at March 10th, 2000, at North Bay Hospital in North Bay, Ontario.

She was 85 years old and had been living in the five-bedroom home in Témiscaming that the government built for the family in 1952.

Neither the hospital nor the family provided the cause of death.

The birth of five identical girls to Mrs. Phalene in January 1940 caused a sensation. The five had developed from a single egg and were the first set of quintuplets known to have survived. The odds of having quintuplets without fertility drugs are one in 85 million births.

ANTHONY RHYS OSBORNE

THERE WAS NO ROMANCE in what happened with Anglette. And while this was infatuation for her, it seemed to him as easy as anything else he did to the girls. He didn't have a strict code about the difference between business and pleasure, and he had no code about the difference between the personal and the professional. And in spite of an early taste of shame, there wasn't much that differentiated for him a specific right from wrong.

The weighty shame he felt once so long ago—upon hearing the sisters utter their shared first word, that first "*No*," that one word that came all in unison—paradoxically had freed him from shame and guilt. He had heard them, and in response, he felt shame. And then, he dismissed it utterly. From that moment, he was without shame. He inhabited this space—all space—without the bothersome ideas of consequence or punishment polluting him. He was outside of it, beyond it. And everything in and around those girls was his.

Things got easier for a time afterward. Anglette made the girls more agreeable and more docile. She acted as a go-between, negotiating tactics for being able to choose their own clothes and then even suggesting that they begin high school. Things had been so good that he agreed at first. It wouldn't hurt him to get them away from those parents who ruined every photograph by lurking in the background like a set of shadowy peasants.

He found a high school—a private school located just outside of Montreal. He had picked a place for children like them. Important. Wealthy. Children not accustomed to the hallways, rules, jostling, late nights of homework and demanding parents that most children suffered. He had already made arrangements for them to live in a dormitory separated from the other students and had hired a chef close by to prepare them their meals in accordance with the diet Dr. LeFevre had created.

It wasn't until he thought through the setup—thought about other children, about boys, about the way in which they would not seem special at all, especially surrounded by a gaggle of teenagers who were better looking or more charming than they were—that he began to question it.

Already, things were not going well financially. There hadn't been many public appearances in the last couple of years (although there had been advertising campaigns and television shows broadcast to America). At their last public performance, the girls sang at the Canadian National Exhibition for the woman who was his Queen, the woman who, when her father had died the year they turned twelve, had become (along with him) their legal guardian.

At the exhibition, they sang a slightly pitchy version of a ballad meant to convey motherly love. His Queen, her face frozen into a tight little smile, looked off into the distance, past them, beyond them, out toward the other citizens of her empire, for whom—he believed—she also felt responsible. He imagined she found them trite and freakish, another in the labyrinth of responsibilities that had engulfed her since her father's death. And he pitied her a little.

In December, he presented the girls with a treatment for *Five of a Kind*, which he hoped would be a kind of comeback picture. The movie was a kind of sequel to *The Country Doctor*, the premise of which had them travelling down to California to cheer up the poor and ailing doctor who had saved them from certain death in the brutal Northwest.

Five of a Kind was a convoluted detective story scheduled to be shot entirely in Canada. The treatment outlined a story in which a young heiress is kidnapped. The Quints (again as the Wyatt Quintuplets) would crack the case and find the girl in the rustic Northern Ontario wilderness. There would be a comedic Mountie, and a handsome young actor up from America would play their father who would assist them as they went about solving the case. In the movie, the Quints were meant to be twelve. By the time production was to begin, however, they would be nearly sixteen. He would have to do things to make them look younger, and more innocent.

The film had come to him from an American friend. As the advertising deals shrank and the money in the liquid part of their assets dwindled—taking care of that many people, himself included, took a lot of money—he was on the hunt again for new revenue streams. The agent had promised this would be a hit. The children who had grown up with the Phalene Five were teenagers now animated with nostalgia for their childhood, and with a little money to spend. And who better than the Phalenes to capitalized on it. The Americans—the agent promised—would love it. Canada at its rustic best, the true north, strong and free. And he hoped that, better yet, the film would entice visitors to come back to Northern Ontario, and maybe, just maybe, they could convince the government to rebuild *Quintland!* This was his hope.

Fabienne said "no" right away. They'd been made other promises for the fall. High school, first of all and most importantly. Secondly, she pointed out, they had been told they could have their own clothes and abandon their lifelong wardrobe of identical outfits. They wanted desperately to go, and Rhys Osborne had promised that, this year for certain, they would be able to attend school with other boys and girls.

Even though they said "no" to *Five of a Kind*, in truth they had no choice. They were still minors and he was their legal guardian. He told Anglette to sell it to them.

"Make them be nice girls. Like you," he said, stroking her face. "Tell them to be good and to behave."

She promised she would. And she kissed the tips of his fingers in a way that made him feel squeamish.

"Good girl," he said, pulling his hand from her lips.

SISTER

INSTEAD OF GOING TO school outside Montreal that fall, my sisters were sent to Toronto, where sets were being constructed and where a pretty blond, who later went on to do a number of Hitchcock films, was cast as the kidnapped heiress.

To be close to the set, they moved back into the Queen Street Hospital, the rooms being outfitted for their purposes. And while *Quintland!* had been their first real home, my sisters were overcome by a melancholy brought on by the sense memory of the antiseptic halls, the wire-meshed windows, and their feeling that they were constantly looking out, looking down at the rest of Canada.

Only a week passed between the time they were moved to when filming began. My sisters were put through rigorous exercise regimens in the same rooms in which they had learned to crawl and then walk. Hours of routines designed by Canada Fitness consisted of squats and lunges and jumping jacks, all while a diet expert from the Hospital for Sick Children clapped her hands in time to classical music—Rhys Osborne's choice. They went back, it seemed, to old ways: people peering at them to make sure that the illusion of sameness stayed perfect for the film's panning effects, which would help to illustrate my sisters as a very real set of carbon copies.

And then Anglette started to gain weight. She was a good ten pounds heavier than my other sisters within a month. Our sisters noticed but never said a word, not even when the seamstress had to let out her dress. Rhys Osborne was furious and put her on a diet. I don't know why he didn't think of it then. He'd been doing whatever he liked with her, whenever he liked.

Anglette felt a certain pleasure in watching herself grow. And she did keep growing. She would take a deep breath each day and climb onto the doctor's scale in their bathroom and adjust the scales until the numbers crept up to a new level she had never before seen. Her fingers became as fat as breakfast sausages and she reveled in their roundness. Her belly filled out, becoming round and smooth. She pushed, took a deep breath, squished, and slowly wriggled into her clothing. How did she even know what it meant. Had she made any connection to her visits to his office and her growing belly?

"I'm pregnant," she whispered one afternoon to Rhys Osborne after they'd finished filming for the day. Our sisters were busy getting into their coats, trying to trick the makeup women into surrendering lipsticks and hairspray that they weren't normally allowed to have.

He looked up sharply. She repeated herself.

His face fell. Rhys Osborne had felt for years entitled to my sisters in all ways but one. And then he felt entitled to that, too. I've spent time wondering if he would have felt the same, done the same, had the Quints been five sturdy boys, had they been pretty girls instead of plain ones, had Anglette had the will or even the desire to say "no" in an echo of my sisters' first words.

The pregnancy was terminated—quickly, quietly, and without fanfare. It was Dr. LeFevre who did the work yet again, as Rhys Osborne felt he could trust no one else. And that doctor (what a marvel!) never asked who, or how, or why. She was lucky, really, Rhys Osborne thought. Other woman he'd known hadn't always had the privilege of a doctor, of a clean room, of a private bed. And so, without my sister's consent, without her asking, without discussion, he put an end to whatever offspring might have come to them.

She cried the morning of the procedure. Cried from the time they left the hospital until they arrived at the doctor's new suite of offices. She cried in the waiting room and she cried as the doctor asked her questions with a kind of distance that might imply he didn't know her at all. She cried when they made her change into a paper gown, when they administered ether, when some nurse, yet another in her life filled with them, lied to her by promising that it wouldn't hurt.

And then she screamed. The kind of scream that every staff member heard, the kind that rattled them and echoed in their core. It was their description of this very scream that would allow Rhys Osborne to be called up on charges years later. That scream had left many of the nurses with restless nights and fitful sleep. They couldn't have all known why she was there, but they talked. They guessed. And they came to know that something real and something imagined had been killed inside one of their beloved Quints.

FABIENNE

WHEN ANGLETTE CAME BACK, they knew. Anglette couldn't figure out how, but she had felt it—that they knew. And she wondered if they all had felt the other, too. The pain had ripped through her as intensely as it had through her sisters. And so they took care of her, bringing her hot tea and towels to put under her hips. Anglette could hardly speak and she lay in bed next to her for hours at a time, holding her hand, listening to her cry and crying herself.

Production on the film was suspended for four days and they all stayed near Anglette, taking their meals on trays in their bedrooms and trying to find ways to entertain her when she wasn't sleeping. And they all said without saying that they felt it all.

The script was horrible. The things she and her sisters had to say to each other made them roll their eyes. And in truth, everyone could see that they weren't nearly as cute as they'd been when they were younger. They weren't able to play the role of ingénues. Even she saw that there was something hard in their faces, something that hadn't been there before. And the camera was not kind, accentuating the accumulated weight of their years.

She wasn't sure why he thought that she would tell. They had all known what was going on—of course they did—whether they talked about it or not. Her weekly disappearance in the back of his car? Even that wasn't a necessary tip off. And when she

would come back, she was quietly different—however subtly—
and it would take her a few days to settle back into herself. Did he
really not understand by now that they knew each other precisely
as they knew themselves? That one was the other? That the notion
of separation and distance among the Quints was foreign, an idea
they couldn't even comprehend. In those long months trapped in
Queen Street, another in a succession of prisons, who else did they
have to lean on but each other? And who else did they need?

But as much as he understood his investment, Rhys Osborne
never understood them as people, as quintuplet sisters. He never
would. They knew everything that had happened with Anglette.
And they'd had enough.

The starting date for school came and went, and still she and her
sisters worked on the picture. Filming was suspended again when
the script underwent a rewrite and the young blond actress went
to New York to audition for another film. All of a sudden it was
November. There was something about the fall that always made
her sad. Where other people felt invigorated by crisp autumnal
breezes, she felt only a sense of dread and smelled dying on the air.
Autumn and a stillness crept into her heart, laying wait until spring.

The sun was fading earlier and earlier and she and her sisters
were bored and restless. They thought about nothing other than
finding a way out. After dinner, when they were alone in their
bedroom, they talked about school, even though it didn't seem a
possibility anymore. They knew that once the film was released,
there would be television shows, magazine interviews, and photo
spreads to promote a movie that they all felt certain would flop. But
they couldn't figure out a way to leave the life demanded of them.

When she said it, it scared them all. "Emancipation." So they
made a decision—to get away. The film resumed shooting that
December and they arrived to the set looking wide-eyed and full
of promise. They had a plan, after all. And as much as they understood anything, they understood performance. Anglette was still
recovering, so the cast and the crew had been informed that she

had the flu. She spent a lot of time sitting with an open magazine on her lap but not reading it.

They'd invited their mother to the set—a rare treat for her if not them. Their mother sat in a chair arranged specifically for her, wearing her best dress and a wide brimmed straw hat regardless of the fact that the sun was hidden behind heavy clouds all day. They laughed to each other about that one.

That morning, though, once they got to the makeup trailer, they were quiet. They had agreed not to chatter.

Anthony Rhys Osborne didn't arrive on set until an hour before noon. He made an entrance, trailed as he always was by two secretaries. He greeted them all, and they glowered at him but said nothing. The first shot of the day was to be a scene in which the five of them burst into the cabin to discover the heiress tied up on a bearskin rug.

The five of them were positioned behind the door, ready to storm in, when the director called to begin filming. After coming through the door, she was to say, "Thank God we found you!"

They stood behind the door, outfitted in fur jackets, each of their heads topped with a wool hat, drifts of Styrofoam snow crunching under their feet. They exchanged a glance, each knowing what was to be done.

And when the director called, "Action!" they burst through the door and she yelled, "*Quel dommage, cette film m'ennui!*"

The second assistant director, a French Canadian, laughed out loud. A grip standing next to him leaned in close and asked what my sister had said. His hand over his mouth, the French Canadian whispered, "Too bad this movie is so boring."

Looking confused, the director called to cut. Walking forward, he scolded her. She stared back at him, willing him to look away, but she said nothing. The director set up the scene again and fell back in his chair. When he again called "Action!" she performed exactly—identically—as they had initially.

The director yelled in her face, screamed that each take cost money and that she was wasting everyone's time.

"*Vous Aussi,*" she said to him.

"What?"

She repeated herself in French, "So are you." Her sisters stood behind her, a phalanx.

But it wasn't the director they were after. No, he was simply collateral. So she was pleased when after the third attempt, the director called Rhys Osborne from the canteen where he was taking coffee with one of his secretaries. The director immediately pulled him aside and explained what was happening. Turning to them, his face darkening, Rhys Osborne addressed them sharply.

"What are you doing? There is money and time at stake."

They stared at him coldly for a moment and then exchanged glances with each other. And when they responded to him, they spoke only in French.

"*This is how it's going to be from now on,*" Anglette said, her eyes narrow and angry.

"*We've had enough!*"

"*You can't punish us enough to make us stop.*"

"*Go ahead. Try. See what we do then.*"

SISTER

STANDING NEARBY, THE DIRECTOR was flummoxed. He had no idea what my sisters were saying or why they said it only in French. But Anthony Rhys Osborne did, of course. As he stared at the girls, his face went pale and then changed to a livid red.

Production was shut down for the day and the crew went home. Rhys Osborne met with the director and they tried to think of some way to work around it. Dubbing the girls in postproduction? Bringing in a French-speaking crew? Punishing the girls until they relented? Unsurprisingly, Rhys Osborne landed on the latter. He began by stripping the bedrooms in the Queen Street Hospital of every bit of makeup, candy, magazines, or any personal effects the girls owned. My sisters stood firm, hissing in French at the movers, calling them all Judases. And when it was done, the room regained the look of quiet sterility it had assumed in their babyhood so that it seemed they were reverse cycling.

When they were brought back to the studio the next morning, Rhys Osborne was irate. He screamed at them, threatened them, and in the privacy of a makeup trailer, he cocked his hand and threatened to slap each of their faces until they acquiesced. My sisters held firm. In response to Osborne's rants and threats, they simply stared at him, blinking slowly and smirking. Finally, my sisters—in French—told Osborne they would return to work.

But when they were brought to the set, they again refused to speak English. Rhys Osborne was nearly apoplectic, and my sisters loved it. Back in their dressing room, Osborne began again with the threats and the tirades. Eventually, my sisters—in French—would commit again to working, and they would return to the soundstage. But they would never speak English. Back to the dressing room. Back to the stage. Back to the dressing room. This happened seven times before the director (who was beyond the point of disgust) pulled Rhys Osborne aside and said that this was not working and that he was done.

The director called the studio. Almost immediately, production on the film was shut down. But my sisters were not allowed to return to northern Ontario. Not quite yet. Rhys Osborne continued to book them for magazine photo shoots and interviews, continued to schedule them at public appearances. Regardless of the occasion or the audience, my sisters' campaign continued uninterrupted. When they were asked a question, any question, by anyone, they answered in French. They could no longer be trusted in radio broadcasts to promote good citizenship. They took to smoking openly, to rolling their eyes. And during French language broadcasts—which Osborne thought could still be profitable—my sisters sat mute, refusing to speak at all. They waged guerilla warfare via language—the best campaign they or anyone could imagine—and Rhys Osborne was furious. He screamed, he cajoled, he threatened, but even then they refused to respond.

And when the papers came from the Canadian High Court requesting that the Quints get access to their trust, he was livid, aware that, finally, all of it was unraveling around him.

Their last public appearance together was for the Canadian Girl Guide 45th anniversary, held at the Canadian National Exhibition two weeks before my sisters were to turn sixteen. They were outfitted in the traditional dark blue uniform with its braided belt, royal blue berets, and blue silk maple leaf scarf. They carried, respectively, the flag of the Canadian Girl Guides, the provincial flags of Ontario and Quebec, the Union Jack, and the Canadian flag. Delegates from troops all over the country filled the arena and my sisters each paraded in, careful not to let their flags touch the floor. They stood silently and waited as a host of dignitaries and special guests made speeches about the value of the organization to girls across the country, about the values of good citizenship, cleanliness, and health.

And when finally my sisters were called to the podium, they locked hands and walked onto the dais.

"These five girls, the remarkable Phalene Quints," intoned the Girl Guide High Commissioner, "who represent the values of girl guiding for young ladies all across the county, will now sing for us 'There'll Always be an England,' a tribute to our founder, Lady Baden-Powell."

As my sisters approached the microphone, they exchanged glances. It was Madeline who leaned forward and said, in French, "*I am sorry, Madame, but we cannot in good conscience sing that song. But we have another.*" Immediately, they began singing the French version of the Canadian national anthem, in part because, particularly when sung in translation, the militaristic violence of the song became even more pronounced. It was their final rebellion.

My sisters were clever, no doubt. They found the way to best exploit Canada's weakness, to make Canada turn in on itself. The media took sides immediately, with the French press lauding the girls for both acknowledging and celebrating their heritage, and the English press, doubting the Quints' loyalty to Canada, accusing them of ethnocentrism.

The trust, set up by some more kindly bureaucrat at the beginning of my sisters' career, was where money from the films, the advertisements, and the promotions went after Rhys Osborne took his significant cut (as he was not just guardian but manager and agent, too). The checks arrived just in time for my sisters' sixteenth birthday.

Movers were sent, again, to the Queen Street Hospital and to our parents' home in Témiscaming to collect their things. And at sixteen years of age, my sisters moved into a penthouse in Montreal and immediately took to shutting themselves off from the world all together. The Girl Guide Anniversary Celebration was the last the general public heard or saw from them until they turned nineteen.

ARCHIVES

Quints graduate from seclusion

Graduation day was an extra special time for the five Phalene sister, who have spent their entire lives in the public eye or in the seclusion of *Quintland!* or in their parents' Témiscaming estate. The completion of their schooling marked the end of an era. In caps and gowns the girls posed for a photo with their parents. Who knows where the girls go next?

ELSA

SHE HAD ALWAYS KEPT in touch with them. The image of those five souls mewling in a basket in their parent's farmhouse had been with her since that moment. They'd written letters to her from the big house. They'd told her about their father's prying eyes, the way he slapped and kicked their mother, the way they felt like prisoners.

She had been back in New York for the three years since the fire. Back at it again, working for lots of different kinds of men. She was a bit older now, and there were none of the indiscreet pats on the backside or brushings-up against her in the elevator that she remembered when she was younger, but she saw it happening to the other girls, the younger ones fresh out of secretarial school, who cast their eyes downward, who blamed themselves when men tried to grope or fondle or kiss. She was relieved that time was over for her. But what else could be done?

She hadn't felt the need to intervene, to try and save them, until the letter came from Anglette, addressed to her, the word "private" scribbled on both sides. She'd said she was in love, said she thought she would marry and wanted to know how and when a girl might know she was pregnant. The words had floored her immediately. She's poured herself a drink before she was able to read about how Anthony had taken advantage of the girl. The news of the abortion came from another sister, who had wondered how she might be able to help them now. She wondered what she could do, really. She pondered it, angry, for the rest of her drink and most of another. And then she admitted to herself that the only way to hurt him was by going after his money. And so she did.

Her disgust for him animated her entirely. Yet she felt shame, was filled with it, horrified that because of her actions, she had inadvertently caused another child's death: Anglette and Anthony Rhys Osborne's unborn.

She took sick leave and then the first flight to Toronto that she could get. In the weeks following Anglette's abortion, she'd written letters to Fabienne first and then the others about how to liberate their financial assets and how to gain access to the money they—*they*—had earned.

She stayed at a small bed and breakfast only a few blocks away from the hospital and went about setting up the things the girls had asked of her. She made certain to find them a reputable lawyer. She made trips back and forth between Toronto and Montreal, and found the kind of people who might really help them. She found them an apartment in Montreal that she leased under her name. She quietly filed papers with the municipal and provincial governments to have the quintuplets' funds released to her, and she went about fixing up an apartment that she thought teenagers would want, that the Quints might want.

She wasn't sure exactly why they trusted her, but they did. And in part because of this, and also because of her own sense of guilt and shame and responsibility, she worked hard for them.

She kept writing to them, telling them that she was there for them, assuring that she would not abandon them. She told them about the place they'd been born, about seeing them as babies, about washing their mother's hair in the sink.

She wanted them to know she cared. She wanted them to see she wanted to help. She wanted to show them the love they so desperately needed. Deserved.

ANTHONY RHYS OSBORNE

ON THE DAY THE Quints left the hospital for good, he stood and watched them from his window. Watched as they stepped into a waiting car. He was surprised to see them go, to see them *really* go. And he was at least equally surprised to see Elsa step out of another. She came toward the hospital and he assumed she was there to see him. He shuffled papers on his desk and waited for her to come up, to make the day right since, as of tomorrow, he too would have to leave the mansion, would have to start over.

The rap on the door came just as he expected it. Would he see her? Of course. They had seen each other on occasion, obviously, in those years since the fire. But he thought now of how much older she looked, and he couldn't imagine that there had been a time when he'd wanted to marry her. She bristled when he reached out to take her hands in his, to hear him tell her warmly how much he had missed her. There was no formality or pause before she told him that she knew what he had done.

ELSA

THERE WAS NO REGRET in her voice as she told him that she was the one who had helped the girls. No moment where she hesitated in voicing her disgust. He smiled then, and she noticed that one of his teeth was chipped and that his lips looked bruised and chapped and that everything about him was disheveled and messy.

"I can't say I'm sorry," he said when she got to the end of the speech that she had carefully considered.

And she wasn't surprised. She hadn't expected him to be sorry. But she wanted him to feel and experience that moment of aloneness that she knew he'd felt in New York all those years ago, and for him to realize that it was of his own making. All of it was.

She watched him well up with tears, and something in that act made her hate him even more. She knew that tears have the primary function to bathe the eye, to wash out debris, and it killed her to see them wasted. His entire face expanded and Elsa could see muscles tense below the skin's surface trying to avoid the inevitable. And yet she felt no pity for him. He took a handkerchief from his pocket and wiped his face.

"You're crying because you don't know how to be caring," she said to him. "Those tears are for yourself and no one or nothing else, nothing more."

"You cut with your words," he said.

It was only then that she felt a tinge of pity, a twinge of thought that she was no better than he was. She moved to put on her coat, prepared to leave the office and to never see him again.

"I'm sorry," she said. But she didn't mean it.

Outside, the snow came in sideways. She had never known that it could snow like that, hadn't known that kind of snow existed. It was the kind that got under her hat, down the back of her coat, and it knocked her down with dizziness.

But it had already snowed twice like that since she'd been in the city, and each time made her more incredulous than the last. She rode in her car through the streets, deserted and wasted, and she knew that, regardless of appearances, the things going on in alleys and behind closed doors were no worse than what she'd just done, though perhaps they were better.

She asked the driver to turn on the radio. As the snow hit hard on the glass, she wrapped her coat more tightly around her, glad she was going to the airport.

SISTER

M<small>Y SISTERS LOCKED THEMSELVES</small> away from everyone for the entirety of their sixteenth year. They hoped that the year of seclusion would give them time to regroup and figure out what they wanted—maybe even come closer to understanding who they now were.

The apartment was on the top floor of a new building and had a view that looked out on the city. In the distance they could even see Mont Royal. But they never left. Never explored the boutiques and cafés near their apartment, never made any friends. The became more solitary—more alone—than they'd ever been before. And they relished it.

But my sisters needed this time, you see, because the act of simply living had itself become so hard.

Calendre's epilepsy became their primary concern and some of the money from the trust went to finding the best doctor they could to keep her from seizing. And they learned to cook, making simple sandwiches and salads from the groceries brought in by maid. They stayed up late at night talking, and when they finally purchased a television, they watched that, too.

They began listening to rock 'n' roll for the first time, indulged in hamburgers and French fries. And more importantly, they relaxed. My sisters had been working—or thinking about work or prepping for work or worried about work—for nearly every moment of their sixteen years. Now, in what felt like a decadent luxury, they let their eyebrows follow nature and their widow's peaks grow in, seeing for the first time the ways in which they looked like their parents.

"Oh look, we do have Mama's eyes!"

"My smile is the same as Ingrid's."

They never called our parents, however. They received the occasional letter from our mother, which included cards from our other siblings and many sterile expressions of love. But they didn't respond, didn't know how to respond or what to say. They had neither seen nor spoken to our mother since the incident on the set of the film, and my sisters imagined that she understood how they had used her, the way their acting out might have looked like some kind of family attachment to outsiders. But how were they to know any better? They didn't know what *mother* meant. They could trust Elsa; they could see she cared for them. But they blamed our mother, and our father—perhaps more so?—for their fate. And as much as Elsa insisted that our mother at least had a conscience, they saw none of it from her and expected even less from our father.

As the months went by, they also began planning for the future, considering what they wanted to do and who they would be, as if they could cobble together identity from scraps of the past. They thought a lot about marriage, and they wondered who would want them. They thought about motherhood but could not imagine a world in which their sisters were not intimately included. They considered careers but didn't know what they had been prepared to do that was real.

At night, when my sisters felt especially anxious, when they had double and triple checked the lock, when they were assured that the building's doorman was on duty, they would call Elsa in New York City. And she would pick up. She always picked up. And one by one, they would get on the telephone with her, each girl going over her own specific fears and those of her sisters. Elsa would listen patiently when she could, bearing witness. But even then, they had nights populated by terrible dreams about Rhys

Osborne, nights where they envisioned him coming through the door, making them dress as sailors, or mermaids, or fairies to promote some project or another. Forcing them to assemble in order to be photographed.

I confess: I loved my sisters more in this year than at any other time. I watched them creating themselves. Watched them learn the things they liked and loved. Move away from the things they hated. Learn about empathy, love, and respect—feelings that had before simply hovered several feet above their heads, close enough to see but not feel.

A second check arrived in 1957 for their 17th birthday. They stomped and laughed and hugged when they agreed upon throwing themselves a birthday party—a real party—and so they rented a ballroom in Montréal. They invited all the teenagers from the local high schools on the condition that photographs were forbidden, as were interviews about the celebration. My sisters purchased five separate—and five quite different—dresses, and my sisters broke into tears as they dressed, each one being able to isolate her own face in the glass for the very first time because of the way in which this moment registered special, delightful, and scary.

My sisters cared nothing about the expense. The hall was decorated to resemble the inside of a carnival—an inside joke meant to reflect the entirety of their world prior. Barker games were set up and the ballroom was littered with bales of hay. A stack of presents teetered above the heads of my sisters, who at five feet had always been tiny. And the boys. The boys seemed to be everywhere—at least that was how my sisters remembered it. The writhing, the flesh, the bodies. Somehow proper in its outward appearance, the bawdy truth of it all roiled just below the surface.

Canada was dying to know the sordid details. What my sisters did that night, and who with. But there was no press to report the details. Know simply that they enjoyed themselves more fully and completely than they ever had in their lives, in part because their guests learned that Fabienne was very funny, Calendre, very shy, that Madeline had a beautiful voice, Anglette loved to dance, and that Eliane was a flirt.

In the wee hours of the morning, my sisters were still in the ballroom celebrating the last of their new year. Nearly passed out in the balcony, Anglette faintly remembered seeing one of our sisters, bottle to her mouth, hair billowing around her, but she couldn't remember which. When she woke up, the music was fading as it coiled through the emptying room, but she could still feel the vibrations in her molars, the way they do sometimes, on a frequency different from the rest of her body. She discovered the rest of our sisters at the back of the balcony, lying sprawled out on their backs, going over the events of the night, making promises that they would always have times like these.

And they did. For two years they had that blissful happiness. And they deserved it. I smiled, watching them then. In a life so contained and mostly so very quiet, my sisters learned to become adults, to make the most of the time they had, and to locate themselves.

Their twentieth year of life was to be their last. I didn't know it at the time, wanting for them to get old, to be able to get all that I would never be able to—husbands, children, a legacy. But there were limits for me and there were limits for them as well.

They had those lovely years, those two lovely, happy years, in that Montreal apartment. They made friends, they attended the neighborhood Catholic Church and Eliane and Anglette began nurses training at a local hospital while Madeline and Fabienne enrolled in a music conservatory.

It was only Calendre who seemed to flounder. She took long walks around their Montreal neighborhood. She kept the house neat and prepared meals while my sisters went out into the city and met people. She stayed at home more than the others, feeling less certain of the world outside their apartment and unsure of what she wanted to do with herself.

Calendre had spent the intervening years trying to make up for the gaps in education they had experienced, and during that time, she had found religion. Elsa could not have been more pleased. She had encouraged my sister to study the Bible and to become more involved with their church. And as my other sisters dated, bought party dresses, and developed a taste for champagne, Calendre edged away from the others as they had eschewed the public eye. She turned inward, spending more and more time at home or church and making less of an effort to join her sisters.

In confession she told their parish priest about the fire she'd set, about her guilt at burning *Quintland!* to the ground, and about the loneliness she felt as her sisters seemed to shift their lives away from her own. I understood; I felt the same way. As much as their lives gave me pleasure, as the connective tissue linking them so closely to each other began to dissolve, I felt as if they moved further away from me as well.

Calendre and I had shared an embryonic sac. She was my own twin, the true other half of me, and I often felt that the loneliness she felt was because, perhaps unknowingly, she missed me, missed the sense of us that made our other sisters feel full, rounded, complete. But I can only guess.

For their twentieth birthday, my sisters hosted another party, this time in their apartment. They had food brought in from a small Italian restaurant in the city and tapped into what lingered of their trust money before they turned twenty-one to buy cases of champagne. And while they mingled with their guests, flirted with boys, and celebrated their newfound lives, their delicious freedom and adulthood, Calendre was in their bedroom on her knees praying for more of it.

It is as though she knew she had to go first. She had always been the most subdued of my sisters, happy to follow their lead, feeling her own enjoyment wrapped up in theirs. But as they drifted in different directions, she felt the tug of solitude as her sisters immersed themselves in the world around them.

And she was, Calendre—first to go. Shortly after their birthday party, she had announced to my sisters that she planned to enter a convent. Naturally our sisters were surprised when she told them she was joining the order. From now on, she would be Sister Marie, and her life, her belongings, and her share of the trust would belong to the Holy Catholic Church. In a different time, they would have talked her out of it. And the idea that she was going to leave them, going to shift her life in a direction that was so remarkably different, stunned them all. She was to leave in three days to accept her orders.

They spent those three days—much as they had at *Quint-land!*—no more than an elbow's length away from each other, this heavy time mirroring the deeper sorrow that would come only the next week. They stayed in the apartment, sleeping and eating together, reading books and magazines and watching television. They spoke very little during those days. They wanted only to feel what it meant to be close to each other in a solitary space one last time. Confinement had always been theirs.

The seizure came the evening before she was to leave the penthouse. Our other sisters asleep in their bedroom, Calendre woke up wanting a drink of water. She thought she heard something, thought she saw someone, thought she felt eyes on her, felt the weight, again, of being observed. And she went into an epileptic fit.

Did I cause it? Did she feel me watching her? Of course I wanted her back. I loved her so much. Her head caught the corner of the kitchen counter on the way down. She died there, alone, her beaten heart quietly pushing blood and then more blood out of her and onto the kitchen floor. My wonderful, loving sister, taken, or perhaps returned, as our other sisters slept in the next room, unaware. No Quint connection pulled another sister out of dream and to her there. So, just like that, and I thought she was mine again.

I thought that when she left my other sisters, I would get her back. I thought that we would be reunited. But where she is now? I don't know. I can only hope that somewhere on this side of things, she knows that I am here, waiting for her. For all of them.

MADELINE

MADELINE FOUND CALENDRE. SHE screamed so long and so loud that by the time the ambulance came, she had to be sedated. Their parents came from Témiscaming for the funeral, accompanied by the younger siblings, who none of them had seen in nearly four years. The government paid for the funeral, and when a reporter approached Anglette at the burial plot, she kicked him as forcefully as she could before being swallowed up in a gaggle of protection by her three other sisters.

She stood next to their parents at the gravesite, and each one threw a handful of dirt on Calendre's coffin. She wished that it had been their father, their mother, one of their other non-identical siblings—or better yet, Anthony Rhys Osborne—in the ground instead of Calendre.

Rhys Osborne was there, of course. Standing in the background, he never approached them. When he gave a statement to the press discussing what a tragedy this was, she stared at him, wanting him to feel guilty, to feel as though he had somehow caused Calendre's death. The paper ran the story without any comment from any of them. Her father had spoken with the reporters at length, thoughtfully blaming himself and then deciding that Rhys Osborne was the real villain. The headlines about their sister's death ended up reading more like a grudge match than a tragedy.

Together, with her sisters, they decided to lock themselves away from the public again. They didn't even invite their parents to the apartment where they all lived. The turned over what was to be Calendre's share of the trust to the Catholic Diocese, and then they waited for a sign to tell them when and how things would be different.

Eleven quiet months passed. The sense of sadness that pervaded their lives couldn't be overcome by boyfriends or new party dresses. They sat in the living room in the evenings, looking down at Montreal and imagining where they would go from here. The place felt empty without Calendre.

In August they received the final installment of their trust, and they decided together that when, that January, they turned twenty-one, they would sell the apartment and go their separate ways. No severed ties, nothing like that. Just expanding outward. It had become harder to be together than what they imagined it would be to be apart. She and Anglette put a deposit on a bungalow in Montreal West, Fabienne found a friend who wanted a roommate, and Eliane planned to move into the nurses' dormitory at the hospital. They planned to move January 1st, to begin 1961 anew, with new lives and new energy.

They could not regain their spirits in those last few months. It was as though the two previous years hadn't happened at all. They fell into a routine, not a fully enclosed solitude, but the kind that sadness begets. They stopped calling Elsa and the letters she sent them sat in a pile next to the door, unopened.

In the mornings Anglette and Eliane went to nurses training, and in the afternoons Fabienne went to her piano lessons, and she to voice lessons. She found the music soothing. It made her forget for a time that this was their life. The voice teacher was a little old man in his seventies, well aware of who she was though she'd given McCoy as her family name. He worked to help her hear the right notes. To get it right. Sometimes when she sang, she cried and he squeezed her arm and told her he understood.

And in the evenings they came home and ate potato chips, or popcorn, or whatever they could find. They all became rail thin and stopped accepting invitations to parties or to the movies. They stopped going to the diners in Vieux Montreal to meet with friends. They stopped having their hair cut, buying new dresses or doing anything whatsoever that wasn't absolutely necessary. All four of them developed hacking coughs and could never seem to get warm. They wore shawls and fingerless gloves inside. And each night they called down and asked if the doorman would come up and build a fire.

They heard from Rhys Osborne in those months. There had been requests for them to talk about their sister Calendre's death, requests for television retrospectives for their twentieth year of life. It felt like someone trying to crawl under their skin. Their lives, as a point of nostalgia for a generation born after them, gave her the creeps, even as she tried to make the house as much of a womb as possible. They made nests of blankets, slept with their limbs intertwined.

"We can't lose another," she said over and over again, as though her sisters hadn't heard her. "Losing one feels worse than losing you all." No one knew how to respond.

Together in the evenings they burned every piece of correspondence that came from him. They refused to speak his name, and when he sent reporters to the apartment, they threatened to call the police, to scream, and she pelted the men with whatever she could lay her hands on.

ARCHIVES

Phalene Reports Rift with 4 Quintuplets

TÉMISCAMING, Ont, Dec 27 — The parents of the Phalene quintuplets said today the four surviving girls ignored them at Christmas and did not send so much as a greeting card.

But in Montreal, Eliane, one of the remaining four sisters, denied there was a family rift. She said the quintuplets had sent Christmas greeting.

"We did send one," she asserted. "Can we help it if they didn't get it?"

August Phalene, their father, blamed unidentified "outsiders" for the girls' rift from the home, especially after they liquidated part of their trusts two years ago, each receiving $250,000.

Eliane was interviewed in the hospital nursing residence where she is in training. Her biggest emotional outburst came when a reporter read a dispatch quoting her father as having said the girls' attitudes had changed after they had received their money.

"Don't believe it, it's not true," she burst out, rolling her eyes.

Mr. Phalene made no effort to hide his grief when he said: "We didn't even receive a card from them. They didn't write, they didn't phone. They did nothing to tell us where or how they planned to spend Christmas."

Asked why she did not telephone her parents, Eliane exclaimed, "We were on duty. It's not easy, this job."

Besides Eliane, Madeline is also in training in the hospital. Anglette and Fabienne recently underwent treatment and check-ups for an undisclosed ailment at the same hospital and were discharged last Thursday.

An informant said that Anglette and Fabienne now were living in an exclusive bungalow in Montreal West. The house is in the name of another staff nurse at Notre Dame de L'Espercance Hospital. Reporters were refused entrance to the neighborhood and a neighbor insisted the Phalene girls were not staying there.

In speaking of his disappointment, Mr. Phalene said: "All our other children were at home on Christmas Day. But not the Quints. They didn't even send Christmas greetings to their brothers and sister.

"A lot of people have asked me why the girls are not home for Christmas. Mrs. Phalene and I have given this thing a lot of thought and we decided it would be better if we didn't try to camouflage things any longer.

"It's not something that just happened this Christmas. We have seen it growing for a long time now."

Mr. Phalene said that "under no circumstances would [he] identity the 'outsiders.'"

"The Quints know who they are. We know who they are," he asserted. "But that's all I'm going to say about them."

All four sisters had been studying nursing or music in recent years.

"For weeks and months they never wrote home," Mr. Phalene said. "And when one of them did write, it was only a few words. Mrs. Phalene had been heartbroken. She doesn't blame the girls; she blames the intruders."

The quintuplets were born in a farmhouse in Témiscaming, Ontario. After a brief time at *Quintland!*, the entire family moved into a nineteen-room house a mile north of the park's gates where their parents still reside today. They lost their sister Calendre earlier this year to an accident in the home.

Hospital authorities said today they had advised Anglette and Fabienne to go home for Christmas

"We did so much to try to make them understand they should," one official said. "But they did not answer. You must remember they now are of age. We have no authority over them."

The girls will be eligible to receive the next payout from their trust on their 21st birthday in January.

SISTER

THEY BEGAN TO LOOK like shadows of themselves, like they were already dead. Their arms like twigs and their eyes sunk deep in their sockets. Their hair was always oily and limp, and one of Madeline's classmate compared her breath to the smell of rot. Both Anglette and Eliane's supervisor at the hospital where they worked suggested more than once that they take time off, eat, heal. But they refused.

By that Christmas both Anglette and Fabienne were ill. A bacterial virus had infected their nervous systems, and so they were on leave from the hospital and the conservatory respectively. Eliane and Madeline continued to work, but on Christmas, they brought their sisters home.

They spent the entirety of Christmas day curled up into a single bed, two at each end, sniffling their way through the evening and into the night. Their telephone rang and rang for hours on end until, finally, Anglette got up and unplugged it. They made misery their full-time job. And I was grief-stricken too, not wanting to let my eyes away from them. So I was as surprised as they were when I saw the article in the paper once again featuring our father.

My sisters learned about the story from their neighbor, who thoughtfully cut it out and slipped it under their door three days after Christmas. In the article, our father slammed my sisters, calling them selfish and saying they had ignored the family at

Christmas. "A lot of people have asked me why the girls are not home for Christmas. Mrs. Phalene and I have given this thing a lot of thought and we decided it would be better if we didn't try to camouflage things any longer," our father was quoted as saying.

And in their disappointment, they couldn't read any more and again took to bed. That night when Fabienne couldn't breathe, terror colored her face and they called a nurse and, finally, a doctor. Anglette went into a panic soon after, also unable to draw air. On Dec 29th, in their home and under the company of nurses and my other two sisters, Anglette and Fabienne died, their hands tightly clasped, in a position that echoed the one they had held in utero.

The apartment went on the market before Anglette and Fabienne had been buried. Madeline and Eliane fled from the place as if to somehow spare themselves. One month later, they packed their little Renault with only the barest of things and headed south into Ontario, winding their way back toward Témiscaming. They were headed home to see our parents. To at least try and make amends for whatever had been said or felt as a result of that post-Christmas article. Madeline and Eliane hoped to find some connection to the last people who they felt might tie them to this world.

My parents hadn't known they were coming, and hadn't expected to hear from them at all. Our mother started awake that night, terrified and clutching her chest. She couldn't fall back to sleep and eventually got out of bed and wandered around the house, trying to figure out what had shaken her. It was only when she'd turned on the radio and started to make breakfast at around seven in the morning that she heard.

Madeline and Eliane, en route from Montreal to Témiscaming, their car had veered—somehow—off the road, slipping and sliding over the icy rural pavement. The car teetered and spun violently before hitting an embankment. My sisters sailed through the windshield together, and when they came to rest, their bodies were no more than a foot apart, their faced turned toward each other, as if looking.

I alone could possibly know this, but while Eliane was driving, she thought she saw the three of them, those missing sisters, standing together, waving at them from around the bend, and she turned the car in their direction, almost without thinking, as though it was the most natural thing to do.

They were all gone. None had lived to see their twenty-first birthday, which was only a few weeks away. A magistrate discovered that the final two Quints—had they lived—would have inherited the remaining money in the trust designated for all five sisters. Upon the death of the final two, most of the funds from the trust would revert to their guardian, Rhys Osborne. Because of this financial reality, an investigation was launched into the circumstances surrounding my sisters' deaths.

But they had been headed home to see our parents. With just the two of them left, they had wanted to make amends, to apologize, to be apologized to. They'd had no idea what would happen, what reception they'd get. But they had retained some hope of reconciliation, of reconnection—or rather, connection.

The four funerals were held simultaneously and without fanfare. They hadn't been relevant to you, Canada, for quite some time, and four years away from spectacle and circus had hardened your hearts against them, the way my heart is hardened to you.

Our mother believed they had ended their lives on purpose.

Our father believed they had been murdered.

Our brothers and sister believed they had gone to heaven.

As for Mr. Rhys Osborne, the primary suspect and a recipient of a large portion of the trust, he believed *he* had been sabotaged.

In fact, only Elsa got it right. She knew, just as she had known the first time she saw my sisters, that they were never long for the world and when they were meant to be gone, they would be.

ARCHIVES

Témiscaming Visitor Bureau 1984

Témiscaming: The Birth of an Industry

Prior to that remarkable event in 1940, the Visitor industry in the city of Témiscaming was generally due to her lumber exploits. Then five girls came and literally so did hundreds of thousands of people. Thousands of tourists to see the Quints in *Quintland!*

Témiscaming was thrust into the limelight. News photographers, writers, commercial entrepreneurs, and even Hollywood directors appeared. With two Phalene movies made, the tourism industry prospered.

Today Témiscaming boasts a great collection of visitor services. From our tour of the Ottawa River, to a newly refurbished downtown, there are still five reasons for visiting Témiscaming —Spring, Summer, Fall, Winter . . . and out great Témiscaming people!

TÈMISCAMING

NO ONE MUCH LIVES here anymore. The International Paper factory burned down in the '70s and by then most people had left town. There are a few families that work the land, and perhaps a local grandma might tell you about the time she saw those kids. Another brags that her mother had tried to breastfeed one of the babies.

Some people's great aunts will pull out perfectly preserved sets of Quint dolls, or buttons, or brochures.

Down at the Becker's, old man Harvey, who runs the place, will brag that he kissed one of them once. But no one believes that story.

It's mostly the old people who want to talk about them. Who want to talk about a time when Témiscaming was *something*. But really, there isn't anyone to be angry with anymore. The town is dead as dead can be. The young people leave as soon as they can, and if it weren't for the museum, they'd hardly remember that there was ever anything special about the place at all.

ARCHIVES

The Phalene Quintuplets Guardianship Act, 1940

...Whereas having regard to the special and unique circumstances touching the birth and survival of the quintuplet infant daughters of August Phalene and Catherine Phalene, his wife, and for the better protection of their persons and estates and of their advancement, education, and welfare, it is in the interests of said children and in the public interest that a special guardianship be created.

By this Act, the quintuplets are declared to be the special wards of his Majesty the King, represented by the Minister of Public Welfare for the province of Ontario, Anthony Rhys Osborne, with the Minister constituted their special guardian.

Any contract with respect to the persons or estates of the quintuplets is declared by the Act to be null and void unless entered into with the consent of the active guardians.

The father . . . shall continue as the natural guardian and as one of the said active guardians but . . . he shall be subject to the provisions of the Act and any order-in-council made here-under, and to the jurisdiction and direction of the said minister in all things and for all purposes in relation to the advancement, education, welfare and protection of the said children and each of them and as to their custody, residence, care and attention, provided always that the said children and each of them shall be brought up and educated according to and in the religious belief and faith of the said August Phalene.

SISTER

IT WAS THE SAME every day, and perhaps it always had been. I chose to remember it differently. Coming to me watery, semiclear, and eerily, my sisters' past is more tangible to me than the future. So when things became different and free will all at once became a viable option, when I wasn't locked into watching them, it made me dizzy and I wasn't quite sure how to handle it. My sisters weren't ever coming back to me. I tell their story to myself.

People who are alive can lie and steal and cheat. People who are alive can shrug off shame. I don't have that luxury. The three million visitors from around the world who took in my sisters at *Quintland!*, our conniving parents, Anthony Rhys Osborne, they are all responsible for the way the story turned out. But the world goes around at ease, unburdened by the groping, ugly stickiness of it all. And when in the end, when it was all said and all done, the wars fought and the loves loved, my sisters' story, my sisters' lives, my utter being—all of it: It wouldn't have even registered as a footnote in the annals of the world.

The farmhouse in which my sisters and I were born is now a museum. It features some of the meticulously taken notes from the days in the Queen Street Hospital, five identical christening gowns hung up, crumbling and devoid of baby. A thick braid that the museum curator claims belonged to Anglette. But more than anything, the memorabilia charts their lives. Framed photographs from magazines and advertisements enlarged and hung on the wall. Tiny teacups and thimbles and commemorative saucers emblazoned with their likenesses.

Visitors come every year from all over the world to wander the museum stuffed with souvenirs and trinkets. Fans and collectors exchange rare finds procured through Internet auctions and congregate on the front porch where our mother used to sit. They shake their heads and say how very sad, say they cannot imagine that such a thing would happen. Could happen. They imagine that—as citizens of the future, of a contemporary world—they don't have the capacity for that kind of sheer cruelty, for that level of spectacle. But the experience of the museum is secondary to the things the museum represents. The objects become substitutes for each of my sisters, for their sheer hubris in living.

I ended up here, in this limbo, alone. That is my father's fault. I had hoped of course to be reunited someday with my sisters. To tell them all the things I saw and all the things I heard that they weren't privy to. I had fantasized about our reunion so many times that when it didn't happen, when it didn't come, I felt as broken as they were. So I am left to tell this story over and over. To those who like me are waiting. Partly a cautionary tale, partly a way to explain that the others won't ever be reunited with their lost mothers, or siblings, won't ever get an ending to their story, will be stuck forever waiting and forever watching, until tired by centuries of sadness they turn anyway, knowing that everything that's been done will be done again, can be done again. Without shame. Or conscience. Or blame.

Memory can be whisked away by a half-century's worth of television, film, and cultural spectacle. Now we can take a look at the why, the what, and the where. We can acknowledge that something went wrong. I have assigned myself the task of meting out responsibility. I want everyone to know the wet heat of fresh blood on their hands, to experience how, as it dries, it becomes sticky. There is blame and shame enough, and I will parse it out.

ARCHIVES

The Phalene Quints Museum

About the Museum

Join us for a trip back in time when Témiscaming was one of the most famous places in the world. The January, 1940, birth of the Phalene Quintuplets in this very farmhouse attracted nearly three million visitors to Témiscaming throughout the 1940s and '50s. The Quints' ebullient joy brought happiness to many people's lives as Canada celebrated the fight and eventual victory as part of the Allied Forces in World War Two.

The Quints brought tourist dollars and more to the region that employed thousands of Canadian citizens from our region and neighboring towns. Both Témiscaming and the world loved the five girls born to August and Catherine Phalene. Their birth is a testament to the Canadian *espoir*.

The museum is a not-for-profit institution and is sustained by our generous patrons to support and preserve an important part of Canadian history.

ACKNOWLEDGEMENTS

With unending gratitude to Hasanthika Sirisena and Leland Cheuk for believing in this book when I had almost given up on it entirely.

To my family: George and Maxine Kelly, Jay and Sara Bremyer, Janice Bent, Adrienne Wallace, Simone Kelly, Anton Kelly, Keisha Kelly-Thompson, Kris Kelly, Seth Bremyer, Camille Kelly, John Thompson, Logan Wallace, Rhys and Tristan Kelly, and Izadora Wallace. Thank you always for your love, patience, confidence, and support.

To all the friends who have given love, support, and critique when necessary: Karen Gentry, Emily Weekley, Chelsea Rathburn, Jim May, Margaret Mitchell, Kristen Chernosky, Ann Marie and Ed Short, Chad and Gwen Davidson, Kelcey Ervick Parker, Charlotte Pence, Greg Fraser, Jamie and Jake Wagman, Alison Umminger, Mike Mattison, Wally Lamb, Stacy Davis, Natasha Walker, Laura Beasley, Adam Prince, Laura Ambrose, Krista Hoefle, Bettina Spencer, Candace Nadon, Perin Gurel, Nafissa Thompson-Spires, Kimberly Mock Nielson, Kathe Roper, Jake Mattox, Amina Gautier, Jade Loicano, EJ Levy, Azareen Van Der Vilet Oloomi, Calaya Stallworth, Meg Pearson, Jason Myers, Robert Foreman, Laurah Norton, Corrine and Alicia Tesson, Maria Thompson,

Debbie Suggs, Keri Perreault Calhoun, Sharon Frezza, Joyce Wilson, and Charlie Clark. Words can't say enough about your support. And I would be remiss not mention the members of my very first writing group, born in the halls of Vista Heights: Carrie Ismail, Pam Sutton, and Rochelle Jones.

To the teachers, friends, and editors who have been supportive of me: Elizabeth Stuckey-French, Karen Lee Boren, and Josh Russell—and to the late Ned Stuckey-French, whose goodness and kindness was boundless. Thank you also to Michael Nye, Evelyn Somers, Matthew Limpede, and Paul Lucas, all of whom have been incredibly supportive advocates for my work. And to my third grade teacher, Anne Sexton, who always let me have time to read and write because she knew it was what I needed.

To my son, Ellison, who deepened my understanding of what it meant to be a mother and who helped push me in a thousand different ways in the creation of this book.

And finally, to my husband, Aaron, my first and best reader, editor, critic and supporter, partner, biggest fan, best friend, confidant, co-parent—my everything. I couldn't have done this without you.

ABOUT THE AUTHOR

Dionne Irving has published fiction and nonfiction in *The Missouri Review*, *Boulevard Magazine*, *The Crab Orchard Review*, and other places. Her essay "Living with Racial Fatigue" was chosen as a 2017 Notable Essay in the *Best American Essays* collection. Her second book *Islands* will be published in 2022 by Catapult.

Made in the USA
Monee, IL
03 September 2021